The Forgotten Orphan

GLYNIS PETERS

One More Chapter a division of
HarperCollins*Publishers*
The News Building
1 London Bridge Street
London SE1 9GF

www.harpercollins.co.uk

First published in Great Britain by
HarperCollins*Publishers* 2020

A catalogue record for this book
is available from the British Library

ISBN: 9780008410742 (TPB Can Only)
9780008363291 (B)

Typeset in Sabon LT Std by Palimpsest Book Production Ltd,
Falkirk, Stirlingshire

Printed and bound in Great Britain by CPI Group (UK) Ltd, Croydon CR0 4YY

MIX
Paper from
responsible sources
FSC
www.fsc.org   FSC™ C007454

The Forgotten Orphan

Also by Glynis Peters

The Secret Orphan
The Orphan Thief

For Charlotte Ledger

Thank you for fulfilling my dream

You are more than just my publisher
x

CHAPTER 1

1940

Maisie Reynolds peered through the grubby window of Holly Bush Orphanage. Another child turned and waved to her from the driveway below. Maisie waggled her fingers in a half-hearted response and leaned her forehead against the cool glass. Another heartbreaking moment for her. She knew the little boy's adoptive parents lived in Yorkshire and she doubted he would ever return to Southampton. His long lashes, gentle smile, and willing personality made him the perfect child to adopt, even at the age of eight.

A familiar ache of want and need burned through her body and Maisie allowed the tears to fall. She wanted the world to stop turning, for familiar faces to stay with her, for people to give her the love and affection she saw the boy receiving from his new parents.

When she was his age, Maisie had known she was not a trophy to parade around the parlour as the new member of a family. With her long, frizzy ginger hair, freckled face, and gangly limbs, many a time she'd been passed over by potential adoptive parents. She'd often been told she was too old and lacked the cute qualities most potential parents sought from the residents.

She noticed some women visibly cringe when she walked in the room, and once a man had questioned her parentage, likening the redness of her hair to that of an ape he'd seen at London Zoo. Maisie had rushed from the room and into the hallway and no amount of cajoling from Matron had made her return. Maisie had suggested it was a waste of everyone's time her being there, and Matron had given a slight nod and released her to kitchen duties. She'd not offered comforting words or reassurance that all would be well. The woman had simply treated the event as she always did, with a bland *'what will be, will be'*. From the age of four, Maisie had listened to nothing else but potential parents and their rejection of her.

For the rest of that particular day, Maisie had not been able to concentrate. All she'd heard were the sneering words of the upper-class city businessman swirling and raging around her mind. She'd avoided as many people as she could, not wanting to subject herself to any more torment and teasing about her stick-thin body. On some days she shook it off, but on others, like today, it tore her apart.

Matron had chosen to ignore such attacks, and so resentment had built a wall around Maisie, a protective barrier, which had also earned her the reputation of having a sullen streak.

Around the age of fifteen, she'd snuck downstairs during the night and found the large kitchen scissors in the drawer by the sink. Without hesitation, but with a steady determination to complete her mission, she'd cut her hair close to her head. When finished, she'd bound her head in a scarf so she looked like a nun she'd once met. It had given her a sense of security, and Maisie had felt sure no one would ever be allowed to see or ridicule her hair again. She'd slipped back upstairs to bed and spent several hours tossing and turning, thinking of ways she could run away. Eventually sleep had taken over, and the following morning the clang of the bell to announce the start of another day had echoed loudly from downstairs. A nervous Maisie had made her way into the toddler room to assist with the washing and dressing of eight children.

When she'd pushed open the door, the nursery attendant Norah Bately had glanced her way and laughed, making snide remarks about the scarf. Maisie had responded with a shrug of her shoulders, and no smile. She'd kept her face as expressionless as possible; it was the only protection she had against the woman. If she'd reacted to the laughter, Norah would have found another way of humiliating her, so Maisie had chosen the safest option: no reaction.

There was no love lost between Maisie and Norah. The woman had never approved of Maisie remaining at the orphanage, an opinion made loudly and clearly during each assessment period. Anyone who would listen to her bitter words was told Maisie was a waste of precious funds.

After many years of watching other children leave, Norah had never stopped to think that the distraught fifteen-year-old had resigned herself to the ranks of the unwanted. During a meeting with Matron one afternoon, Maisie had wept as she declared she'd be forgotten and would end up dying at the orphanage. She'd never be loved and would remain an old maid. Matron had said her personal view was that if a child needed a home, she would always endeavour to find one, no matter how long it took . . . but she couldn't force people to like someone. She'd told Maisie to accept her lot in life.

Even after witnessing Maisie's distress, Matron had made no attempt to hold her close, to comfort her and reassure her she'd never be forgotten. As always, Maisie only experienced indifference. From the day her twin brother Jack walked away holding the hands of a new mother and father, Maisie noticed the matron had a deepened coldness towards her and no matter what she did to try and please the woman, Gloria Mason only found satisfaction in treating her as her personal lackey. Years of pleading with the woman to find her brother, to send her to him so they could be together again, fell on deaf ears. Quite often it earned her a slap or two, hidden beneath Gloria's loud assertions that Maisie had become hysterical again and therefore deserved her punishment.

Over the years, Maisie had begged people to write letters on her behalf, and as soon as she could write for herself, she'd written endless letters to Jack, pleading for him not to forget her, and to write back. She begged Matron to address them and forward them to him, but she suspected they never got sent.

As the second world war was announced in 1939, the more she pleaded with Matron to check he was still alive. They were seventeen and with war on their doorstep, Maisie wanted to reach out before it was too late. Each time she asked for news, Matron would tut with impatience and firmly state there was none, and that Maisie should move forward and forget he existed.

But Maisie found it hard to think that Jack could forget her, or the day they'd arrived as new residents of the orphanage, scared and desperate. For hours they'd clung to each other for comfort before they were separated into their new living quarters. She refused to believe he'd forgotten he had a twin sister. She certainly could never forget the day five weeks later when Jack was dragged to a small van screaming for her as she screamed for him. She'd bitten and clawed at Gloria and the staff who held her back, not one offering comfort to a child so distressed she didn't eat for a week. From that day, Maisie drew up a wall of survival as she mourned the loss of her brother. She went to school, spoke with only a handful of children, and allowed life to spin her into its web, tying her to a life of misery. She fell into a pattern of existing and the years melded together, one after the other. As she reached her teenage years, she tried to make plans to run away but with no money and no one to turn to outside the orphanage, Maisie let the ideas slip away.

The only time she'd known affection was when she turned twelve. Life before the orphanage had faded into memories she struggled to cling onto: a woman shouting at her and Jack to be quiet; a man making the woman scream. Neither she nor Jack knew if she was their mother. She was just a woman who threw bread with dripping scraped over it their way whenever she appeared in the small room where they slept.

Often, when a child at the orphanage wet the bed, the smell dragged Maisie back to that room, to its dank smell and the damp feeling against her skin as she and Jack huddled together in fear. These were memories

Maisie pushed to the back of her mind as swiftly as they appeared. As she grew older, some days were a struggle of loneliness and loss. The world around her seemed cruel and unkind, black and steeped in sadness.

During these dark times, Maisie drew upon the only memory of affection she had – someone giving her a warm hug and a tender kiss on her lips.

It had been her twelfth birthday. Her friend Simon had held her in a clumsy embrace under the walnut tree and placed his lips on hers. Simon never commented on her tangled hair, or her inability to walk gracefully. He told her he saw her as a special girl in his life. She was bereft when he left the orphanage to live with old family friends. He'd written a few times, telling of the wonderful life he enjoyed in Scotland, but to her distress he never wrote again, and Matron mentioned that his guardians had spoken of leaving the country due to whispers of another war.

She had never forgotten Simon, or their tender kiss – the impact of such tenderness and affection could never be swept from the mind of someone so desperate to be loved.

Every day from then on, Maisie had made it her duty to comfort the other orphans by embracing them from the day they arrived, and offering them friendship instead of the official efficiency Matron was apt to prefer. Her days became busier as she comforted more and more victims of the second war who had been deprived of parents in the most dreadful ways. The orphanage took them in until relatives claimed them or until they were evacuated to safer towns and villages.

Maisie knew their willingness to embrace her in return wasn't genuine affection on their part, but of the necessity of comfort during confusing times. But Maisie didn't care; she took what was on offer. Her only regret was that no sooner had she inhaled sweet baby perfume, or shared a giggle and clutched the chubby hand of a toddler, they were snatched away into large cars by women wearing fur collars, and swept into a new life.

Today, Maisie's mood was dark. Envy had snuck into her heart and no matter how she tried to suppress her envy, she found it hard. She chided herself for begrudging an eight-year-old boy a new life, but she resented the time she spent in hope, and the hours she was worked to the bone without thanks. Envy wormed its way inside her gut, and she clamped down on her emotions in order to protect herself yet again. She wiped away the tears, drew back her shoulders, and headed out for another round of chores. Each day she asked to be released from the orphanage to enable her to join up in a wartime unit of some description, but each day Matron gave her reasons as to why she couldn't. Closeted in the orphanage for so many years, Maisie believed all she was told and accepted she was to remain a resident until she received her call-up papers or reached twenty-one. Neither could come soon enough for Maisie. She found it unbelievable that it was 1940, and at the age of eighteen her life was no different from when she was nine, always looking out of a window waving goodbye to yet another child.

Walking along the corridor of the baby and toddler home she tried to find something positive in her life but failed miserably. Just then, her thoughts were interrupted by Norah.

'What a face on you. Miserable mare, what's eating you?' Norah taunted.

Maisie felt no reason to explain her sadness so ignored her and the other unkind taunts the woman threw her way.

Maisie walked towards a baby girl holding out her arms from the confines of her cot.

'Hello Deedee,' Maisie said and lifted the child into her arms for a cuddle.

Norah gave a loud tut.

'Her name is Deidre.'

'I know.'

'Well, Miss Know-it-all, call her by her given name, not by some ridiculous pet name you've invented. Go and wash her. She stinks.'

The tiny blonde child snuggled close into Maisie. Norah was right; the urine-soaked nappy gave off a strong whiff of ammonia, but the touch of another human being was worth the nose tingle to Maisie, and she staved off the dark thoughts that threatened. Deedee had the attributes Maisie wished had been bestowed on her – a tiny, pert nose, rosebud mouth, and snow-white hair which dropped into curls around the child's neck. There was something angelic about the baby. She was a child who'd not live at the orphanage forever, but one who'd be adored by doting parents and Maisie feared it wouldn't be much longer before she had to say goodbye. She was the kind of child Maisie dreamed of having of her own one day – not Deedee herself, but one exactly like her. Gummy smiles and chubby fingers to brighten a gloomy day.

'She should have been called Angel,' Maisie said softly as she walked to the bathroom.

'And your parents should have named you Freak. No wonder they left you here. Your poor mother must have died with shock seeing you slide out.' Norah's vicious words were followed with a cruelly cackling laugh.

Maisie, not giving in to the taunt nor the pain inside her chest at the mention of her parents, retorted in a voice loaded with venom, her hatred towards Norah spilling out.

'And you should have been named Witch or Devil to match your evil tongue.'

With force, Maisie slammed the bathroom door behind her to block out the sounds of cursing and more snide comments.

The time had come to for her find a way out of Holly Bush. Norah's nastiness was getting worse each time she spotted Maisie. It was time to find a life that matched her dream of a husband and family. To find comfort and happiness, to have children of her own to nurture and never let them out of her sight. To hold someone and share with them the abundance of love she held inside.

Although Maisie had dreams of life away from the orphanage, she didn't know where to go to find it – or if she ever would. She leaned against the door and closed her eyes. She imagined holding a child much like Deedee and feeling the love of a man prepared to protect them both. The more she sank into the dream, the stronger her determination to leave grew. She could not allow the likes of Gloria Mason and Norah Bately to destroy those dreams.

CHAPTER 2

The next day, Maisie received a request from Matron to see her in her office promptly after chores. She straightened her dress before knocking on the office door and entering.

'Matron, you asked to see me?'

'Maisie. Yes, sit down.'

Over the years, Maisie had grown to judge the moods of the woman she'd known most of her life. Stern, sharp, insensitive, and cold, all words Maisie felt summed up Gloria Mason. There was nothing matronly about the woman. Today, her body language spoke of disapproval.

'It appears you have put in a request for an evening excursion to attend the cinema, and the money from your allowance to fritter away on such a waste of time,' Matron said.

Maisie fidgeted in her seat. This was the first time in months she'd asked to spend an evening in Southampton and she knew she'd have to sit and listen to the same lecture as always. But it would be worth it because her friend Charlie and his girlfriend Joyce had asked her to join them, and they were always good fun. There were also rumours swirling around that hinted the orphanage could be closing, which would mean Maisie would be made homeless and her future would be even more uncertain. She knew she'd go to the cinema regardless of Gloria Mason's decision because she was determined not to miss out on happier times.

Matron gave a loud huff and puff. Her plump cheeks swelled, as did her over-large bosom. She plonked herself down onto her seat behind her desk.

'Just this once. I'll not have you gallivanting around town and giving the orphanage a bad name.'

Maisie gave a false smile of gratitude as Matron counted out the coins from her allowance.

'Your ticket money and bus fare. Be home on time.'

Maisie scooped up the money before Matron had the opportunity to take it back.

'You know I always do my best to get home on time and never gallivant around town. I'm not a child anymore,' she said.

Gloria gave another disgruntled huff and pointed to the door.

'I repeat, be home on time. No alcohol or servicemen, understand?'

'Yes, Matron.' Maisie sighed out her reply. She resented the suggestion that she brought trouble to the orphanage's door. Her behaviour was, and had always been, impeccable. She was wise enough not to antagonise Matron, as the woman found enough faults already in her good behaviour, so goodness knows what she'd do if Maisie did break the rules.

Walking to the bus stop later that evening, Maisie took in the shadows around her and longed for springtime when the world always looked brighter. Pretty flowers were now replaced by vegetables in most gardens, but many wildflowers still grew along the hedgerows. She preferred living semi-rural rather than the city, but always enjoyed the excitement of a visit to the cinema. Matron never allowed her to attend dances, but Maisie promised herself that the first time she was a free agent, she would dance the night away as often as she could.

As she stepped off the bus, she spotted her two friends, Charlie and Joyce, waiting for her outside the cinema and waved to them. She received a warm smile back from them both.

'Hello, you two lovebirds, how are you both?' Maisie gave them both a hug. 'It's been ages. Old Moaning Mason gave me the usual third degree about coming out, but I was going to break the rules this time anyway. Quick, let's get inside where it's warm.'

Maisie and Joyce linked arms and waited whilst Charlie bought their tickets.

Her friends were an odd-looking couple, Joyce short and petite with a thick thatch of jet-black hair which she styled into a quiff fringe that framed her olive-skinned face, against Charlie's height, pale skin, and white-blond cropped style; prior to shaving his hair to fit under his ARP cap, he'd had a thick crown of blond curls. Charlie always made Maisie feel short, even though she was nearer five foot ten than five feet, like Joyce.

She envied Joyce, not for being the girlfriend of Charlie – he was more of a brother figure to Maisie than boyfriend material – but she envied her for even having a boyfriend. Maisie had never experienced that joy. Just the thought of sharing her hopes and dreams with someone who wanted the same, who wanted her in his life, lit a flame inside Maisie. She wanted to experience the secret hand touch in public, the snatched kiss and loving whispers in her ear as she'd witnessed so many others experiencing. She longed to dream with someone about the life they would lead together. Maisie didn't have a clue where or when this desire would ever come into fruition. Stuck in a rut at Holly Bush certainly didn't offer any opportunity for that. In the meantime, her dreams would have to be her companions.

*

'Well, that was fun,' Joyce said and giggled as they left the cinema together after the film.

'It was marvellous. I haven't enjoyed myself so much in ages. Thank you both for inviting me along.'

Charlie stood between them and took Joyce's hand.

'How's it going at the big house?' he asked.

Maisie gave a soft sigh.

'There's a whisper about that the orphanage is closing down. Holly Bush is to be taken over for the war effort. I'll have to leave.'

Joyce swung away from Charlie and grabbed Maisie into a firm embrace then stepped back.

'That's dreadful news. Oh, Maisie, you've lived there nearly your whole life. You've got nowhere to go. What will you do?' she asked.

Charlie stood quietly. Maisie saw the smile leave his face and she felt guilty for ruining a pleasant evening.

'Oh, I'll be fine,' she said, flipping her right hand in a dismissive wave. 'I've got plans to enlist. I'll have to do something. Probably as a nurse, using my skills with the children. Or I'll find another orphanage or evacuee programme as a placement. Don't be sad for me. It will be my opportunity to get on in life. No more being dictated to by a grumpy matron. And I'll get to leave Holly Bush.'

Maisie wished her inner feelings were as sound as her words of bravado. She hated to admit out loud that she was scared of what her future looked like. Homeless and penniless: two words that churned over and over in her mind. She had a background of nothing and a future of the same. And if she did get to leave, would it be a better life or a repeat of the one she was so desperate to leave? Looking at Charlie, she knew she could confide in him but it wasn't up to him to resolve her situation, it was her task alone. Maisie knew the closure of Holly Bush would mean she would have to take control of her own life and make her own decisions. The thought scared her as she was fully aware that there were people out there ready to take advantage of a naïve girl.

'It's for the best. Don't worry about Maisie Reynolds. I bounce back, right? I'm a survivor.'

Charlie nodded and Joyce rubbed the top of Maisie's arm in a reassuring way.

'Whatever you do, you will do it well, Maisie. I do hope you don't leave the area though; we'd miss you. Wouldn't we, Charlie?'

Charlie gave another nod. His face still showed disappointment.

Maisie gave them both a beaming grin. 'Let's go. I've a bus to catch.'

After they'd said their goodbyes, Maisie watched the lovers walk away into the darkness. She spent the time waiting for her bus watching people leaving the cinema hand in hand, arm in arm, and sneaking kisses when they felt they were safe to do so. Soldiers, sailors, uniformed men and women, families, friends, all enjoying each other's company. Another pang of envy washed over her, and she huddled deep into the collar of her coat. She was convinced her limited social life meant she'd never find a partner in life. Charlie and Joyce had met at a dance, and a couple of the women who worked at the orphanage had met their husbands at social functions held by the church. The desire for a family unit of her own overpowered her thoughts of a single life. She knew at eighteen that she'd not witnessed much of life outside the orphanage, but she'd read enough books to know she wanted a hero to ride in and whisk her away. Books were her escape; they were the place where she had learned that love could overcome cruelty, and Maisie wanted all the love she could find.

'Excuse me ma'am. What time is the next bus to Aldershot?' A soft voice cut into her thoughts.

Maisie turned to peer at a uniformed man outlined by a faint light from his cigarette. His accent wasn't local. She doubted it was British, although she wondered if it was perhaps just a regional accent she'd not heard before.

'It's late. Ten minutes already. My feet are freezing.'

The moment she said the words about her feet, Maisie regretted them. Drawing attention to her thick woollen stockings was the last thing she wanted. They were

18

plucked and had seen better days. The man stood beside her, not as tall as Charlie but still taller than her. She could see he was broader than Charlie and although not too close to her, he smelled pleasant – a hint of masculine soap, clean and fresh. His cigarette had a woody fragrance which blended with the damp night air and added to his attraction. She felt the urge to sidle closer, to benefit from the shelter of his body against the wind but remained rooted to her spot for fear of making a fool of herself. The man drew on his cigarette again, puffed out the smoke which spiralled into the night sky, and tugged the collar of his coat around his neck.

'Time for me to walk it then. See you around.'

'It's a long way,' Maisie said, in the hope he'd wait it out for the bus. 'To Aldershot. A long walk. They've taken down the signposts to confuse the enemy. I take it you know the way?'

The man gave a slight laugh. 'I do, thanks, and I'm used to hiking. I've got good boots on and capable legs,' he said and slapped his thighs.

'I could do with a pair of them – boots, not capable legs. Not that I intend to walk home. I'm sure the last bus will be through soon. Be careful in the dark.'

Maisie saw the outline of his hand touch his cap. The farce of them chatting in the dark made her giggle.

'Are you laughing at me, young lady?'

'No. At myself. Telling a soldier to be careful in the

dark. And who knows, I might not be so young,' Maisie replied.

'You were thoughtful, thanks. Goodnight Gran'ma. See you around.'

She saw his outlined arm sweep upwards into a salute. It frustrated Maisie that she couldn't see his face. His voice was soothing and friendly and he sounded young.

The clip of his boots echoed into the night and Maisie turned her attention back to the delayed bus. With no one else waiting at the bus stop, she was beginning to suspect that the service had stopped running. She hesitated, debating whether to call out to the soldier to wait for her, to ask if she could walk with him part way. Her sensible side told her to get home sooner rather than later and to stop daydreaming about strangers.

With a sigh, she took herself off through the dark side streets back towards Holly Bush House, all the while thinking of the soldier and envying his boots the more her feet ached. Her shoes were sturdy and sensible – something she'd always hated – but now appreciated far more as she had another few miles to walk.

Slipping in and out of the treelined pathways across the common, a familiar wail ripped through the silence of the night. Maisie froze and listened. Sirens screamed out their warning, and unidentifiable outlines of people moved towards each other, forming a small crowd on the common ahead of her. Maisie turned full circle; there was nowhere to hide. Not a safe haven in sight. Male voices barked out instructions above the droning sounds of the approaching enemy planes and Maisie's breath came thick and fast. What was she to do? They were closer than she'd anticipated and as the first of the bombs slammed their target with mighty force, Maisie's body shuddered with fear. Inhaling until her head spun, Maisie decided to turn back to town and run to Charlie's house from there, rather than walk any further. Disorientated by the blasts, she had no idea where the bombers were dropping their loads, though she could hear the defensive rat-a-tat sound of the local guns fighting back. Maisie started running. A plane screamed across the sky above her, low and menacing. Another revved its engine and was so low she felt the rush of wind as it skittered across the sky. White pellet-like flashes flicked where clouds had once been, and Maisie realised the sky had cleared, leaving them exposed. The German pilots were off-loading their unused bombs from an earlier raid, saving fuel for their return journey.

'Go away! Drop in the ocean and die!' Maisie screamed out as she ran faster. The pain in her calves and thighs told her she would have to find shelter and rest them a while. A stitch formed in her right side but she dared not stop running.

Another explosion brought her to her knees, and Maisie cursed the bus that had never arrived. She looked towards the night sky. It was now bright like daylight, alive with pilots twisting their planes in and out of the firing line, focused on gaining victory, determined to destroy the enemy.

Lying as flat as she could, Maisie waited for a break in the return fire. She crawled forward, dragging her bag alongside her. She was exposed – out in the open and in danger. A spray of bullets pounded the floor nearby and she let out a scream.

'For Crissakes, there's someone out there! A woman,' a male voice shouted out to his companions in the distance.

'Sounded like a girl,' another called.

Maisie staggered to her feet and waved her arms. The lights from the ack-ack guns flickered around her and she yelled out, 'Here! I'm over here!'

More bullets skimmed around her.

A floating sensation followed by waves of nausea caught Maisie unawares. Her legs lost strength and as she tried to compose herself, another round of enemy fire rebounded against what sounded like metal. She listened to the cacophony surrounding her and clamped her hands over her ears.

Eventually the lights receded and the sky activity calmed. Maisie lowered her hands. A bright orange glow highlighted the city and vast plumes of smoke hurtled towards the sky until Maisie could no longer see anything beyond the smoke. The group of men in the distance no longer called out to her. All she could hear were orders about helping the wounded and she knew their attention was no longer focused on the distant scream of a female. She was on her own. For the first time, the thought of returning to the orphanage seemed a welcome reprieve.

More large clouds of white-grey smoke billowed from the left side of the common and she pulled on her gasmask, the stench of rubber making her gag. Maisie's thoughts flew to the remaining young children and babies of the orphanage. With her gone, the task of putting the babies in their protective chambers and persuading the little ones that Mickey Mouse on the side of their masks made them magical, would take much longer than normal. Norah would be rougher and harsher than ever before.

Suddenly, the ground shook and another loud explosion erupted a few yards away. Maisie could feel her body flying backwards but she could do nothing about it. She thudded to the floor, landing on her right hip. She sat up, and could make out the mound of her bag several feet away, but she was completely disorientated. She pulled off her mask and wiped away the beads of sweat underneath.

Once she caught her breath, she started her journey again. This time she left off her mask. She needed to take deeper breaths and the mask hindered her attempts as she ran. Moving fast towards the edge of the common, she maintained a steady pace, avoiding the open areas.

The freezing temperature burned her lungs which made walking hard and a cold wind made the skin sore around her lips. The natural instinct to lick them was instantly regretted. She dried them with the cuff of her sleeve, wincing at the pain.

The closer she got to the residential side of the common, the more she became aware of the commotion that lay ahead.

Where the bombs had fallen in the distance, they'd started many fires and Maisie found herself yearning for the heat from the flames they produced. Her thoughts overrode the guilt she felt for thinking that deadly flames could, or would, be a comfort.

'Pull yourself together, Maisie Reynolds, you wicked, wicked girl.'

She sat on a wall to rest her legs, rubbing at her bruises with shaking hands. She was just debating which route to take back to Holly Bush when a voice disturbed her concentration. 'Maisie? Is that you?'

Maisie turned her head towards Charlie who rushed towards her, flicking his flashlight on and off as he tried to find his way towards her in the dark. She noticed he was no longer dressed in his tweed suit but in the uniform of the Auxiliary Fire Service. He smiled down at her.

'I'm fine, Charlie. Not hurt. Just resting. Catching my breath. I can't stop shaking.'

'Resting? Lucky you. I'm on my knees.'

'Really? I'd hate to see you when you're standing,' Maisie quipped. 'Joyce get home safely?'

Charlie yawned and rubbed his eyes.

'Yes. Just before this lot fell. How come you're out walking? No bus?'

'Last one must have been the eight o'clock,' Maisie said.

'I had to rush home and change. If I'd know I could have— Down! Get down!' he yelled and pulled Maisie to the ground.

A burst of bomb blasts shook the ground and Charlie grabbed her hand and held it until the attack subsided.

'Get yourself gone, Charlie. I'll be fine. Don't let me stop you going home to rest,' she said, her words rushed and her voice full of concern.

'Rest? Can't go until I've been down there.' He pointed towards the city where the flames licked even higher. 'Buggers dropped on the airplane factory. They've missed it the past few nights but got a couple home tonight. Firefighting has to be done. You heading back to Holly Bush? I'd take you, but . . .' Charlie gave a fleeting glance towards the city again.

Despite the duty that drew him away, Maisie sensed his friendship, his concern. They'd been friends since school when he'd saved her from a teasing gang of children. Several of their old school friends now worked in the factories and her heart gave a jerk-flip of anxiety.

'I'm holding you up. I'm heading back to the children. They need me. You've an important job to do. I'll be fine, honestly.'

Maisie nudged him forward.

'You treat those little ones as if they're your own. Lucky to have you, they are. It looks as if it's getting worse down there. Stay safe, Maisie. If you don't think you'll make it home, head for Glebe Court, over there.' He pointed across the common. 'It's where the public shelter is and much safer than here. Head down that road, past the large shed, see it?' He pointed out to his right. 'Highfield Lane. But be safe, not foolish. See you soon.' Charlie bent and gave her a peck of a kiss on the cheek. 'Take care, and get home safe.'

'Will do, and you do the same. Night, Charlie.'

Maisie heard him whistle his way down the road and his tune remained with her in the darkness. Ahead of him, the flames flickered higher and the smoke grew thicker and darker. Maisie sent a small prayer to the sky asking for safety for the whole of Hampshire, and beyond. She then switched her thoughts to her own predicament as she made her way home. The war had hindered so many things, destroyed so many lives. Was it about time she settled for what she had – a roof over her head and food to eat? Or was it time to find out more about how she could help the war effort? The children in the home had others to help them, and Matron only used her as an extra pair of hands. Maisie glanced around and wondered about those caught in the bombings. Who helped them? How could she find out about supporting the victims of the raids?

Another rain of bullets and bombs fell and a frightened Maisie upped her pace. Adrenalin raced through her body as she ran, her mind focused on survival as she made it to the quieter area of the allotments just behind the orphanage. With a determined stride to safety, Maisie told herself there were more urgent things to think about than how she could escape the city and follow her daydreams. She needed to find a way of being useful instead of *used*. She made up her mind to start the very next day.

CHAPTER 3

'And there she is, the laziest girl I know. Enjoy your holiday?'

The sarcastic tone of Norah Bately grated on Maisie. She was tired and not in the mood for Norah's snide remarks. Rather than disturb the house, she'd spent the night curled up on two chairs pushed together.

Sliding off the chairs and onto her feet, Maisie stretched her body. She ignored Norah and went to the sink to fill the kettle. She lit the stove, keeping her back to the woman still ranting on about her night away.

'Sleeping around town with the soldiers, were you? Trying to earn your way out of here? Ungrateful. That's what you are: ungrateful.'

Norah often tried to goad Maisie, but Maisie tried her hardest not to rise to the bait. But, exhausted after all she'd been through last night, Maisie wasn't in the mood for listening to the spiteful tirade. Finding new courage, she bit back.

'I've never, *never* been ungrateful. You know that, so why are you so horrid? You make my life so miserable. Just leave me alone!'

A snort of indignation was the only reply from Norah, and the woman pointed to the door.

'Stop snivelling and get back to the job you were given to do before you chose to gallivant around town. I cannot abide the sight of you. Go and clean yourself up and stay out of my way.'

Maisie stood her ground and sipped from her mug, all the while staring at Norah over the brim.

'I'm speaking to you, madam,' Norah said.

Maisie raised a daring eyebrow at her, and it was Norah who eventually left the room.

Determined not to be browbeaten by Norah ever again, Maisie gave herself a virtual pat on the back for finding the courage to stand up to the woman. The previous night had scared her into rethinking her life. Although she'd been fired up to seek out a war-effort position this morning, she decided it best to wait a day or so before throwing out innocent questions about where people went for help after losing their homes. It would give her a clue about where she could apply. She would also speak to Charlie about where she would be best placed, and even where she'd find a wage and accommodation.

Getting caught up in the bombings had changed her mindset. The enemy frightened her far more than the likes of mean old Norah Bately.

When she'd finished in the kitchen, Maisie headed for the dormitory and bathroom. Once freshened up, she went to collect her chore list from Matron.

Tapping on the door, she waited for the usual trumpet sound of Gloria Mason's firm voice, but all she heard was a mellow, 'Come.'

Puzzled, Maisie cautiously opened the door.

'I've come to collect my worksheet, Matron,' she said.

Gloria beckoned her inside and Maisie stood waiting in front of the large desk for whatever Matron had in store for her. Quite often she received instructions for jobs no one else could be bothered to do; she pondered on which delight she'd be given today. Washing windows? Scrubbing toilets?

'I didn't hear any banging at the door so I assume you arrived home on time. Today I need you to help me. I'm not feeling well and it's something you can handle alone,' Matron said as she rubbed her hand across her brow. She slumped back in her chair with a deep sigh, pinching the bridge of her nose as if in an attempt to ease a pain somewhere.

Maisie was taken aback. In all the years she'd known Matron, the woman had never had a day's illness. Today, Maisie had to agree that she looked pale with dark rings framing her eyes. She was also grateful Matron hadn't heard her arrive home but she knew Norah wouldn't miss the opportunity to mention she'd slept downstairs. She thrived on telling Matron awful tales about Maisie.

'I was a little on the drag as the bus didn't arrive and I had to get home during the bombing raid. It was horrible. I didn't want to disturb you all so I slept in the kitchen,' she said, keeping her voice calm and steady.

'Stop your chatter. As I said, I'm unwell and my head won't cope with your voice chipping away all day,' Matron said, putting her hand to her head again and rubbing at her temples.

'What's the matter? Do you need the doctor? I'll fetch him,' Maisie said with genuine concern in her voice.

'You will do no such thing. It's my business. You will spend your day emptying the filing cabinets in here in readiness for our departure. As I understand it, the new residents will take over the moment we leave,' Matron snapped back at Maisie and rose to her feet. She brushed Maisie's hand aside when she swayed momentarily.

'I'm going back to my room to rest. Hopefully this headache will disappear in an hour or so. In the meantime, pack away the files into the boxes over there.'

Maisie turned to where Matron pointed and saw several wooden packing crates.

'Keep everything in alphabetical order.'

'Where are we going?'

'The children and I will be moved on. You? I'm not sure. You're too old for me to be worrying about anymore.' Matron gave a dramatic wave of her arm. 'I'm too ill to even think about you. Just do as you're told.'

Matron slammed down a set of keys onto her table and left the room. Maisie simply stared at the back of the door.

The rumours were true! Her home was to be ripped out from under her and Matron did not care one bit. She'd kept control of Maisie's life for eighteen years and now she was walking away without a single thought of where Maisie was to go. Anger bubbled inside Maisie, but it was followed by sadness, and the feeling of being discarded like an unwanted cat or dog. She meant nothing to Matron . . . to *anyone*.

Unable to face that while she was still shaken by the previous evening's near-miss during the bombing raid, Maisie opted to work her way through her crisis. She had a mammoth task ahead of her. Not only did the files need organising, but she could see the room needed a declutter and thorough clean too. If the freezing wind weren't howling around the windows, she'd have lifted them all open and blown fresh air into the room.

Maisie prepared a large crate and opened the first of the large cabinets. Perhaps she could turn this into an opportunity? With Matron out of the room, she'd finally get the chance to find answers to the questions she'd been asking for years. Where had she come from? Who were her parents? No matter how often she asked the questions, Matron had always ignored her or found a reason not to answer. It was part of the insidious emotional torture that had long frustrated Maisie. Why, when records were to hand, couldn't Matron find time to answer her questions? If her mother had never wanted her and Jack, and if she were unmarried, then so be it, but Maisie could never understand why her requests were met with hostile responses. A sudden thought came to her. With access to the files, she'd be able to find Jack's paperwork and in it would be information relating to his new home. Maybe she could find him! She tugged open another drawer and flicked straight through to the R section until she found the file bearing her name: Maisie J Reynolds.

The J confused her. She'd only known herself as Maisie Reynolds; a middle name had never featured in her life. She pulled the folder from its resting place and opened it to the first page. It bore her name and age on entry to the orphanage.

Where the family name had once stood out as clearly as the first name, the page was rubbed and smudged. She held the paper up to the light in the hope of seeing the surname more clearly. Was this her mother, or simply the person who'd handed her over?

Then it hit Maisie. Was it wrong to forget the face of

the person who gave birth to you? As hard as she tried, she could not bring her mother's face, the woman who'd fed her scraps of food, to the fore. Why couldn't she remember her? Had she ever loved her mother as a child should? Maisie simply couldn't remember having feelings for anyone other than Jack and the thought sat heavily in her chest, like a bulky mouthful of bread trapped in the gullet.

A creaking floorboard alerted Maisie to someone coming along the corridor. She snatched up the file and moved towards the crate in the hope of hiding it, but time was against her. Matron re-entered the room and looked at the papers Maisie held in her hand.

'Have you finished?' Matron demanded.

'It's going to take longer than five minutes if you want me to do a good job,' Maisie replied, trying to keep the sarcasm out of her voice. She placed the file on top of the cabinet.

Matron walked over and Maisie placed her hand back onto the file. Gloria's face creased into a disapproving frown.

'Hold your tongue girl. Your file, I assume?'

Maisie nodded. 'There's not a lot of information in there but I think I'll keep it as it is mine. There's nowhere else for it to go. You never know, I might need it for the future. I've not received call-up papers yet, but might need this when I do,' she said.

Matron took a step forward and stared Maisie down, her teeth grinding beneath her jawline.

'It is government property to go to the local council and of no use to you. Now, hand it over. As regards to call-up papers, you won't need to worry about those. Your work here is important enough for them not to want you.'

Not wanting to antagonise the woman, but frustrated by her attitude, Maisie spoke again, this time more forcefully. 'But the file is mine,' Maisie said, holding the file closer to her.

With a hissing reply of impatience, Gloria balled her fist and shook it at Maisie. 'Don't be childish. It is not yours, and nothing in there reflects your life as you know it. It is *my* file, or rather, the property of the orphanage.'

'It has my mother's name inside,' Maisie whispered, unable to raise her voice. The pain of having to battle to find out such meagre scraps caused her throat to tighten against a pending screech of indignation.

'Don't be ridiculous. It has a smudge. It does not mean anything to you personally.'

Matron had been known to strike hard when her temper was roused, and Maisie could see the Matron's face reddening, a sure warning sign, but still she clutched the file to her chest.

'If it is of no importance, why are you so het up about it?'

With a forceful step towards her and a push, Matron launched herself at Maisie, knocking her against the cabinet. She wrenched the file from Maisie's hands and with a triumphant roar held it high.

'There'll be consequences for this, Maisie Reynolds!' she yelled and went to sit behind her desk. Maisie stepped forward and stood with her arms out in question.

'Why? Who would know? Tell me, who would care?'

The pleasure in seeing Gloria flinch when she slapped her hand onto the table in response, gave Maisie a thrill. She repeated the act.

'Don't make out I'm a fool. I know I had a mother, and I know she'd be named on official papers when she brought me here. This can't be all you have on me! Where are my true files?'

'You were not brought here by your mother, and this file sums up your paltry life.'

'So, who did bring me here? Why has my mother's name been rubbed out in the file? Who would be able to help me find my family? You've never liked me. Never tried to find me a loving family or home to go to. You tore Jack and me apart. Can you be any more unkind? You destroyed my life and now you use me as an unpaid skivvy.'

Frustration clutched around Maisie's throat and she choked on her words as they rushed from her mouth. Maisie was no longer prepared to take the scraps she was offered, to have her past hidden from her by the people who should have protected her. It was her right to know who'd given birth to her, to know what had been so ruthlessly hidden from her.

She stared Matron down as the woman crossed her arms over her bosom in a defensive gesture. Maisie knew she held the trump card and also that if she stopped her onslaught now, she'd never learn the truth about where she came from.

'You always pushed me to one side, never praised me. When people wanted a child, you held me back, or pushed me into the faces of people who'd no intention of taking on an older child.' Maisie snatched in a breath, giving Matron no time to intervene. 'I was a four-year-old child and you were all I had. I trusted you. How could you treat an innocent child in that way? Call yourself kind, I—'

Maisie stopped her verbal attack when she saw Matron's hands go to her chest and clutch her blouse close to her, her face scarlet, and her lips blue and twisted with pain.

'Matron? Gloria?' Maisie called as the woman slumped to the floor.

Unsure whether to run for help, or run to Matron, Maisie faltered for a few seconds before rushing to Gloria's side to check she was still breathing. On hearing rasping noises from her mouth, Maisie ran to the door.

At that moment, the dreaded sound of the enemy-pending siren burst out over the town. Outside the window, Maisie watched the figures of staff members running towards their allocated units. Maisie looked back at Matron. Her twisted face with one eye staring back told her something was seriously wrong, but there was nothing Maisie could do. Gloria was too heavy to lift, the staff were needed to get the young ones to safety, and deep inside, Maisie couldn't deny that she wanted Matron's cruelty gone from their lives. However, instinct told her she must do all she could to save her and so, with renewed strength, she dragged Matron into the hall.

'Help! Norah! Help! Somebody?'

The ground shuddered as the bombs dropped around them, near enough to suggest they were a sitting target and they needed to get to safety.

'Norah!'

The silence inside the house was deafened by the screams of retaliation from planes outside. Maisie sank to her knees. This was it; this was the end of her life. A life of struggle and loneliness. A forgotten life. A forgotten daughter. As the high-pitched sound of a bomb homing in on its target sounded outside the window, Gloria groaned and Maisie crawled over to her. Now was not the time to abandon someone in need, but to offer them comfort. No matter their past deeds. She muttered words of reassurance to Matron, despite the rising fear that she would never get out alive.

Was this really how her life was meant to end, lying on a floor with a sick woman who'd shown her nothing but unkindness? Who'd refused to help her move forward into a safe and happy future? The file! If she did get out of this alive, Maisie was determined to have her file, even if there was nothing of importance inside but a scratched-out name; it was part of her – a record that she had existed.

She scrambled to her feet and rushed back to the office where Gloria had dropped the file. She rolled it up and pushed it into the elastic of her skirt. Now for Jack's. She returned to the cabinet and flicked with speed through the R section but was met by disappointment. Jack's file was not there. She ran back to Matron.

'Where's Jack's file? What have you done with my brother's file? Where is it? Maisie shouted and railed at the woman who lay staring back at her, her eyes blank. It was too late; Gloria Mason had passed away and Maisie yelled out her frustrations until Norah Bately and other members of staff pulled her away. Maisie was convinced the woman had died holding on to secrets about her and Jack's background. Was it to save herself from having to explain why she split up twins? Or was the simple truth exactly what she'd always told Maisie: she was not desirable enough to be someone's daughter?

By the time Gloria's body had been removed and Norah Bately had stepped into the chaos, Maisie had resolved to find Jack's file, to find out the truth about who they were, and where they'd come from. And there was nothing Norah could do to stop her.

CHAPTER 4

'How's it going up there?' Charlie asked, referring to Holly Bush Orphanage.

He called across the hut to where Maisie was laying out cups and saucers in readiness for the first batch of firefighters taking a break. Many had been drafted in from other areas to support the local teams. The city refused to buckle under the ferocious attacks but the struggle to survive wasn't easy.

'Oh, Norah enjoys whipping me with that spiteful tongue of hers, but I've found a trick. If I get on with the ironing, she leaves me alone. So, as you can imagine, I do a lot of ironing.' Maisie laughed for the first time in a long time. Her life had become a living hell since the authorities had asked Norah to step in and run the home until its closure. Today, Maisie had ignored requests to clean toilets and instead announced she was off to carry out her war duties by making and serving refreshments for the firemen and others working to beat out the fires in Southampton. She knew Norah could not refuse Maisie permission to join Charlie and his team, so no argument was offered on her part. The offering of tea was the least Maisie could do and it helped give her a feeling of being useful. She was happy to be in a place where she could hold her head up with pride and not suffer constant putdowns.

She took jugs from a shelf and filled them with watered down milk. With a small smile, she produced a small bag of sugar from her basket. It was her personal ration. She'd grown used to drinking tea without it, and instead of surrendering her share to Norah, she wanted to give it to people who she felt deserved it more.

'You coming to the dance on Saturday? Providing that lot,' Charlie pointed to the sky, referencing the enemy bombers that wreaked havoc on their lives, 'leave us alone. Over 600 bombs dropped in two nights, according to my dad. The docks are a right mess – all the food storage areas are destroyed. Butter melted across the docks, coal went up in flames. A true disaster. And we've not enough firefighters if anything like that happens again. Dad reckons there'll be more. We need something to cheer us up!'

'I can't get away, Charlie. You know that. Not to a dance. I can come here, yes, but for me to have fun . . .

God forbid. Norah would never let it happen. It's like a prison up there since she's taken over.'

Charlie pulled out a chair and stood on it, rearranging a blackout curtain across a window.

'Get away from the place. Look at the state of you. White as a ghost and old before your time. Move out, Maisie. Why stay?'

Shaking a teacloth open, Maisie stared at him, then laughed.

'Really? Why stay? Well, for one thing, because it's the only home I've ever known.'

Charlie jumped from the chair and stood in front of her. 'Open your eyes, girl. They get money from you for food and board, don't they?'

Maisie nodded.

'How many times have you been to the cinema and used that allowance? Four times? They're cheating you, Maisie. Don't shake your head, it's true. Think about it.'

'You're probably right, but where do you suggest I go, Charlie? How do I find an alternative life?'

Charlie pushed a stack of chairs against the wall, their screeching feet on the floor making Maisie wince. Her head ached from lack of sleep and the constant nagging of Norah.

'Well, all I'm saying is get away as soon as you can. Have fun.'

'I do. I come here, to be with friends. This is fun.'

'Yes, and we appreciate that, but it isn't a life for a girl like you. You should be dancing on a Saturday night,' Charlie said, before unlocking the hut door to let in a stream of tired, dirt-streaked faces in of sustenance.

'If only, Charlie. If only.'

Looking around the room at the many people who worked tirelessly to fight fires, rescue people from the rubble, and support the city in so many ways, it was hard for Maisie to feel sorry for herself. These people never had time for self-pity; they fought demons every second of every day. They fought the enemy by surviving – and by helping people like herself to survive. She refocused her mind and started serving tea to those who deserved her attention. Charlie had a point about going out and having fun, but Maisie's free time was precious, and she chose to spend it where she received gratitude and friendship.

Since Norah's promotion, more and more of the orphanage's staff had left and Maisie had no choice but to take on the extra workload. Norah lounged around the office pretending to be busy with administration and other important tasks, but Maisie suspected she took advantage of the privacy to sleep. For all Charlie's encouragement about leaving, Maisie knew she had to stay a while longer for the sake of the children. This was her duty and contribution to the war effort – keeping orphans safe, making sure they didn't experience the bullying and cruelty she had.

No sooner had Maisie stepped back into the orphanage later that day, than the sirens sounded out around them again. She sighed. There was no respite from the war and its restrictions. The constant attacks were taking their toll on everyone and no matter how many times the bombs dropped, the fear was the same.

Maisie rushed to the children and gathered them about her. She heard the voices of the other staff and children from the other houses making their way to the shelter.

'Get them moving faster, Reynolds!' Norah shouted from over her shoulder.

Maisie noted the woman carried a flask but no child. Unlike Maisie, Norah always put herself first.

Increasing her pace, Maisie bustled about her small group giving words of encouragement for them to run and see if they could catch Matron. Their little legs wobbled as they ran, and her arms ached with the weight of Deedee and another tiny baby.

The children screamed at each shuddering thud and flashing light around them. They ducked beneath the bombers much like mice under the shadow of an owl or hawk.

Another blinding light flashed across the courtyard and appeared to bounce away from the gardens. Maisie continued to urge the frightened children to run and followed on behind them, but their walking speed never increased. They were toddlers in the new stages of walking and were not able to run, even when it was for their lives. Maisie inwardly cursed Norah, but was grateful to see another member of staff run to the aid of the little ones. Norah stepped to one side to let them pass just as another white flash of light blinded them, and Maisie heard Norah mutter the Lord's prayer. Even the hard-hearted feared death. Another flash lit their pathway and this time the explosions were closer to home. Too close.

As they reached the entrance, a woman rushed forward and took a child from Maisie. From the corner of her eye she spotted a dark shadow on the ground ahead.

'Norah! Quick Jane, take Deedee. Norah's fallen over.'

Maisie ran to the static mound and found Norah's body twisted on the floor. She knelt by her side and encouraged her to get back up on her feet. Norah gave no sign of moving and when Maisie tried again, she knew there was nothing she could do for her.

A woman in charge of one of the other houses ran to Maisie's side. 'You need help? Oh, there's a sorry sight. Where'll we put her? What's the plan?' the woman asked in a rushed voice.

Maisie turned to her and stared in disbelief. The woman stood with her legs squarely planted and her hands on her hips. Another plane droned overhead, and

Maisie wasted no time in realising what the situation required. She had to take charge. There was no Norah to ensure their safety and standing in front of her, Elsie gave no sign of taking control. It occurred to Maisie that they were all used to receiving daily orders and during her years in their company they were never required to make the decisions. No amount of standing around would make Elsie do anything different. Taking a deep breath, Maisie realised it would be up to her now. This was her opportunity to show them she was not one of the children, and Maisie Reynolds might be young, but she was capable. This was her time to step up and make them see her for a change. It often felt as if they moved around her as they would a piece of furniture, knowing it was there but not really noticing its presence. Well, now, no more. Keeping her voice calm but firm, she touched Elsie's arm.

'We'll move her over there, to . . .' Maisie was going to add, *to safety,* but realised the foolishness of her words. She pointed to the smaller building to their right. It was used to store old beds.

With difficulty, they lifted Norah's body, flinching at each flashing light as they came, and placed her body onto a damp mattress in a dank room. Maisie shivered with the cold and shock.

'That's that then. It looks like a stray incendiary. There's bad luck for you.'

Maisie, amazed at the matter-of-fact way that Elsie spoke, just nodded.

'We'd best go rescue the others. The kiddies are a handful at the best of times,' she said, but before she'd finished speaking Elsie had disappeared.

Maisie turned back to look at Norah, reassuring herself that she was definitely dead, then turned and left the room. As much as she disliked Norah, dying as she had was not what Maisie would have wished for anyone.

Loud chattering noises from inside the basement shelter were a welcome distraction and Maisie settled into a seat. After a while, she noticed the four staff in the shelter were chatting to each other and completely ignoring the children, several of whom were shaking with fear. Using the same commanding voice she'd used with Elsie, Maisie spoke over the noise of the children.

'Might I suggest we try and get them settled? Calm them down a bit? Lessen the noise perhaps?' The noise of children never bothered Maisie, but the sounds of their sobs did; these women had a duty of care, and she was going to ensure they carried it out. No more slacking when it came to the safety and wellbeing of the children. None of the women seemed to have the foresight to understand their situation, to realise that there was no one in charge, so Maisie tested the waters with her suggestion. All four women broke off their chatter and began moving amongst the children, patting heads and muttering words of reassurance. Maisie couldn't believe her eyes. An eighteen-year-old girl had made four women more than twice her age listen. Could she do this?

'Jane, Elsie, the two of you get some sleep, and I'll wake you in a couple of hours to take over from,' Maisie pointed to two women sitting side by side, 'Lil and Mo. There's a large bag of darning on the end of the bench – Norah told me to put it in here this morning – so we'd best get it done.'

Again, she stared in amazement as the women carried out her instructions. She took up a small pair of socks herself, one with a hole in the toe and stretched it onto the small darning mushroom. She sat back, fighting off her own drowsiness. Now was not the time for her to fall asleep.

For seven hours they huddled in their safe space, occupying the time with naps and nursery rhymes. The room smelled of body odours and mould, and Maisie hugged Deedee to her chest during feeding time, crooning soothing words over her head. Maisie dreaded the day when the baby would be adopted or moved on to safety, though she knew it would be for the best. Holly Bush was no place for a child to grow up – Maisie knew it firsthand – and the war only made matters worse. She recalled being locked in the shelter as a punishment even before the war, when it had been used as a storeroom. She'd managed to avoid entering it again until Matron had made her clear it out in readiness for the start of war. It had been a cruel and endless task of clearing and scrubbing. Once, the door had closed on her and she had stood frozen with fear. Her heart had pounded and bile had threatened to rise. The ghosts she'd imagined as a tiny child had returned. Even now, when the room was filled with people, the flickering shadows on the wall taunted her. If it wasn't for the war, she'd not be sitting there recalling some of the darkest days of her life. Maisie longed to be one of the names on the evacuee list she'd seen that morning, to find some-where safe and start afresh, but there were children in the shelter who would need her now more than ever. The children who weren't listed for adoption, waiting for their turn. In the days to come, Maisie vowed, she would write down the qualities of each child before they were packed away for fostering or onto another orphanage. She wanted to be the one who wrote something of their character in the hope it would lead to a better life.

When the all-clear siren sounded, a great squeal of delight from the children filled the room. Instructions were bellowed out by the adults and once again it fell to Maisie to bring order to the situation.

'Take all the children back to their own houses and feed them. I'll deal with the babies and toddlers in the main house. I'll make a call about Norah to the police station, and we'll take it from there. Is that all right with everyone?'

The other women nodded in agreement and Maisie could see the relief on their faces. The burden of Holly Bush was not theirs; someone else had stepped into the breach and let them off the hook. She doubted they even cared about her age or capabilities, but they were not Maisie's concern; the children were her priority.

Back in the kitchen, the warmth of the gas stove flames underneath the kettle filtered across the room, but Maisie was convinced she'd never be warm again. She rubbed her hands together and blew into them. She'd busied herself feeding the children and putting them to bed for a nap and, to her joy, they'd settled down to sleep. This had given her time to freshen up and make the telephone call which could not be put off any longer. Norah's husband would be expecting her home in an hour.

'What a start to December. How about you, Maisie? How are you dear?'

Startled by the sudden appearance of Mo, but mainly by the fact that anyone had taken her feelings into consideration, Maisie glanced at her and gave a slow nod.

'Tired, as we all are, but managing. I've just got to make that telephone call and then I can relax a little. Will you keep an ear out for the little ones upstairs please?'

Half expecting the older woman to take over and say she'd make the call, Maisie's heart sunk when the woman headed for the stairs. It was now her place to restore order to Holly Bush House and for the sake of the children, she would do all she possibly could.

'Of course, dearie. You carry on. You've a lot on your plate. Losing Norah must be such a shock. You've known her all your life, poor lamb.'

Thoughts tumbled around Maisie's head, and none were charitable. She could not shake off the fact that she felt nothing but relief at the death of Norah.

Is there something wrong with me? Why am I thinking like this? Am I going mad?

The kettle let out a hiss of steam and Maisie walked to the stove. She went through the motions of mashing tealeaves and poured out a cup of tea.

'Thanks. Here, take this up with you. I'll be in the office.'

She turned back to the teapot and poured herself a cup, taking it to the office and placing it on the desk. Composing herself, she telephoned the police station to explain their situation.

After the call, she went upstairs to relieve Mo in the nursery.

'I spoke with the police about Norah. I wasn't sure who needed to know. The undertaker will come when they're free. Norah's husband will be informed. It was definitely a stray bomb; the target was the spitfire factory and docks . . . again. A tragic accident. We'll have to make a few—'

Mo jumped to her feet and stretched her arms above her head interrupting Maisie.

'Right, that's me done. The little ones are still asleep, so catch a nap for yourself. I was going to tell Norah today that I'm not coming back. I've got a cleaning job in the hospital, better hours and pay. As she's not around, I'll tell you. Good luck, Maisie. You're going to need it by the bucket load. You handle the babies well enough, so I'm sure you'll cope.'

Caught unawares by Mo's statement, Maisie took a moment to think – this was not the right time to lose another member of staff.

'The little ones rarely wake, and the only baby for overnight milk is Deedee. I just hope they get a replacement for Norah soon, especially now you're leaving. I don't suppose you could—'

Mo raised her hand. 'Not a chance. I've had my fill of little boys running riot. It was bad enough bringing up my own. I took this as a temporary job. I'll come by for my wages at the end of the week; you should have them ready by then.'

She smiled and waved goodbye. Maisie stared at the children and envied their lives: sleep and eat. What she'd give to have that life again. Or would she? Had she ever had a life where she slept as soundly as these little ones?

Sitting in the office with the door open and one ear

trained for the sound of a baby's cry, Maisie sat staring at the worksheet for the days ahead.

With Norah dead, a new rota needed to be drafted and the council informed. She explained to the remaining three staff members that they were now one down, and someone needed to be with the undertaker when he came. With no volunteers, which didn't surprise her one bit, Maisie found herself in the unenviable position of signing official papers and paying her respects to a woman she had despised. She tried to explain that legally she was not considered adult when it came to official duties because she was still only eighteen, but the undertaker wasn't interested. So long as he had a signature to release the body, he was happy. He'd got several hundred more to deal with, thanks to the endless bombing raids.

Once Norah's body had been taken away, Maisie gathered the remaining staff to discuss all that needed to be done. To make their job more manageable with such a skeleton team, she suggested moving all the children into one house. But Maisie began to grow more and more disheartened by their lack of willingness to engage with the children. Unlike during her own childhood, these children were now free of two cruel dictators and Maisie was determined to improve things. She took it upon herself to write out a routine for the day for the twenty remaining children and their carers. At first the women grumbled when Maisie explained what she'd like to happen each day, but once they noticed an hour's break for each of them, they relented. Neither Gloria nor Norah had granted the requests for longer breaks. They had kept to the fifteen-minute morning and afternoon regime. She also reminded the women that a temporary matron would probably arrive any day and they'd revert back to the old routine, so they'd best make the most of hers.

Pleased with her efforts, Maisie took herself upstairs to check on the children. The room was cold – freezing cold. Breath vapours rose from the mouths of the children and something snapped inside Maisie. For years the conditions in the orphanage had favoured only the residential staff – mainly Matron – and the bedrooms with their high ceilings were cool even in summer. The children had been through a tough night and Maisie decided to leave them to sleep rather than follow the usual rigid routine. Chills wouldn't leave her body, and she shivered. A short nap in the warmth was all she craved. She tiptoed from the room and into Gloria's old bedroom next door. A welcome rush of heat where the coals still glowed out a golden warmth in the hearth wrapped itself around her like a warm blanket. With a shovel and coal scuttle, Maisie transferred the hot coals into the fireplace in the small dormitory. The warmth soon spread, and after she'd dragged her mattress into the room to keep watch over the children, Maisie fell into a more relaxed state and finally settled into a guilt-free sleep.

CHAPTER 5

'Do you really dish out the orders, Maize?' Charlie asked as he blew into his cup of Bovril, his hands wrapped around the tin mug for warmth.

'I do,' Maisie replied, and winked as she sipped her own drink.

They stood in the kitchen of the orphanage, enjoying a rare visit together. Charlie had sent a message saying he hoped all was well and Maisie had invited him to visit when he could.

It had all come about when a member of the council telephoned the house and asked if she would be happy to remain in charge of the orphanage with its few remaining staff until someone new was found to take over. The man had gone on to say that he understood if she refused but would be grateful if she'd take into consideration their desperate situation in the city. Finding a new manager and the capacity to train them in the running of the place at short notice, and for such a short time, was more than they were able to achieve at present. Maisie, with her newfound confidence and wanting to be of use, did not hesitate to agree. The man on the telephone had also told her to keep a record of all spending and to add her name to the salary book; she was to draw her own salary, which would be whatever Gloria or Norah had recorded for themselves. He couldn't remember the exact sum but felt sure it would be a satisfactory wage for a girl of her age and she deserved it with such commitment to duty. He'd asked if she understood the workings of the ledger, and although Maisie had never seen it, she'd replied that she was more than capable of working it out. Mathematic problems were a passion of hers. She'd crossed her fingers when telling the white lie; although she enjoyed mathematics, she much preferred English lessons. She mulled over the words 'commitment to duty' and a warm glow of pride shimmied through her body.

Running Holly Bush was a new experience for her, and certainly kept her busy, but she thrived on it, as did the staff. They seemed happier in their work and the children loved the attention they now received. The council sent word that they were working on the official closure date, including the date when the children would be moved. In the eight days since Norah had died, Maisie had waved off one baby and four toddlers. With each adoption, she tried to feel happy that the little ones would be taken to safety, but there were times her feelings overwhelmed her. She missed the children, even though they'd only had a short time together, because they made up the pieces of her patchwork family. Occasionally, she imagined that Deedee was her own child, and wondered what would happen if she kept her name from the adoption list. The cost of being found out was too great and more importantly, she would be standing in the way of Deedee being adopted by a real family that would love and care for her which was, after all, what the precious little girl deserved.

'I bet they gave you hell the first time you told them what to do.' Charlie's voice cracked with laughter.

'I was so surprised when they didn't. I was waiting for one of them to start bossing me about but it never happened. For some reason they looked to me for guidance. I think because I know the place so well, they assumed I'd be happy to step into Norah's shoes. I think they're just happy someone else is taking the bulk of the work. And if I'm honest, it's best to be in control rather than controlled.'

'True enough. You'll be able to save to get out of here when the children have gone. Any idea where you'll go?'

Maisie shook her head.

'I've heard a rumour that the place is to be used as a medical centre for army personnel,' Charlie said.

Maisie looked at him wide-eyed. 'Really?'

'Yup. You might be drafted to stay here seeing as you know the place so well. Be prepared, Maize, you might not get away until the war finishes, but at least they'll treat you right.'

Maisie worried over his words. If the rumour was true and she was drafted to stay there, what would she do? She had no medical skills, nor would she want to tend wounds. Scraped knees were one thing but war wounds were quite another. Surely Charlie had it wrong; they couldn't make her stay.

'By the way, I heard a bunch of Canadians have moved in to the Aldershot barracks. My chief is taking a few of us to get information about who does what and where they can get help whenever they're off camp. Easy job for me after this week. We want them helping, so we must make them feel at home. According to my dad, there's a new lot arriving in a couple of months.' Charlie grinned at her as he moved to the back door. 'I'll let you know when and you can come along to share your smile with our chums from abroad.'

Maisie threw a dishcloth his way.

'Actually, I might shock you and say yes,' Maisie joked.

'I'll remember. I take it you won't be joining us for Christmas Day now?' Charlie asked.

Maisie gave a slight shrug of her shoulders. 'I can't. I've arranged our shifts so everyone gets time at home. The only person who doesn't get time off is me. The children need a happy day before they leave. Forgive me?'

Charlie gave her a bear hug and she squealed. It felt so good to laugh again.

'Of course, you're forgiven. Just don't forget to rest. If I get five minutes I'll come up and see you, but I've got to visit Joyce's family, too. I'll try.'

Maisie shook her head. 'You concentrate on Joyce and your family. I'll be far too busy to stop. Enjoy your day and come see me another time.'

'Righty ho, don't work too hard. Good luck with this place,' Charlie said, moving his hand in a sweeping motion around the room.

'What are you like at dusting ceilings? It will save me climbing a ladder!' Maisie said with a laugh.

'Cheeky. See you soon. Don't be a stranger. Joyce misses you.'

'Send her my love and be careful out there.'

Returning to the office, Maisie made a start on clearing the filing cabinets and stacking the filing boxes to one side.

'Is it all right to mop in the kitchen now? I didn't want to disturb you earlier, what with your young man visiting. I've finished over in the other houses.'

Maisie looked at the cleaner Val, poking her head around the door. With the busy days running into one another, she'd forgotten Val came to do a deep clean once a week.

'He's not my young man – more like a brother. Charlie and his girlfriend are the only friends I've got. They mean the world to me.'

'Do you have a young man?' Val asked.

Maisie giggled. 'Do I look as if I have time for courting?'

'May I just say that the others are impressed with you. When they told me it was you running the place, well you could have knocked me over with me feather duster. The last time I came in this room and Matron Norah was on duty, I had a paperweight thrown at me!'

'She didn't hurt you, did she?' Maisie asked.

Val shook her head and Maisie gave her a gentle smile in return.

'Good. And I promise I don't throw things. I'm just grateful for the help.'

'How are you managing all of this, Maisie? It must be hard work,' Val said.

'I haven't got to cope alone for too long. It won't be long before the children are moved and this place is taken over for the war effort. I just have to keep a level head until then.'

'Makes sense to ask you to take the helm, but if we

weren't at war you'd probably be away from here, am I right? This war is madness, thanks to the Germans and politicians with loud voices.'

Maisie smiled. She knew nothing about government and wasn't prepared to get into a conversation about politics when there were more pressing items on her agenda.

'We've a week until Christmas and I want to try and give the children a gift each to take away with them. We orphans don't have many possessions, and Christmas was never celebrated here when I was a child. Matron didn't believe in frivolities. We sang carols, said our prayers, and were sent to bed as normal. I remember one year we were treated to a visit from some dignitaries who brought large baskets of food and delicious cakes, which they handed out willy-nilly. Most of us were sick because of all the rich foods and she never allowed them to come again.'

Val stood listening and Maisie saw sympathy in her eyes – the kind which embarrassed her.

'I forgot you were a child of Holly Bush,' she said.

'I still am, Val. My name is still listed as a potential adoptee.'

Val grinned. 'Well, I'll adopt you. How about that?'

'I'm a handful, according to notes I've read about myself. A nuisance child, unruly and wild,' Maisie said and burst out laughing.

Val laughed with her.

'Who the heck wrote that? Were you unruly and wild?'

'Matron hated me for some reason, and no, I was a reader and loved learning. I'm the quiet one in the corner. If she riled me, I'd answer back, but other than that, I thought I was one of the good ones.'

Val leaned against her mop. 'Listen, my girl has far too many things and she's not using them. I'll get her to have a clear-out and we can wrap them up for Christmas and maybe you can hand them out. I'll have a word with my friends; they'll donate, I know it. Leave it with me. I'll take charge of the presents. One less thing for you to worry about. Now, I'd best finish my floors and head home.'

Val moved closer and looked Maisie in the eye. 'You have a big heart and will be rewarded for this one day.'

Maisie gave a shy smile and watched as Val left the room. The day was off to a good start. She sat at the desk preparing lists of things to do and worked through the salary ledger with a lifted spirit. Things were looking up and she was enjoying the newly calm environment at Holly Bush, despite her organisational skills being tested to the limit.

Though the bombers disturbed their evenings and their sleep, adding to Maisie's workload, Christmas Day brought nothing but happiness to the home and all the sleepless nights were soon forgotten.

Val and five neighbours arrived to hand out gifts, causing a joyful racket that Maisie had never heard in the main hall before, especially when homemade biscuits were shared around. Two of the staff brought along large hampers donated by the Women's Institute filled with meat jellies, jams, and small loaves. In the afternoon, one member of staff arrived with the mayor and his wife to deliver six large bags of clothing. Maisie stood back watching each event with tears in her eyes. The tears turned into sobs when she was handed a Christmas gift of her own. It was a box containing a tortoiseshell hairbrush and two small combs for dressing her hair. It was an adult gift, and a thing of beauty. Val patted her back.

'I thought you'd like it. You deserve it, girl.'

'I'll treasure it forever. It's beautiful. Thank you,' Maisie managed to whisper in reply.

1941

As the days progressed into January, it became obvious there would be no new matron and, gradually, fifteen children were reduced to ten. New parents eagerly snatched the hands of their adopted child, and not one questioned Maisie's age or authority to deal with their case, all keen to leave the dreary place behind and enjoy their new family member.

Fortunately, all the adoptions were completed with minimal fuss but the day Deedee was adopted was always going to be painful. Maisie couldn't be happier for the child, but she would miss her terribly. The mayor and his wife had fallen in love with Deedee when they'd visited at Christmas and knew she was the perfect child for the mayor's sister and brother-in-law from a rural village in Cornwall. They were both teachers and lived quiet lives a short distance from the sea. The mayor contacted them and put the wheels in motion with the correct authorities, and a process which would normally take months took less than three weeks. The handing-over day arrived and Maisie dressed Deedee in the prettiest outfit she'd found in the bag of clothes. The mayor's sister beamed when she met Maisie and cried when she held Deedee for the first time.

'She's the sweetest thing. We think her nickname suits her, and we'll call her by it rather than Deidre. We'll write and send pictures. My brother told me how fond you are of her, Maisie. She'll be told of you, I promise. My husband has brought his camera and if you like, we can take a photograph of you together and we'll send you a copy.'

Maisie smiled at the woman who she knew was the perfect choice as a mother for the baby. 'I'd love a photograph of us together. You will be so happy together. She looks a lot like you; I can see why your brother got in touch with you. Christmas Day was a wonderful occasion here and Deedee got the best present an orphan could ever wish for, believe me.'

Deedee's new mother smiled up at her. 'Thank you, Maisie. I promise we'll give her the best life and protect her always.'

After posing for one or two photographs, and allowing them to take pictures of what was once Deedee's home, the couple gathered her few belongings in readiness for their journey home. Gathering in the driveway, the family hugged and rejoiced together, and Maisie could clearly see the love they shared. Deedee was a lucky little girl. Her new parents brought her to Maisie for one last goodbye, and she bit back the tears of parting. She shook her head when the mother held her new little daughter out for Maisie to hold.

'It's best I don't,' Maisie said, her voice cracking with emotion.

'Please, come and visit us one day so we can prove she's got a good home. We'd love it, wouldn't we, darling?'

The woman's husband nodded as he took Deedee from her arms and headed for their car. It was the moment Maisie had dreaded for over a year, but somehow the usual sadness of saying goodbye was helped by meeting the new parents of her precious little friend.

'Thank you. I'll take you up on it when I can. It's a

long way to travel but the journey will be worth it. Take care of yourselves. Stay safe.'

One by one the children left Holly Bush, and when the last child left at the end of January, Maisie cried with relief. Each one of the children had a new home or had an evacuee placement; not one had entered another orphanage. The only name remaining on the list was her own. She left it there for several days before inking it out forever. Maisie Reynolds remained an orphan but no longer held out hope for a new set of parents. Those days were behind her. What she wanted now was to follow a new path of happier days. The mayor had agreed to speak to the council about Maisie remaining at Holly Bush as a housekeeper until the handover, after which she was free to leave. He signed formal papers releasing her from the status of a resident of the home under council care and wished her well.

It was over and at last Maisie felt she'd stepped into adulthood.

CHAPTER 6

1941

In a hand-me-down dress from Val's daughter Edith, and with her hair freshly washed, Maisie walked to the bus stop. Val and Edith had arrived in the afternoon to keep her company and help her get ready for the dance. Back when Charlie had first mentioned it, it had seemed impossible that she might get to attend, but so much had happened to change her circumstances since then. Fortunately, they were chatterboxes which left Maisie to concentrate on the evening ahead. Her nerves twitched with nervous excitement.

Val's persuasive manner had enabled her to convince Maisie to help man the refreshment table at the dance. Although it wasn't the night out Masie had imagined, she realised it would give her something to do rather than standing around looking lost.

Val had offered for Maisie to stay over with her after the dance so she didn't have to battle with the restricted bus service; Since she would be back home first thing in the morning, Maisie had agreed. She ensured Holly Bush was securely locked up and looked forward to her first night away from the orphanage since she had arrived fifteen years previously.

The bus rattled its way past bomb craters and endless trails of rubble. A ripple of guilt shimmied through Maisie's mind. How could she be heading for a party when others had lost so much – their lives included?

Music drifted from the hall where Maisie was used to serving tired firefighters their tea, and she soon forgot her qualms. Val grabbed the girls by the hand and ushered them inside via the side door, where Maisie put her bag to one side and waved to Charlie. He stood by the entrance doors and, along with other colleagues, shook the hands of their guests. Val was not shy about expressing her opinion that some of the guests were very handsome indeed, and Maisie agreed. A few stood out in the crowd, especially the younger ones. She was surprised to see so many young faces had travelled so far. Then she reminded herself that the majority of young British men were away fighting so it was no different.

Charlie left the welcoming committee and headed over to greet her.

'Anyone seen my friend Maize? Tall, skinny, red hair?' he teased.

'Stop it, you.' Maisie gave him a friendly punch on the arm.

'Seriously, Maize, you look lovely. I can't stop long. I promised I would take over from Dad on fire watch. This lot will be gone in an hour. Friendly group. Enjoy yourself. Happy Valentine's,' Charlie said and gave her a wide smile.

Maisie had forgotten that the previous day had been a day for lovers. It had never featured in her life before, and therefore meant little to her beyond foolish, hopeless dreams.

Everyone moved around the room and many new friendships were formed with each new song that was played. She watched couples whisper and laugh together. The Canadian servicemen had a swagger about them, an air of confidence she'd not noticed in men before this evening. They treated everyone as their friend, and she lapped up the attention they lavished on her as they approached the refreshment table. Maisie stood eavesdropping on conversations just to hear their soft accent.

At one point, Maisie scolded herself, and Edith, for comparing Charlie's lean physique to that of one or two of the more muscular soldiers of the supporting forces.

To Maisie it felt disloyal. A betrayal. Yet, she still giggled and had her say whenever a young serviceman glanced their way. The giggles and comparisons increased and neither girl could help themselves. Maisie thought it was just as well Charlie was out of earshot; he might not have enjoyed hearing some of the girlish thoughts they shared.

'Behave, both of you. I'm heading out to welcome them to England, and you'd better ensure they are fed and watered. No leaving the table area or underage drinking, understood?' Val waggled a finger at both her daughter and Maisie and teetered off in the direction of a group of servicemen ready to embrace the female company.

'There she goes, doing her *duty*,' Edith said, her scathing, sarcastic tone not lost on Maisie.

'She's kind-hearted. I'm sure they appreciate her friendship,' Maisie said, but no sooner had the words left her mouth than she realised what Edith meant. Val was *over* friendly where the men were concerned.

'My dad probably appreciated her *friendship* but I'll never know. From what I gather, he visited the canteen at the docks for a week, and by the end of the year she'd lost her job and gained me. Who knows how widely my mother spread her friendship. I'm off to have fun. See you later. If she asks, you can play the innocent.' Maisie was shocked at the way Edith spoke about her mother.

Maisie was left bewildered by both women. She was certain Edith had snuck in a dig at her at the end there but she wasn't sure.

Taking a moment to study the room, she noted that the majority of the occupants were soldiers in uniforms of varying descriptions. There were also a few uniformed girls, and several women decked out in civvies. Everyone was chatting and smiling. All except one. A Canadian soldier. He stood leaning against a wall to Maisie's left and stared into space. His face never bore a smile, and no one pulled him into conversation. With only a slight hesitant glance towards Val who was now giggling with two soldiers, Maisie made her way over to the serviceman.

'Hello. Welcome to England,' she said and held out her hand.

She gave him widest smile.

'Thanks,' came the reply, but no smile followed.

'You look a little lonely,' Maisie said, determined to make him feel welcome.

'I like my own company and listening to the music.'

'Your voice is familiar. Have we met before?' she asked. 'Not that I go anywhere, so it was a silly question really,' Maisie said, rushing her words with an awkward shyness.

The soldier never replied and instead returned his gaze to staring at the roof.

'Well, forgive me for trying. I'll leave you to it.' Maisie

didn't hold back her indignation and with a huff she turned away from him. She returned to the refreshment table and joined the others who were all busy offering jugs of weak orange squash. She'd seen some people pull small silver flasks from pockets or bags and pour the contents into their cups. She guessed it was alcohol of some sort since the dancing and chatting increased along with the noise levels.

'I'm sorry.'

A voice cut in to a quiet moment between songs. Maisie turned her attention away from laying out cups on a tray, to acknowledge the speaker. She knew it was the young man she'd spoken to earlier by the softness of his voice.

'Sorry for being rude or for liking only your own company?' Maisie asked tartly. She didn't need to retaliate in any way, but she wasn't going to let him walk away so easily. He was not many years older than her, possibly two or three, certainly no more. She liked that his complexion was fresh-looking, not spotty like Charlie's, and it was free from facial hair. Trying to avoid eye contact, Maisie glanced across his shoulder, and out into the crowd.

'Lots of company out there for you to enjoy. Here, have a squash.' She thrust a glass towards him and realised her mistake. Now she'd have to look at him, to see those large blue eyes stare back at her. Something about them made her want to know more about him. They invited her to ask.

His hand took the glass, but his eyes never left her face.

'Thank you . . . um?'

'Maisie. Maisie Reynolds, I—'

'Maisie from the orphanage who has to go home now. Goodnight, soldier boy,' Val's slurred voice cut into the conversation and Maisie jumped guiltily.

With a dismissive flick of her hand towards the Canadian, Val followed it with raised eyebrows and he laid down his glass, turned heel, and left.

The burning of embarrassment scorched Maisie's cheeks. She looked at his back hoping he'd turn around, but when he didn't, she swung around to Val.

'Why did you do that? You treated me like a little girl! And why tell him I'm from the orphanage?'

'Well you are. Nothing to be ashamed of, is there? Anyway, you're too innocent to be flirting with the likes of him. Mind you, he's not that much older than you girls by the looks. Talking of girls, where's the other one? Mine.'

Maisie shrugged her shoulders. She wasn't prepared to tell Val where Edith was – not that she really knew, but Val had annoyed her by saying she'd been flirting.

Flirting?

Maisie didn't know the first thing about flirting, and

it angered her to think that her being friendly to a stranger would be seen as such. He could have become a friend. Then it dawned on her . . . he was the man at the bus stop in Southampton. His voice was so familiar, and it was the only place she'd heard a different accent. She wanted to go to him and tell him. To ask if he remembered.

Shake away the thought, Maisie. Why on earth would he remember?

The sound of Val's voice berating Edith cut into her thoughts, and Maisie sighed. Tonight was not turning out as she'd imagined. Singing, dancing, laughter – all things she'd never really experienced – were happening in front of her, rather than to her.

'Get your coat,' Val's voice demanded, and Maisie grabbed her belongings, taking one last look across the room. She saw the young Canadian back in the same place, his leg propped onto the rim of a chair as he stared at the roof.

Was he as lonely as her? Did he want more from life too?

Don't be daft. He's already crossed the world to be in another country. He's busy fighting a war. What more could he ever want?

Maisie's inner thoughts challenged her. She wanted to ignore Val and stay longer, to enjoy the evening as she'd imagined – and if she was to be honest with herself, she wanted to speak with the Canadian again. He intrigued her. He made her experience feelings she'd never felt in the past. His quiet, almost moody personality drew her into wanting to know more about him.

Go with Val and forget tonight. Forget the stranger. He's not interested in you.

Charlie had long gone and she'd only Val and Edith for company and their squabbling irritated and embarrassed Maisie as she headed out of the door behind them.

They continued to bicker on the walk home. As grateful as she was for the overnight stay, once inside Val's home she suddenly felt suffocated. The rooms were small and filled with photographs and bric-a-brac. Laundry was draped on a clotheshorse in front of the fire, steaming up a large mirror on the wall. The fresh laundry smell reminded her there would, without an ounce of doubt, be a pile of ironing waiting for her the following day. As she climbed the stairs in the small terraced house, she realised she'd spent the majority of her life inside a mansion. Turning the corner onto the landing, she had a flashback vision of doing much the same as a little girl. She stood still and let the memories flood her brain. Edith was yelling at her mother from inside one of the rooms, and it brought back memories of two other women shouting in much the same way. She recalled hearing loud screeching voices inside a small room. She remembered thuds when objects hit the adjoining wall and the deep voices of men bellowing at them to be quiet. A flashback of a hand slapping her face made Maisie shudder. Her earliest memory was crying due to hunger and the noise around her – and then a stinging slap across her face with instructions to keep her mouth shut. For a moment, Maisie screwed her eyes shut against Val's voice berating Edith's. She took breaths to control the shock of the memory until eventually, her breathing settled into a calm rhythm.

The small box room where she was to spend the night was crammed with knickknacks and spare bedding. Maisie undressed and snuggled under the red and gold paisley eiderdown, far more luxurious than the coarse blankets of the orphanage. Her mind drifted back to the welcome party and she wished Charlie had stayed longer, but she knew he'd rushed off to see Joyce when she finished work. Joyce's job was somewhere in the city outskirts and something so secret to the war effort that she was not allowed to speak about it. Although curious, Maisie and Charlie knew not to pressure her into telling them. Both Joyce and Charlie worked hard and deserved fun in their lives. She loved seeing him smile. He was a popular lad amongst the ARP team and Maisie felt fortunate to have him in her life.

She thought again of the young serviceman wanting to be alone. He and Charlie were two different young men possibly wanting different things, but the war had interfered with both their lives. Maisie drifted off to sleep knowing that she wanted a different life from the one she had, and soon the opportunity to find it would present itself. She curled under her covers but the strangeness of the room held her back from falling asleep. For so many years she'd shared a room with many others and always under the roof of the orphanage. To tempt sleep her way she tried making up names for the young Canadian she'd spoken with at the dance. It amused her to think he'd made such an impression when all he'd done was ignore her attempts to befriend him. Perhaps she was too young for him, or her hair colour and style were off-putting; perhaps she had come across as pushy. She pondered these and many other scenarios as to why he hadn't considered her worthy enough to talk to, and, if Val hadn't interrupted his apology, whether he and Maisie might have made it to the dancefloor.

CHAPTER 7

Maisie lifted boxes of old files onto a table and began the task of replacing old folders with new ones and marking them with dates from before the Great War. Children abandoned by desperate mothers after the death of their spouse featured heavily in many of the first pages she read.

All the time she worked, she kept her mind focused on finding Jack's file.

Four days of clearing and packing had brought her no closer to finding anything of use, and Maisie wondered whether Gloria had destroyed it, or perhaps it had been given to his new parents. Maisie resigned herself to letting go of the search since everywhere led to a dead end.

She was relieved to see the endless rain of the previous days had eventually stopped. The air was warm and damp on her on her skin. She needed a few lungfuls of fresh air so instead of taking the bus to town, Maisie headed to the common to see if Charlie was on duty. She met him just as he and his father were leaving for the Aldershot barracks.

'Come with us. We'll be back by four o'clock as we're on fire duty at six,' Charlie coaxed. His dad nodded his approval.

As eager as she was to see the place, Maisie hesitated.

'I won't be allowed inside. I'm not on any official duty or listing,' she said.

'True, but come for the ride out, it's better than heading back home or walking through town. That place is heartbreaking. Bombed to its core.'

Jumping into the truck, Maisie settled between Charlie and his father. Maisie relaxed and listened to the father and son's conversation. It dawned on her that the life she'd led had stifled her worldly knowledge. Her education had prepared her for homemaking and not much else. Charlie's father spoke about the political situation and Charlie surprised her with his knowledge of the mechanical workings of a tank. He chatted excitedly about his second medical exam to check whether his previously injured knee would no longer prevent him joining the engineers.

Maisie was boring. She heard herself speak and was bored by what she had to offer. In an impulsive moment, she searched for anything to speak about in order to try to sound interesting.

'I meant to tell you, I found my personal baby file a few months ago. I have *J* as my middle initial.' The moment the words were out of her mouth, she felt foolish. 'What I mean is, I didn't know. I don't know what it stands for. Haven't a clue,' she said.

'You don't know your middle name? Didn't know you had one?' Charlie asked.

Charlie's dad tutted.

'Who doesn't tell a child their full name? Maybe the initial is your mother's name? Was there anything about your family in the file?' he asked.

'That's the odd thing, there's nothing. All the files I've seen of the children I've sent on their way are full of information or official papers. Mine has one sheet with my name on it and the name of my mother scrubbed out.

'How frustrating,' Charlie said.

The vehicle came to a standstill outside a set of large gates.

'Here we are then. You stay here, miss, and we'll be back shortly. The weather is fair for the moment, so take a tarpaulin from the top box over there and sit on the grass until we return. I warn you, don't move or they'll shoot first and ask questions later. Understand?'

Disappointed she couldn't join them and see what

the inside of the camp looked like, Maisie did as she was told, tugged down a tarpaulin and watched as they drove away. She spread out her temporary seating on a grassy verge sheltered by the back of a tin hut that opened on the inside of the camp and sat down. Barbed-wire fencing surrounded the large field opposite, and people moved around at varying speeds, going about their business. Maisie made a game of guessing whose job was what, just to while away the time.

'Odd place to have a picnic.' A male voice interrupted her thoughts. She recognised the voice, and her stomach gave an excited flip. It was the Canadian soldier from the dance.

Although weak, the low spring sunshine shone in Maisie's eyes when she lifted her head to look up at him. This time he wore a smile. A beautiful wide smile. The hairs on Maisie's arms tingled and her hands itched to reach out and touch his lips. His smile was infectious. Captivating.

'Hello again, Maisie from the orphanage. What brings you here, to sit outside an army camp – other than to make the residents sweat a little?'

Maisie noticed a particular tone in his voice. Something about his question suggested she was loitering in the hope of capturing the attention of the soldiers. She bristled slightly but then relaxed when she saw him give a mischievous wink.

'Cheeky. I'm waiting for my friend Charlie and his dad,' Maisie said, and struggled to her feet.

Extremely conscious of her shabby appearance in hand-me-down clothes, Maisie gave a bright smile to compensate. She hoped he wouldn't notice her brown knitted stockings with plucks, or the thin skirt and blouse covered by a cardigan in forest green that was too large for her and a tweed coat that was too short. Never before had Maisie felt ashamed of what she wore. It had never occurred to her to want to look any different in her clothing during the day; it was usually her wild and unruly ginger curls which caused her the most embarrassment.

She took hold of the hand he proffered and shook it. 'It is Maisie from the orphanage, but sadly, she's not sure who you are as you didn't have an embarrassing friend to speak out on your behalf at the dance,' she said cheerfully, reminding him of Val's rude interruption.

'Harry Cameron at your service, ma'am. Cam to my friends.' The soldier saluted. 'And you were right, we had met before. You had cold feet as I recall. Grandma at the bus stop.'

The sun still stung her eyes so Maisie stepped to one side, taking advantage of the shadow Harry cast.

'I knew it! Nice to meet you, Harry, and if I was enjoying a picnic, I'd offer you something to eat, but sadly I'm just along for the ride.'

'I told you, it's Cam to my friends. That night in Southampton, did you get your ride home?' Cam asked.

'The bus didn't turn up and it was a long walk home during the bomb attack.'

Cam raised his brow and shook his head.

'I hitched a lift with some guys heading back to barracks. You weren't so lucky. Shame I can't hang around a bit longer and keep you company but I'm on a mission – walking with weights.' Cam indicated a backpack on his shoulders, with his chin.

Maisie peered around to the backpack.

'It looks heavy. Have you carried it far?' she asked.

'Roughly ten miles. Farnham Castle and back,' Cam replied.

'Carrying all of that?' Maisie waved her arm from his feet to his head. His gasmask was strapped to his leg, and the bulky backpack looked as if it housed all his worldly goods.

'Yes ma'am. Sixty to seventy pounds heavy, and even heavier in the rain.'

Maisie had no idea how much sixty pounds would feel like on her back, but guessed it would not be comfortable. Cam's politeness at stopping to say hello must be causing him some discomfort – not that he showed it in any way. She stepped to one side and pointed to the front entrance of the barracks.

'I think you'd better keep walking before your legs

give way. I feel guilty now. Besides, the drizzle is back again.' She held out her hand, palm skyward.

Cam nodded. 'I've another hill to climb this afternoon so I need to rest a bit and find something to eat. Nice to meet you again, Maisie. Take care.'

'Bye Cam,' Maisie said and raised her hand to wave. She watched his straight back support the weight of his load, his shoulders as broad as his bulky backpack and admired his strength. His backpack finished just above a well-rounded rear, and Maisie noticed the firm thighs supporting the weight. He was a sight to be seen. At the gates he turned and waved, and she felt her cheeks flush warm with embarrassment at being caught out watching him.

Disappointed that their meeting had been cut short, Maisie waved back. She wanted to know more about Harry Cameron, to listen to his accent, to enjoy his calm and relaxed company. He interested her, and as he side-stepped to allow Charlie's father drive out through the gates, she couldn't help but compare Charlie and Cam once again. She decided that she liked his rugged physique more than Charlie's taller, skinnier one.

'Climb up. We've got a treat for you,' Charlie called out to her, and Maisie clambered into the truck. It was in Maisie's mind to suggest that she'd just enjoyed a treat but thought the better of it; neither man would understand what she meant.

'Apple pie, and a can of condensed milk. We were given one each, but we thought you'd like one to take home,' Charlie's dad said and handed her a small package wrapped in cloth.

'That's very kind, but . . .'

Maisie's words were cut off by Charlie's dad raising his hand to stop her talking.

'No buts. My guess is that you don't get many treats, Maisie, so we want you to have it.'

'Your guess is right and thank you both. I'll enjoy it this evening.'

Laughter rang out in the truck and Maisie enjoyed the relaxed atmosphere. Charlie's dad insisted on taking her back to the orphanage when the rain began to fall more heavily the closer they got to Shirley. The moment the large building came into view, Maisie's heart sank. Her day was over. She had no one to share her thoughts with and she so desperately wanted to talk about Harry Cameron with someone.

With the *Music While You Work* programme on the wireless in the kitchen, Maisie looked at the display of cosmetics on the table in front of her. Val and Edith had moved away from Southampton and, after a clear out, Val had insisted Maisie should have whatever they didn't want to pack and take with them. Maisie was now the proud owner of a bottle of red nail polish, a tube of red lipstick, some rouge powder, a box of face powder with a puff, a mascara cake – which she apparently had to spit on before it was of any benefit to her lashes – and a nail file. Val had brushed aside her refusal to accept them and tapped the side of her nose, declaring she had friends in the right places to get more, despite rationing.

Maisie thought the waste was not going to be an issue as the very thought of it all on her face was not appealing. Her own lashes were already dark, and she'd often been told it was unusual for a redhead as they often had fair lashes. She pushed the mascara pat and the powder to one side and pondered the rouge. Her cheeks were usually ruddy at the best of times, so she also reduced that to the ranks of 'not today thanks'. The nail polish and lipstick were the only items that appealed, and she busied herself filing her nails into an almond shape and applying two layers of the polish. She sat reading as they dried and glanced across at the lipstick debating how best to apply it, and wondering whether it would clash with her hair. Once satisfied her nails were dry, she fetched a mirror and applied a light layer of the lipstick to her bottom lip. She'd seen Val pout and push her lips together to smudge top to bottom, but just as she was poised to do the same, a knock rang out along the hallway. Someone was at the front door. Taking a moment to wonder who it might be, she searched for her handkerchief to wipe away the lipstick as she went to open the door.

To her surprise, the visitor was Cam. He stood there smiling with beads of sweat across his brow and his backpack on his shoulders. Maisie's heart jumped a beat and she quickly ran through what she was wearing: clean skirt, blouse, no socks or stockings, barefoot, tidy hair and neat nails. She gave an inward sigh of relief.

'I hope you don't mind the intrusion, only I'm lost and . . .' He frowned at her. 'Have you cut your lip? I think it might be bleeding,' he said with concern in his voice.

'Lipstick. I was removing lipstick. A new shade to try,' Maisie said in a flippant tone, as if lipstick played a large part in her daily routine. She dabbed again at her lips with the handkerchief to prove her point.

'Oh, I see. Anyway, I know this is an unannounced visit, only I missed a turning across the common and found myself here. Without road signs, I wasn't sure where I was. I passed through a vegetable garden and ventured across the lawns once I saw this house, and didn't hesitate to knock when I saw the name engraved above the doorway. What luck eh?' Cam's words came out fast and rushed and his face flushed as he spoke. Somewhere in the back of her mind, Maisie sensed he was only telling half the truth. It excited her to think he'd gone out of his way to visit her.

'Luck and fate, I'd say. You look hot and bothered. Would you like a glass of water? Take a rest, perhaps?' she asked, hoping the answer would be yes. She'd hoped for someone to chat to about Cam, and now the luck was all hers because she got to chat *with* him again.

'I'd not say no to the water and I will stay a short while. I can justify my tardiness to my sarge by explaining how I got lost, but not for sitting in the company of a pretty girl.' Cam laughed and Maisie stepped aside to let him in. She wasn't going to waste a minute of their precious time standing on the doorstep when she could be sitting inside and enjoying his company. He unhitched his belongings and removed his cap. She noticed his head was soaked with sweat.

'Feel free to run your head under the tap in the kitchen. I'll fetch you a towel. You'll catch cold.' She wasn't sure why she added the last bit as it made her sound like a fussing old woman. So she followed it through with a light-hearted laugh. 'An old wives' tale, I'm sure, but it's no bother and better not take the risk. Back in a mo.'

Maisie pointed him in the direction of the kitchen and took the stairs two at a time. She hastily daubed cleansing cream across her lips and gave them a rinse with her flannel then she grabbed a towel and sped downstairs, just in time to see Cam shirtless and dipping his head under the tap. His bronzed muscles moved across his shoulders as he rubbed his head. She admired the fact that the cold water didn't make him flinch away and remained focused on what she realised was her first sight of an adult male's bare torso. Her body tingled. When he finished, he kept his head over the sink and ran his fingers through his hair to rinse away the excess water. Maisie knew she could wait for him to raise his head or she could make a bold move. She opted for the latter and moved forward, reaching out and touching his back.

'I've a towel for you,' she said, hoping her voice didn't sound as breathless as she felt. 'It's here. She tapped it on his right hand. As Cam reached out, their hands touched. For a few seconds neither one of them moved. Cam was the first to break the moment. He pulled the towel to him and rubbed his head. When he stood up and turned around, his face was covered. Maisie hoped her own face wouldn't give away her thoughts when she saw his muscular chest in all its glory. It was outlined with shapes she'd never seen before and a pleasurable – and most welcome – ripple surged around her body.

'I'll get a glass . . . for your drink.'

Cam wiped his chest down and Maisie forced herself to turn away and look in the cupboard for a cup.

'Feel better?' she asked.

'Thanks,' Cam replied.

Without making eye contact, Maisie moved to the sink at the same time as he reached forward to get his shirt. She turned on the tap and, to her disappointment, when she'd turned around he was fastening the last button.

She gave a soft smile. 'I don't know how you do it.'

Cam drank down the water.

'Do what?' he asked as he handed her the glass.

'Walk so far,' she replied.

'Some walks are worth the extra mile.'

A dam burst in Maisie as he stared at her, and she felt her cheeks flood and burn. She'd read his silent message loud and clear: he hadn't got lost. He'd sought her out. He'd deliberately taken the route to the house just to see her.

She looked back at him with a new boldness and smiled.

'Feel free to get lost and freshen up here anytime – well, before we're invaded by nurses.' No sooner the words were out of her mouth than Maisie regretted them. If he did revisit, what chance did she stand against the glamour of nurses? He could have his pick of women. Why on earth did she think he'd be seriously interested in her? Maybe his mixed message was her mix up. Maybe he meant the glass of water and a wash, not her company after all. Whatever the reason, she'd had the pleasure of seeing more of him than she'd ever anticipated and would remember it for a long time to come.

'I'll see you again sometime. And thanks.'

Maisie watched as he hitched his backpack onto his back and strapped it into place. It was easy to see how he'd built up his muscles.

'You're more than welcome. Mind as you go.'

Maisie watched him walk across the lawns towards the allotments, and it came to her that he'd not asked for directions back to barracks. He really had gone out of his way to visit her! A small smile played on her lips and the rest of her day was spent reliving the memory of Cam and his muscles taking a wash in the kitchen sink.

The following morning, the crunch of tyres on the gravelled drive alerted Maisie that visitors had arrived. She put down the papers she was packing away and peered through the office window.

There was a loud thud on the front door, followed by a male voice giving loud instructions to someone about taking the filing boxes away.

Maisie pulled open the front door and, to her surprise, a stream of servicemen stood in a row on the driveway.

'We've come to collect the official files to go to the council offices,' a man in uniform barked out at her. Maisie suspected he resented working on what he perceived to be civilian affairs.

'They're in the office ready for you. I just have to

check them off as they leave,' she said and fetched her clipboard.

The servicemen trooped through and passed boxes to one another in a steady stream from the office to the front door, then onto the drive. Each box was stacked into the back of an army vehicle by a young soldier under her watchful eye. Maisie watched until the last box was set down, and the truck doors closed.

'All recorded,' she declared.

The soldier nodded his thanks. 'I'm to give this to the housekeeper. If you can pass it along please?'

Before Maisie could tell him that the letter was for her, he and his team were driving away.

She ripped open the letter which informed her that there was to be a visit from a delegation of inspectors arriving at two o'clock the following day. The building was now under government control. It had been requisitioned by, and handed over to, The Ministry of Works. The guardian housekeeper was to be on hand to provide access to the property.

Suddenly, it dawned on Maisie that she needed to establish her presence in the house. She needed time to find a new home and a job; being thrown onto the streets by government officials was not an option. She needed to secure a salary that was decent enough to survive.

If she wanted to stay, she needed to present herself as

settled, organised, and capable. She needed to be too valuable for anyone to force her out before she was ready to leave.

Straight away, she set about putting her plans into action. She moved her belongings into the bedroom that had been set aside for the matron. Why she'd not done it before was beyond her. She'd slept in the same bed in an empty dormitory out of habit, which she realised now was ridiculous. She sorted through the piles of bed linen for spare sheets and blankets. Placing them in the blanket box at the end of her bed, she then gathered up all the toiletries she could find and placed them in the bathroom opposite, along with a large quantity of various sized towels. She finished upstairs and went down to the kitchen where she organised all the non-perishable food items into the lockable pantry. She set aside her own supper, including the remaining apple pie, and then went on to search the laundry pile for spare clothing. After the clothes rationing had been brought into play the previous June, staff had donated old clothes to be altered or remade into new ones for the children. Quite often, for example, a man's shirt became a shift dress. Maisie selected a pile of the best items, found Gloria's old sewing box, and put them all in her bedroom. After eating her supper and devouring the last crumb of her apple pie with no guilty feelings at all, Maisie went to her room and sat beside the blazing fire she'd built. Her nerves were restless, but she concentrated on unpicking a jumper and rewinding the wool until her eyelids grew heavy. She undressed and clambered into bed, not daring to think about what the next day would bring.

Would this be the last day at Holly Bush?

Sitting at the desk, Maisie enjoyed the light from the window. It was always bright in that part of the room and whenever she'd stood there ironing, Maisie had often fantasised about reading or writing at a desk in that spot. She doubted the office would be accessible to her when the new residents arrived, and she wanted to make it look as if the area was her normal place of work.

Surprised that she had managed to get a good night's sleep given her nerves at what the following day might bring, Maisie enjoyed watching the dawn battle for attention behind fast-moving clouds. She had until two o'clock to enjoy the peace and quiet. Still shocked that such a large establishment could be left in the hands of a girl as young as herself, Maisie wondered what Gloria and Norah would have made of the situation as she ran her fingers across the keys hanging from their hooks. She laughed to herself when she imagined the looks of shock on their faces. Maisie Reynolds in charge of Holly Bush House! She loved that the word 'orphanage' would no longer be used to describe the building.

After firing up the boiler for hot water and using up

precious coal, Maisie drew a bath to the marked level, which had been painted on shortly after war broke out, and washed herself down with lily-of-the-valley soap. Drying herself on one of the larger towels instead of a thin rough one like she'd normally use, she followed through with washing her hair. The curls bounced into their natural positions and Maisie left them to dry without brushing.

She studied herself in front of the long mirror. It took a few minutes to appreciate that all her childish features – including her tangled hair – had now disappeared. Curls replaced frizz, and she had firm neat breasts, a trim waist, and shapely hips which all complemented each other. Her skin was no longer pale and wan. Instead, it had a peach-pink glow, and her limbs were defined by rounded, muscular mounds. She rummaged through the clothing that was neatly ironed and hanging in the wardrobe and selected a heavy cotton pinafore dress in navy blue and a pale blue floral blouse with navy woollen tights. March hadn't moved into the weather for bare legs, plus it gave the impression of a uniform of sorts. She picked up a copy of *Wuthering Heights* and laid it on the table; she'd come back to it later. First, she wanted to do a final inspection of the other buildings, and await the arrival of those who held her future in their hands.

CHAPTER 8

At two minutes past two o'clock, Maisie stacked the last of her dishes away in the cupboard, dried her hands, and went into the hallway to greet the occupants of a large black Ford car which was pulling up outside. Four men wearing dark suits and trilby hats, and carrying brown leather briefcases, stepped from the vehicle and gathered together, turning this way and that, taking in their surroundings.

Composing herself as they approached the building, Maisie waited for a knock on the door but stepped backwards in surprise when a key rattled in the lock, and the door swung open. She stood stock still, dumbstruck and fearful.

'. . . And the staff have all left aside from a . . .'

The man at the front of the small group stopped in his tracks and stared at Maisie, who in turn stared right back. He moved to one side to let the others enter, and each one took a second or two to register her presence. One man who was so short he had to look up at Maisie, held out his hand.

'I assume you are Mrs Douglas. It's kind of you to help with refreshments. We'll not bother you for long. I know you have a train to catch, but if we encroach on your time, we'll leave the key under the mat when we leave, in readiness for the removal team tomorrow. I believe the medical teams are arriving first. We were under the impression you were leaving earlier than expected. Now, as you can see gentlemen . . .'

He turned away from her before Maisie had an opportunity to enlighten him that whoever Mrs Douglas was, *she* wasn't her and she had no intention of going anywhere. She watched open-mouthed as all four moved into the temporary office. Unsure whether to follow or to stay where she was, Maisie thought she'd wait for an appropriate moment to interrupt them.

Heading back to the kitchen, she was setting up cups and saucers when the kitchen door opened and another man peered inside.

'Ah, tea. Could we have the keys for the other buildings please, Mrs Douglas?'

Maisie frowned. Didn't she look too young to be a Mrs?

'I'm afraid you – and possibly I – have been misled.

I'm Maisie Reynolds, general house—' she broke off and started again. 'Well, I suppose I am the housekeeper, and also a former resident. I've no idea who Mrs Douglas might be. I'm sorry.'

The man fiddled with the edge of his thick moustache, his face etched with confusion. He followed up with a semi-smile.

'I did wonder. You are younger than we'd anticipated, but the war has brought forward many young married couples, so we assumed you were she, so to speak. Never mind. At least there's someone on hand to make us a cuppa.' He guffawed out a laugh.

Maisie reached down for the keys and handed them to him.

'I'm skilled in that area, that's for sure. I'll take a tray of tea into the office for you at five,' she said, offering him a warm smile.

Without replying, the man left the room and Maisie glanced at the clock. Another forty-five minutes to herself. She heard footsteps on the stairs and above her head. They were in her room. The familiar click of the bathroom door sounded out, and the creak of the floorboard in the long dormitory room. She picked up her book and continued reading but could not concentrate on the words. Eventually, the ping of the clock told her reading time was over and she kept her promise of tea in the office.

All four men were huddled around hastily drawn pictures and markings laid out on the table. Maisie hesitated as to where she should place the tray, but luckily one of the men made space. Setting it down, she poured four cups and handed one each to the men.

'I'm sorry we have no biscuits. I have a little bread, if you're hungry. Or I can find something to cook, but there's very little here, I'm afraid.'

All the men drank from their cups as she spoke, and she stood there unsure of what was expected of her. The man she assumed was the head of the group placed his cup back on the tray and gave her a smile.

'I understand you are Miss Maisie Reynolds. My colleague told me of our misunderstanding. Forgive my earlier mistake – foolish of me. Your name rang a bell when my colleague here told me, and I realised we have information here with regard to employment for you as a temporary measure. Your time in the care of the orphanage is over, as I understand it, and you have nowhere to go while you await call-up papers. You make a good cup of tea, I'll grant you that. Ideal housekeeping skills.'

The rest of the men nodded politely and gave encouraging smiles as they also put down their cups. Maisie felt awkward and confused but knew her future was in their hands, and she wasn't prepared to leave the room until she had answers.

'You mentioned something about medical teams arriving tomorrow. Is this to become a hospital?' she asked.

'Of sorts,' the man said. 'We've handed the building over for medical rehabilitation and recovery. The Emergency Hospital Service is in need of support. Beds for general ill-health are not always available due to the large number of injured from the bombings. With its many rooms and units, it makes this the ideal property. Servicemen will be moved here as a priority from the end of the week, and it will be monitored by the Ministry of Health from there. Our job is done. Inspection complete. Satisfied, gentlemen?'

With mutterings to the positive, the men went back to shuffling papers and placing them back into their briefcases. Cool, calm, and collected. Not one of them gave her a thought.

'But I'm still here. What happens now?' she asked.

'I beg your pardon?' one of the men said.

To Maisie's horror, the tears she'd held back flowed down her cheeks.

'What happens to me?' she whispered.

The man who appeared to be the senior person turned to face her. He coughed politely before speaking.

The other three remained stern-faced and unemotional.

'I'll return tomorrow and we'll discuss the way forward. I'm afraid I don't have the time now. Nine-thirty. Does that suit you, Miss Reynolds?'

Wiping her eyes with the back of her hand, Maisie nodded. He spoke with a softer voice and she felt reassured that he'd do as he said.

'Good. Do you have food?'

Maisie nodded.

As he walked past her, he stopped and laid his right hand on her shoulder, giving it an awkward tap.

'We'll help. Don't worry,' he said.

Maisie stood there, bewildered and bemused, as she watched them pull away from Holly Bush. Everything felt surreal. A dream with no ending.

After clearing up the tea things, Maisie curled up on the comfortable chair in the kitchen with blankets around her feet and shoulders and read into the evening. She nibbled at her supper and pondered on the outcome of the following day. Just as she reached scenario two, she heard the familiar wail of the siren warning of enemy planes heading their way. The thought of sitting in the shelter alone didn't appeal and she made the bold decision to stay where she was and risk riding it out in comfort. She pulled the desk away from the window and made a makeshift bed underneath. Outside, the noises grew louder. Planes thundered across the sky much closer than in previous attacks. Flashbacks to the night Norah died caused Maisie's breath to hitch in her throat; fear clawed its way into her chest. The pounding of her heart became unbearable, to the point where she wished it would stop beating – anything to end the fear of death.

The force of the first bomb shattered through the trees. Tiles on the kitchen wall fell away and splintered onto the granite floor. She felt the thud of one bomb, then another and judged them to be a short distance away. Droning over the property was the thunderous pounding of the never-ending engines and it penetrated her skull and beat a tune of despair. The walls of the big house shuddered, and wooden beams creaked as they threatened to twist from the security of their thick iron nails. Maisie's ears popped and she forced a yawn to clear them. Attack after attack from both ground and sky ripped her nerves to shreds, leaving them unable to support her body. Eventually, drained of all emotion except fear, she curled into the foetal position, wrapping her arms across her body to give herself the comforting strength she'd always hoped another person would offer her at the end of life.

She'd heard that when death came for you, your life flashed before your eyes, and you thought of nothing but those you loved. Maisie had no life to recall, and as for those she loved, they were non-existent.

Flashes of light flickered through the narrow cracks around the edges of the blackout curtains, and Maisie flinched at each one. She scrunched her fists together and her jaw ached when she gritted her teeth. To know you are to die, and to hear your attacker pound through the skies with relentless force was enough, but to die alone? Maisie had never dreamed that the end of her life would see her alone. Even the German pilots who'd trained their bombs on her small part of the world died with colleagues, with friends.

When the kitchen window shattered across the floor, Maisie accepted her lot. She made peace with all those whom she felt had done her wrong, and once again repeated the only prayer she knew. Then came the silence. Whirring engine sounds drifted out of earshot and the wind's whistle settled. But the silence was short-lived. Next came the sound of fire bells clanging and voices in the distance drifted through the darkness. Maisie shivered as cool air blew in through the shattered window and across the kitchen. A red glow across the tips of the trees at the end of the driveway told her that a large fire burned in the Shirley area. No doubt the enemy planes were targeting the Southampton docks and Spitfire factories again. She'd heard Charlie and his father discuss the dangers when they drove to Aldershot.

The light from a small torch guided her towards the door and upstairs to her room. A few glowing embers from the small fire she'd made before the evening's attack had started were a welcome sight. Without undressing, she climbed under the covers, thankful that the windows in the room were intact. Tomorrow she'd prepare to leave Holly Bush. Remaining was no longer an option. She needed to do something useful towards the war effort. To fight against the enemy in her own small way.

CHAPTER 9

Sleep had eluded her after the bombing, and her nervous tension about the pending visit from the council official left her tense. To her surprise, a group of soldiers turned up unannounced and began an organised unloading of vehicles.

She rushed downstairs and unlocked the front door.

'Morning ma'am. Sorry about the noise.'

'Oi, mind the bleedin' door mate.'

'You mind your manners, there's a lady be'ind ya.'

Maisie listened to the banter between six soldiers who were moving large wicker boxes from the back of an open-tailed vehicle marked with a red cross.

'Morning miss. Got the kettle on yet, gal?'

'Kenny, stop that bleedin' whistling.'

The joy of hearing happy voices bouncing from the

walls lifted Maisie's mood to a higher level. She gave them a beaming smile.

'I've got to clear glass away from a broken window and then I'll get onto it,' she said.

Placing the kettle onto the stove, it occurred to Maisie that making tea was a task she performed so often. Her job description should read, 'tea-maker'. She swept the glass to one side and set up a table of tin mugs for the men.

'Tea's up,' she called through the doorway into the hall. Without warning, a sudden rush of bodies moved down the hall and the six soldiers raced into the kitchen. She stood to one side and allowed them the freedom to help themselves. One of the group gave her a toothy grin.

'Cor, you're a gooden' gal. The fodder's on the next run. Some for each house, so me sarge said. We'll fix the winda when we're done. Planes?' he said, without drawing breath.

Maisie assumed he was in charge of the group. He had turned to another soldier and chattered on before she had the opportunity to respond. She listened to the group, trying to pick out words from their strong accents. Eventually, she caved in and asked where they originated from.

One young man was Scottish, and she soon learned that nobody understood him. The group leader and another soldier were from London. One came from Birmingham, one from Norfolk, and Kenny the whistler came from Suffolk. She tried to remember their names as they introduced themselves but settled on knowing the leader's name was Will.

She also learned Kenny was the joker of the group. She liked him. She liked them all. They were a mixed bag of fun people yet each one showed her respect.

'When's the rest of your lot coming to work?' Kenny asked Maisie while he cleared the glass into the yard.

Maisie laughed and took the broom from him. She watched as he went to fetch a large piece of board and held it to the window frame whilst his Scottish colleague held a hammer ready to cover the damage.

'I'm it, I'm afraid. There's only me,' Maisie replied.

The Scottish soldier mumbled something but with large nails gripped between his teeth, all Maisie could do was throw a questioning frown to Kenny.

'I think he said something about slavery,' Kenny translated for her.

The Scotsman turned away from his hammering, removed the nails from his mouth and looked at her. 'Where's yer fowk? Wark?'

Without the nails in his mouth, Maisie just about understood his questions.

'I've lived here since I was four. I'm an orphan. It was an orphanage. I've become part of the furniture.'

Kenny raised an eyebrow and let out a low whistle.

'Sorry. Didne realise,' said the Scot.

'Now you know,' Maisie said. 'If I'm truthful, I'm a bit concerned about what's going on here today. It's happened so fast and one of the officials who came yesterday said they'd be back today to talk with me, and that you weren't due for several days.'

Kenny clambered down from the ladder.

'Can't help you there, I'm afraid. We got orders for the delivery today. Right. Well, we'd better get finished before the next run,' he said before leaving the room.

Another three truckloads of items arrived, and Maisie kept out of the way. She'd decided that since it was several hours past when the council worker was due, she'd take a walk to the common. When she reached the edge, she could see smoke spiralling from Shirley and the Southampton area. She heard the soldiers mention that over two hundred people had been injured in the night bombings, many dead and hundreds left homeless. She thought of Charlie and hoped he was safe.

Not wanting to see any more, she turned on her heel and walked back to the house. Several more trucks and cars lined the driveway and as she walked towards the building, a warm sense of peace washed over her. She now lived in a temporary rehabilitation unit, not an orphanage – until someone told her different.

Dodging large crates and pieces of furniture, Maisie

slipped around the back and into the kitchen. An enormous stack of tinned foods and other items, either in sacks or wooden crates, partially filled the room.

A young soldier stood counting the boxes and ticking them off on a list.

'Sorry about this. It arrived all at once and we need to feed them'—he thumbed towards the hallway—'once it's unpacked. We'll be out of your way, but I warn you, we'll be back.'

'How many will be eating?' she asked, dreading the reply. She couldn't tell how many men were on site.

'Twenty.'

'What will they be eating?' Maisie asked.

'Spuds, carrots, onions, all with a bully beef teaser.'

Bewildered by the confusion around her, Maisie decided she'd wait until she was told to start cooking. She'd cooked for six in the past, but only as part of what Matron had called 'kitchen education', and even then she'd only managed to fry eggs and bacon.

'Right. And a bully beef teaser is what, exactly?'

It was a question she had to ask, for if she was expected to cook it, she'd need the recipe.

'Basically it means open a tin of corned beef and cook the rest.'

Not wanting to appear ignorant, Maisie didn't reply, and instead turned to look at a large hot water urn on the kitchen bench.

'Now, that's a useful item.'

'It's full and hot if you want to use it. I'll be letting them in to use it soon, so best get in quick. They'll stampede through like kids in the sweetie shop.'

Maisie laughed. 'Yes, I witnessed their attack this morning.'

She edged her way around the boxes to the locked cupboard. She took the key from her pocket and proceeded to prepare a pot of tea from her ration collection.

'What's all that in there?' the soldier asked, and moved over to her side, peering into the cupboard.

'It's, er, well, um, my orphanage rations.'

'I see. So, they're not official . . . military?'

Maisie shook her head.

'No. They're mine.'

Realising she sounded selfish – or worse, greedy – Maisie hastily added, 'but I'll share them.'

'There's no need. You can put your own allowance in there and we'll use the remainder of the cupboards for the official stuff. I'll find out your allowance as I've not had to work it out for a female before. All I know is that you get a bit less.'

Pouring the tea, Maisie handed him a cup.

'Cor, I haven't had tea in a china cup since I went to say goodbye to my gran. Thanks.'

'I didn't want them to get broken,' Maisie said.

'Don't blame you. Heirlooms are precious nowadays. So many things are lost thanks to the Jerries.'

Unsure if a reply was expected, Maisie said nothing. She was saddened to realise the soldier thought the cups had been handed down by her family, but she decided they *would* become her personal property as there was no one left to claim them. She washed them up with care and placed them and the tea items back in the cupboard.

'Wait!' the soldier said before she could lock the door.

She froze and took a second to turn around.

He stood holding out a packet of tea.

'If you're going to be generous with your rations, I can be the same with ours,' he said and gave her a beaming grin and a wink.

'Thank you . . .'

'Jim. I know you're Maisie because there's only one female here and your name has been mentioned a few times. All good.'

When Jim left to gather a group of soldiers to put things away in the kitchen, Maisie ventured into the hallway and went to look around the rest of the building. The transformation was astounding. Her room had a 'No Entry' sign nailed to the door, and it was an indignant Maisie who ignored the instruction. She pushed the door open and, to her relief, the room was as she'd left it that morning.

The dormitory was set out as a large storage centre

for endless boxes of what looked to be medical equipment, and the bathroom also had a new sign. 'Female Staff Only'. In the old storage room, she noticed four unmade beds and all the clutter removed, giving the room a lighter, airier feel. She assumed the nurses would be on the same floor as her.

Downstairs, the frantic moving of furniture back and forth had finished. She volunteered to unload boxes of unused orphanage accessories to make the stark rooms more attractive. Maisie started inside Matron's old office first, delighting in changing the appearance from somewhere she'd once dreaded entering to a room offering relaxation and comfort. Large armchairs were placed looking out onto the grounds and all other furniture had been removed. When she'd finished adding a cushion here or draping a shabby chair with a checked blanket there, the room looked comfortable and inviting. The old dining room – the temporary matron's office – was now a room of official standing. Large filing cabinets lined the walls, a set of weighing scales stood on the opposite, and on the desk there was a heap of bits and bobs but she found a place for each item. Once finished, she gathered up a mound of stethoscopes and draped them from some old coat hooks.

Further down the corridor were three more rooms and Maisie saw they had also been made into comfortable seating areas. One room had shelves which she filled with books, and for the other she hunted out packs of cards and board games. Beside each chair she arranged small coffee tables that she'd dragged from the back of the old cupboard in the hallway and stacked the games on each one. She enjoyed the praise from the soldiers, who took it in turns to try out the chairs pretending they were lords of the manor. For a brief time, Maisie had fun in her home. She doubted it would last but she absorbed the feeling so she could look back on it for comfort on a dark day.

She wandered back to the kitchen and, to her delight, it was tidy, every cupboard filled with foodstuffs. A large sack of potatoes stood near the sink so she grabbed a peeler and set to working out how many potatoes were needed for twenty hungry workers.

By the time Jim returned, a flushed-faced Maisie had peeled her last carrot.

The large ovens heated the kitchen when both were lit, but with daylight dwindling, Maisie dared not open the back door for air. She needed lights on.

'What the . . .?'

'Something wrong?' a puzzled Maisie asked, as Jim stooped to look inside the ovens.

She had gravy which was browning in a large pot of Bovril-flavoured water and she stirred furiously. On the table were large metal tins, jugs of different sizes, and plates piled high next to a mound of cutlery.

'What are you doing?' Jim asked.

'Writing a book. What does it look like I'm doing? I'm trying to turn out supper for more people than I dare think about. What have I done wrong?' Maisie wiped her hands down her pinafore and waved them palm up in question.

'You, dear girl, have saved me and three others a massive job!'

'There you go, that's what happens when the government leaves an orphan in charge. She never quite gets the answer to any of her questions and has to muddle through life guessing. How was I to know you were going to do the cooking?' Maisie managed a laugh.

'I also hear you've transformed the rooms, which will save the ladies a fair bit of work tomorrow. You're a grafter, I'll give you that. Thanks.'

Jim saluted her and walked over with his arm outstretched.

'Jim Waddeston, cook for king and country. Soon to be part of the new Army Catering Corps by demand of the Quartermaster General. Trained at catering school, St. Omer barracks, Aldershot – at your service, ma'am.'

Maisie wiped her hands again, and took his, shaking it hard.

'Maisie Reynolds. No great chef, and no mind reader either. Formerly resident of this large establishment, brought down to earth by a sack of spuds for not knowing who's who round here.'

Jim's laugh bellowed out and he slapped his hand across his knee.

'You forgot to add Queen of Sarcasm. Brilliant humour you have there, Maisie. Keep it up. It will get you through life.'

Maisie pouted. 'I think I'll need a lot more than humour. Right, these bully beef teasers are ready. I'll drain the veg. Where are they eating?'

'Bully beef teaser?'

'My name for them. Well, yours really,' Maisie said as she pulled out large tins of corned beef covered with mashed potato.

The kitchen was filled with delicious smells and Maisie's stomach grumbled.

'Load up those tins and I'll send some lads down. The new sleeping and eating quarters are in House Two. This looks good enough to eat, so's best get it over to them fast!'

An hour after enjoying her own meal alone in the kitchen, Maisie made a start on the washing up. Although the day had come with some strange moments, she'd enjoyed each and every one of them. There there were a lot of people in the house once again, no one humiliated her, no one shouted at her, and not one person had bullied her into work. She'd been a free agent. To someone else, everything she'd done that day would have felt like a chore, but for Maisie she saw it as a sign of moving forward and doing her bit . . . and it made her feel good inside.

Jim marched down the corridor towards the kitchen. She knew it was him because his boots had a distinctive click, unlike the others.

'Leave those. We have spare hands for washing up. You're wanted in House Two. By the march, left, right.'

Maisie giggled. She removed her pinafore and patted her hair into place.

'Move it, soldier,' Jim quipped, and Maisie followed him across the yard and into what was once a ground floor dormitory. Beds no longer filled the space in row after row; instead, their place was taken by long tables pushed together. When she entered the room, a loud cheer went up and many of the soldiers bashed their cutlery against their plates or stomped their feet.

Will, the most senior of the men, held up his hand for silence.

'Miss Reynolds, we'd like to thank you for our meal. An unexpected night off for some, and the meal went down a treat. Here's to Miss Reynolds's bully beef teaser!'

Unsure what to do with such praise, Maisie gave a little curtsey and a grin.

'You're welcome.'

Will gave orders for his team to clean up and go about their duties. He instructed Maisie to join him in the room now known as the quiet lounge.

'We'll be heading off back to barracks soon and I wanted to thank you personally. We're a mixed bag, and some of the lads are overseas tomorrow, hence them hanging around camp and needing a distraction. You gave them a homecooked meal, and they'll not forget it when they're eating from an old tin can and dodging bullets.'

A shiver went through her and a sadness swept over her. She didn't know the men, but their friendly banter didn't deserve to be ripped apart by enemy bullets. She wondered how many of them were leaving loved ones behind or if, like her, they went to war with no one to lie awake thinking of them.

'Who is coming here to run the place? I'm still waiting to find out what's happening about my position.'

'Medical teams will arrive tomorrow. It'll be quieter than today and you'll have a few nurses to chat with – and a new boss, no doubt.'

Outside in the corridor she met Jim and he smiled and gave her another jovial salute.

'I've put a few things aside for you in a box. Lock them away. Good luck, Maisie, and thanks.'

Walking into the kitchen, she was sad to see the soldiers had left, but pleased to see all the pots and pans gleaming on the table. The box Jim had mentioned sat on her desk and on top of that sat a copy of *Rebecca* by Daphne Du Maurier, a book she'd not read. She flicked through and saw mention of an orphan girl. She smiled and held the book close. It was a gift, a treasured gift. The book might have come from the library, but Jim had selected it with her in mind. She'd never part with it. She also had no intention of parting with the four bars of chocolate and a packet of biscuits she found inside the small box underneath the book. Those, along with the china cups, would be stored in her bedroom for safe keeping. In the silence of the house, she mused over the strangeness of the day. She also thought of Jim's words about her having a new boss. How could she have a boss when she wasn't employed by anyone yet? With the orphanage closed she had no income coming her way. Tomorrow she'd have to sort out the situation once and for all.

CHAPTER 10

Peering through the window through which she'd once watched children leave to enjoy new lives, Maisie sat in awe watching uniformed nurses arriving. There were four in the first vehicle and three in the second. She loved the crisp whiteness of their aprons, and the swish of the capes they wore, and they had her admiration for keeping the tall, starched white caps from falling from their neatly coiffured heads.

Unsure as to what was expected of her, she remained seated. She stretched and yawned, all the while watching the efficient activity below.

Another yawn forced her away from the window. She needed fresh air to stay awake. The bombers had attacked with full force overnight, and listening to their constant drone and bombing distance, Maisie knew Southampton had fallen victim yet again.

Not wanting to get under the feet of the new arrivals, she pulled on her coat, grabbed her bag and headed downstairs and into the kitchen. Upon opening the kitchen door, she was greeted by excited chatter and all eyes turned towards her. The chatting stopped abruptly. Maisie felt slightly intimidated and held back from entering.

'Ah, you must be our civilian housekeeper. Come in. Don't stand in the doorway.'

A robust woman in uniform stepped forward and addressed Maisie. Before Maisie could reply the woman thrust out her hand in readiness for a handshake. Maisie winced when the firm grip of the woman crushed hers and shook it with great enthusiasm.

'Captain Bloom. Senior sister,' she said, her voice deep, firm, and commanding respect.

'Maisie Reynolds,' Maisie said and eased her hand away from Captain Bloom's.

'Apologies for not arriving yesterday when the hard work fell your way. The bombs blocked a few roads,' the captain tutted, then gave a brief smile. 'I must say, I've had a quick look around and you've done a wonderful job. We were informed of your hard work and we're grateful. You've made it homely. Just what is needed. You will find we are a mix of staff. Some navy, some army, but we're all here to do a job. To care for our confused and bewildered. We're not here for long, just long enough to establish the running of the place and then others will step into the breach. The Red Cross, I believe.'

'What am I supposed to do?' Maisie asked.

'Just your job, as you do. Keep house.'

'Cook and clean?'

The captain shook her head.

'We all cook and clean for ourselves until the first patients arrive. I then requisition the appropriate staff for those jobs.'

Still unable to think what her position in the house really was, Maisie said nothing until a nurse started clearing items away from Maisie's desk.

'That's mine.'

'Beg pardon?'

'The desk, it's mine. Until the window blew out, it had the best light. The things on it, they're mine.'

Not wanting to sound like a needy child, Maisie desperately wanted to keep the desk. She knew her days of quiet reading in the kitchen were over, judging by the giggles and squeals coming from two of the young women who were stocking baskets to take to the other buildings now known as Two, Three, and Four. Aside from the one they stood in, Maisie only knew of two other buildings and so assumed Four was the tiny cottage on the edge of the land, once lived in by the gardener and his wife, before both took up military posts at the start of war.

'Nurse Drage. When our male support arrives, see to it Miss Reynolds's items are taken to House Four.' Captain Bloom barked out her instructions to a petite blonde woman.

'Yes, Captain.'

Maisie went to raise her hand for attention, such was the effect the captain had on her, but when it came to it, she managed to speak firmly and clearly.

'I've lived in this building nearly all of my life. My room is upstairs, and I . . .'

Pulling off her cape and draping it over her arm, the captain spoke in an even firmer tone.

'Then it is time you had a change of environment. Change does one good. I have been shown the plans and I've made decisions about the way this place will work best for all concerned. Four will be your home from now on. We will not disturb you whilst going about our duties. Your bedroom will become mine. For the best. For the best. Take the time to pack your things, and they'll be moved by the end of the day. Now, where to start . . .'

Knowing the captain's speech was her dismissal, Maisie left the kitchen and went to her room. Life had become extremely confusing.

She apparently had a job, which no one had actually given her and no one had told her what was expected of her, nor whether she would be paid. If she'd guessed correctly, she was to move into a tiny one-up-one-down cottage with a small outhouse built onto the side for good measure. She had no idea what it looked like inside as she'd never been in there. How exciting to have a place of her own! Somewhere to retreat to after a day's work. She'd grown accustomed to being alone over the past months and after hearing the giggling from the new residents she felt maybe the captain had done her a favour. Once again, her thoughts went to the opinions of a Norah and Gloria on the matter. They would have had something to say for sure. Bemused, she began folding her clothes into a linen basket when a knock on the door disturbed her train of thought.

'I'll be busy for the rest of the day, Miss Reynolds, but would appreciate it if you could find fresh linen for the staff bedding. I noticed they are not made up yet. Tardiness is not tolerated, but I'll let it go just this once.'

There it was. The voice of authority belittling her yet again. A sharp retort trapped itself in Maisie's throat. The woman's tone was one of disapproval and reprimand. She responded in a polite voice.

'They are airing. The mattresses haven't seen the light of day for some time. I didn't want the bedding to be damp for the new residents.'

The captain took a step backwards. Maisie could see she was struggling with how to treat Maisie. She was a civilian and the precise rank and hierarchy of the situation had not been made clear, but it hadn't been a request, as far as Maisie could make out.

'Thoughtful. I must say, I am surprised you were employed for this job at your age, but I can see why going by the quality of your work elsewhere, hence my surprise at the lack of made up beds.' The captain spoke in a much friendlier manner and Maisie knew she'd earned herself a modicum of respect.

'I'm just as surprised,' Maisie said, not adding that she still didn't know who'd employed her, where her salary was coming from, or what she was supposed to do. She was not prepared to rock the boat just yet; she'd wait until she'd made herself too useful to remove. Maisie was in survival mode.

'I tell you, Charlie, the woman landed me with a job. The cottage was a mess. It's taken me days to clear the cobwebs. Don't get me wrong, I love the little cottage. It's incredible to be given my own home, but when I asked for help with the cleaning, they were busy elsewhere and had no one to spare. After all I've done for them!'

Perched on the step of the entrance hall, Maisie watched Charlie inspect the fire hoses for cracks. He'd listened to her rant on for a good five minutes, not interrupting her once. Finishing his inspection, he turned to her and gave her a beaming grin.

'Finished?' he said.

Maisie let out a loud sigh.

'I'm sorry, I've run on a bit, haven't I?'

'Just a little. You are fired up today, but I think I can understand why. It isn't Captain Bloom, is it? Is there no clue as to who your employer is yet?'

With a quick shake of her head, Maisie jumped to her feet and began pacing.

'None. The official chap still hasn't turned up. I telephoned but their building is out of action and switchboard couldn't help. The new people have assumed I'm the housekeeper, as I said earlier. It's all very confusing. That said, I am getting better food and I love having my own home. I daren't say anything in case I get kicked out, and then where would I go? My income no longer exists so I can't save for anywhere. It's all rather odd.'

'Strange affair, Maize. Strange. My dad said my Auntie Vi has a room if ever you need it. She's nice, my Auntie Vi.'

'That's sweet of her. Please thank her and I'll bear it in mind if I need help. Oh, talking of sweets, here. Mints from the army lads who came the other day.' Maisie handed Charlie a small twist of greaseproof paper with six sweets inside.

'Thanks. By the way, I've heard there's to be a party for some of the local kiddies and as you're good with children, perhaps you'd like to come along to help. I think nurses are in cahoots with the lads at the garrison and arranging it. The Canadian chaps have been very generous by all accounts. We got an invite to bring a couple of children from our street. Come along. Your nurses are bound to be going.'

Maisie thrilled at the thought that she might see Cam again. Even fully dressed . . . Maisie smiled to herself.

'I'll be there. I have no one to ask. I'll check and grab a lift with the nurses if I can. If not, I'll beg a lift from you.'

For the first time in her life, Maisie realised she really was a free agent, and could make her own decisions. The war had certainly brought changes to her life and she wasn't sorry about them. All Maisie could think of now was the party and what other surprises might be around the corner.

CHAPTER 11

Over-excited chatter greeted Maisie when she entered the main building where the party was to be held. The noise came from children and adults alike, and Maisie's heart went out to a couple of the little ones who were standing together, no smiles on their faces, just a look of bewilderment.

She rushed over to them and ushered them into the hall. She knew what it was like to be on the outside of everything and she wanted them to know that it was their party too and they had a right to have fun. Her heart went out to them. Thanks to the severity of the enemy bombings, their little lives were to be uprooted and they were to join the ranks of the other evacuees around the country. She smiled when they didn't need a second telling and ran off to join the other children who were receiving treats from groups of men and women.

Amongst the group, she spotted the face of Harry Cameron and everyone else in the room no longer mattered. She watched as he laughed and smiled with the little ones. He was so at ease with children and it sent shivers through her body. He didn't care what the other soldiers thought as he raced around playing chase with them. To Maisie it said a lot about his personality; he had a caring soul. She resisted the urge to run to him and beg him to chase her, to add fun into her life, to be her friend always. Charlie and Joyce joined her, and Charlie nudged her arm.

'It's rude to stare,' he teased.

'Stare? I'm watching the kids enjoy themselves.'

Joyce giggled and Maisie gave her a swift glance.

'What's so funny?' she asked.

'I think it's one big kid who's caught your attention, Maisie.'

'I don't have a clue what you're on about. Go and play with the children and leave me alone. Go, shoo.'

Maisie thought about what they'd said, and knew she'd watched Cam for longer than was proper, but the image of him part-naked at the sink simply would not go away.

She shifted her attention to the nurses from the house. They flirted, flicked their hair, giggled, and preened in front of the soldiers. Their intentions were clear. They were husband hunting. She watched their moves and smiled as each one gained a partner for the evening. Maisie moved towards the refreshment table loaded with glass bottles, jugs, and cups.

She selected a bottle, flipped off the lid with an opener, and poured it into a glass. The brown cola liquid hissed and fizzed. She watched the bubbles settle and she sipped it, watching Charlie and Joyce dance with some of the children skipping around them. The couple made every attempt to look elegant, but his gangly limbs and her short ones made it impossible for an onlooker not to smile.

Suddenly Cam was beside her, and he raised his head and jutted his chin to indicate her friends.

'They're a fun pair to watch.'

Maisie's stomach flipped and turned with excitement that he'd noticed her, but she dared not look his way, so continued sipping her drink and pretended to be focused on the dancefloor.

'They are, and the kiddies love them,' she replied.

'Have they been a couple for long? Married?' Cam asked and reached across her for her bottle to top up her glass, forcing her to look his way. Her hand shook and the liquid fizzed and spilled over the rim onto her hand. Maisie lifted her hand to her mouth to remove the drips.

'No. They met a year ago, but I've a feeling Charlie is like the cat that's got the cream. He's the happiest I've seen him since we left school. Joyce is lovely. All heart. Goodness knows what she'll do when he joins up. I've an inkling they'll marry.'

'Good to hear. There's a seat over there. Come join me,' Cam said and pointed to a table to their left. He touched her elbow and Maisie nodded.

'So long as I don't cramp your need to be alone and stare at the ceiling,' Maisie said, and gave him a grin.

Cam led the way into the shadow of the stage and she heard him laugh.

'Sorry about that. I was a little homesick that night.'

Cam pulled out a seat and waited for her to get comfortable before sitting next to her.

'It must be hard to be so far away from your family.'

A loud scream of laughter filtered above the music and distracted them. Excited children raced around chairs in the hope of not losing their chance to grab a seat. A memory caught Maisie with unexpected force, and she gulped her drink creating a choking event. Cam jumped from his seat and rushed to her side to begin patting her back. Tears coursed down Maisie's cheeks. Some for the memory, and others at the courtesy of the extra fizz racing into her windpipe.

The last time she'd played a game of Musical Chairs was with her brother Jack before he left. They'd raced around as the final two with just one chair to claim between them. As the music stopped and Jack raced towards it, he'd slowed down to allow Maisie to win. Everyone had cheered him and both had earned a lollypop. It was the only party they'd had together and the last one she'd been allowed to attend. It seemed like a lifetime ago and Maisie felt the urge to try and track Jack down strengthen inside her.

'Still with us?' Cam asked with concern in his voice.

Her coughing subsided but the tears still trailed their way to her chin. She dabbed them away with her handkerchief.

'Sorry. Bubbles. They reminded me of my brother,' she managed to gasp.

Cam gave her back a gentle tap and returned to his seat.

The noise on the dancefloor subsided and a trail of children were ushered towards the door. The party for them was at an end. For a brief moment in their little lives they'd been able to let off steam and forget the war. Maisie knew they would wake the following morning and take a long journey into another new and bewildering life.

'Poor little things. It's so sad. Soon they will leave their loving parents and it will be so hard on them. I can't remember my parents but I have vague memories of being left at the orphanage and it was frightening,' Maisie said, shrugging her cardigan closer around her shoulders.

Cam looked at her and leaned his head to one side in question.

'Oh, I thought you worked at the orphanage, or maybe you were the daughter of someone who worked there. I didn't realise the orphanage was your home. I'm sorry,' Cam said.

'Sorry for what? For not knowing I'm an orphan?'

'For you losing your parents, or for them perhaps not wanting you,' Cam said.

His words jolted her. She'd often wondered about her background and the reason she'd been sent to an orphanage but she'd never heard anyone say it, other than when Norah had spat it out as a cruel taunt.

'They might have wanted me – us, Jack and I were . . . *are* twins. I really don't know. I just say it, but who knows, maybe they couldn't keep me. I'm sure they are – or my mum at least, isn't dead. I have a vague recollection of someone who may have been our mother from before the orphanage, although it is a blur of a memory really,' Maisie said and shrugged.

'I didn't mean to upset you. I'm sorry. Let's change the subject.'

Willing to drop the subject and not go through the painful process of explaining that her brother Jack had been wanted but not her, Maisie settled back into her seat.

'What's Canada like? Is it much different to Britain?' Maisie asked and took a careful sip of her drink.

'It's large. Filled with beautiful mountain ranges. I'm from a small village in British Columbia called Lions Bay. It's at the bottom of two mountain peaks, mostly known as the Two Sisters. I live near the sea, which I love. I did think about joining the Navy like my older brother but I would much rather sail for fun, which we often do – *did* – as a family during the summer months. My sister is around the same age as you and she's a war-office typist. Mom keeps house and Pops is an engineer and is busy with helping the war effort,' Cam said. Maisie noticed the wistful look in his eye when he spoke of home and family.

'Is it a hot country?' she asked.

'In the summer. Cold in the winter. Colder than England. Deep snow – and I mean deep.'

Cam intrigued her and she was determined to find out more about him. He showed no sign of wanting to leave so she continued asking her questions.

'What is it you do over there?'

'I'm proud to say I'm now a paratrooper both in Canada and England. I've passed all the tests the British have thrown at us and I'm attached to a unit here. They sure know how to work us hard. Jumping from planes is the easy part. You Brits have grit, I can tell you.'

Wide-eyed, Maisie stared at him.

'My goodness, I think you paratroopers must have a lot of grit too, if you have to jump from planes. Why on earth would you want to do that? I can't think of anything I'd enjoy less!'

'It's exhilarating. What more can I say? It's something I have to do. What do you do in your spare time, Maisie?'

Maisie thought for a moment. She had nothing to offer which would interest him. No leaping from plane moments.

'I make tea for the firefighters,' she said.

Cam nodded in approval. 'And?'

'That's it. I don't get a lot of spare time now the nurses have moved in, and before that I was busy with the orphan children. I certainly didn't have time to go sailing, but what little I had or have, I fill by helping others. I get a lot of pleasure out of helping people,' she said with a shy smile.

'Is there anything particular you'd like to do?' Cam asked.

Rubbing her finger around the rim of her glass, she smiled up at him.

'I'd like to improve my writing. Maybe write stories or poems one day.'

Cam gave a slight frown.

'Why don't you now?'

'I don't know. It seems a waste of valuable time sitting around writing. I'd feel guilty.'

'Chase your dreams. Never feel guilty for wanting to improve your life, Maisie.'

Maisie smiled. 'I hold back because I think I need to have more life experiences to write about. I've led a sheltered life. Nothing exciting has happened for me to . . . well, to *feel*, and the poetry I've read has deep, powerful meaning. It's uplifting.'

Drawing breath and taking another sip of her drink, Maisie hoped she'd not bored Cam and searched his face for a sign he was ready to walk away. It pleased her when she saw him settle back into his seat and cross his legs.

'Poems don't always have to be uplifting. They can be melancholy or mood-altering.'

'I can alter moods, that's for sure,' Maisie quipped back and Cam gave a laugh.

'You have to have confidence in yourself. Besides, why not write poems? You don't have to show them to anyone. Do something for yourself. Write about past lovers.'

Maisie was thankful she didn't have a mouthful of drink when she burst out laughing. She clamped her hand over her mouth to stifle more giggles that were threating their way forward.

'Did I say something funny?' Cam asked.

'Past lovers? The last time I was kissed was a peck on the lips when I was twelve. Yes, you said something funny.' A flush of embarrassment washed over Maisie.

The reference to her innocent and lonely past made her fear that he saw her as a child rather than a young woman. She rose from her seat. 'I think I'd best pay attention to the children. That's why I'm here, to make sure they all get back home safely.' She smiled.

As she walked past his chair, Cam reached out and grabbed her hand, and when Maisie went to pull away, he drew her closer. Without warning, Cam placed his lips on hers and sent a wave of nerve-tingling flashes around her body. It was a soft kiss – but plenty powerful enough to take her breath away. She felt the warmth of his body through her clothing and enjoyed the comforting embrace he offered. She knew what was beneath his shirt and she let her imagination run riot.

Cam released her from his arms.

'I hope that helps towards your poetry. I confess it would have happened anyway; you gave me the perfect excuse to steal a kiss. I'm also leaving in the morning. I've another important training session and I'm not sure when I'll return.'

Maisie's heart skipped a few beats, before a feeling of sadness swept over her. She touched her lips.

'It was . . . inspirational. I've never met a kiss thief before,' she said.

Cam bowed theatrically. 'Always willing to inspire, ma'am.'

With disappointment, she saw Charlie heading their

way, and before the conversation was not hers alone, she leapt at an opportunity.

'Write to me. Would you write and tell me how you're getting along, please? I never get letters and I hate it when the postman delivers to everyone else. It's a purely selfish request I know, but it would mean a lot. Address it to Holly Bush, Shirley; it will find me.'

Cam nodded. 'It would be my honour. I'll do what I can.'

Feeling foolish for asking, Maisie gave him a wan smile.

'Of course, only if you're not too busy jumping from planes.'

One of the nurses waved her over and she waved back. It was time to leave if she was to get a ride back home with the nurses.

'Thanks for a lovely time,' Maisie smiled at Cam.

'Anytime, and thanks for the kiss,' Cam said with a cheeky wink, and before Maisie had the opportunity to say another goodbye, he walked away.

'Have fun?' Charlie asked as he joined her and the nurses who were saying their own farewells to new acquaintances.

'I did. Joyce not here?' Maisie hoped her flushed face didn't give away her response to Cam's kiss. Her body still tingled with excitement. It was a new sensation which, if asked to explain, she'd struggle to describe. It was like the ending of a loud piece of music, the heart-pounding moment when you waited for the cymbals to crash against each other bringing the pleasure to its crescendo. For Maisie there was no question that she wanted more.

'Powdering her nose. Scratch that, here she is.'

Joyce and Maisie embraced.

'I see you had a good time. Even better than the kiddies, I think,' Joyce said and nudged Maisie's ribs.

'I had a nice time, yes, thanks,' Maisie said, embarrassed that she and Cam had been spotted kissing.

When it became obvious that the nurses were lingering and her lift was to be delayed, Charlie offered her a lift home. Not wanting to sit around alone, she accepted.

As they reached Charlie's truck, a soldier called out to Maisie.

'See you around, Red.'

Buoyed up with the excitement of being with Cam, Maisie gave her hair a flirtatious flick, mimicking the nurses earlier, and called out to the group of soldiers from where the voice had shouted out from.

'Not if I see you first, soldier.'

The moment the words were out of her mouth she regretted them because she saw Cam smoking a cigarette, watching her. She gave him a wave, but he never returned it. Her heart sank when she saw him frown, throw the cigarette stub to the floor, and grind it out before walking away.

Glynis Peters

Maisie kicked herself for playing the fool. Cam looked hurt and she regretted her actions. Now she looked cheap and easy, ready to throw herself at any man who looked her way.

Charlie, keen on getting home before it got dark in case there was another bombing raid, urgently tugged her arm and pulled her up into the seat of the truck. He had a theory about the flying times of the enemy, and often boasted about his accuracy. As they rumbled their way out of the garrison, Maisie looked out of the window, desperately hoping to see Cam again, but the gates opened and they pulled out into the road ahead, leaving the base behind.

A deep-seated confusion set in. Was this feeling she had inside, the one creating rippling waves of excitement whenever she thought of Cam, lust? Was he interested in her or did he see this as an opportunity to seduce a British girl? Would he write to her? Her mind buzzed with questions.

Once home, she removed her dress and pulled on her dressing gown. A cup of cocoa and a good night's sleep would round off the evening, and she hoped the image of disappointment in Cam's face as he walked away would disappear. She touched her lips and recalled his kiss.

What she wouldn't give for another . . .

CHAPTER 12

No sooner had she got into bed with her cocoa than the sirens sounded outside and the thought of leaving her comfortable position was most definitely a negative one. Snuggling under the blankets, she tried to ignore the high-pitched squeals and flashing lights filtering across the sky from behind her blackout curtains. She tried to shut out everything that was disturbing her thoughts of Cam and his earlier kindness when he'd held her close. However, the barking instructions outside in the yard that came from Captain Bloom and included her name made her fully aware that her presence in the shelter was expected with immediate effect.

Tugging on her outdoor shoes and grabbing her bag of assorted sewing, knitting, books, and a pack of cards, Maisie headed outside.

'Thank you for putting in the effort to join us, Miss Reynolds.'

Maisie said nothing to feed the sarcasm of the captain. She hesitated before entering the shelter, but soon ducked her head when the captain nudged her forward.

'Inside, girl. Find a seat.'

Maisie made herself as comfortable as she could on a bench beside a nurse she'd only nodded at once in the past.

'Not a fan of enclosed spaces. You?' the young woman asked, inhaling and exhaling at an alarming rate.

'No, I'm not a fan either, and I *hate* this shelter,' Maisie said with feeling.

'Yes, the raids are getting more and more frequent. I'm Pat, by the way.'

'Maisie, and I spent time down here before the raids. Before the war,' Maisie muttered.

Pat gave her a quizzical look then nodded.

'Of course, you lived here before we came, didn't you? Was this a storeroom?'

Maisie didn't reply straight away. She tried to control the hammering in her chest which had started when they entered.

'A staff member was killed outside by a stray bomb and I had to lay her to rest in here until she was taken away. I used to be shut in here as a punishment if I'd upset our first matron. On my own, in the dark, from the age of four.' Maisie's eyes followed the flickering shadows around the wall. 'It's not my most favourite place to spend an evening. The other shelter is far too small though and we'd never fit inside.'

Aware that the talking inside the shelter had stopped, she looked about and noticed all the faces were looking at her. Maisie's cheeks warmed with embarrassment. The captain coughed loudly, clearing her throat in readiness to speak.

'Most of you won't be aware of Miss Reynolds's position here. Until recently, this was her home. We've invaded and moved her around without thought. It's nobody's fault, but if we are to blame the circumstances then the blame must be laid at the door of the enemy.'

Mutterings of agreement echoed around the shelter. The captain waited until they'd stopped. Maisie kept her head down, looking at her scuffed shoes, comparing them to the shining ones of Pat.

'All we can do now is offer compassion to those who will be joining us, and friendship to young Miss Reynolds here. She's been landed with the task of housekeeping for us. It is a monumental task which, I'm sure you will agree, she's performing admirably. Open your doors and your hearts to her and you will find ironed sheets will always be yours. Am I correct, Miss Reynolds?'

Giggles rumbled around the shelter.

Grateful that the captain had lightened the mood and

broken down the awkward barrier that Maisie had built between the nurses and herself by being shy and unsure, she lifted her head and smiled.

'If you have any mending, my door is always open. And if anyone could tell me what to do with this, I would be eternally grateful,' she said and touched her hair.

'Nothing. I'd do nothing. You've got a beautiful style which suits you and the colour is gorgeous,' one nurse gushed.

The rest of the nurses shared their agreement, and Maisie found it strange to have praise heaped upon her in such a way.

'It's frizzy and orange. She's just being polite,' Maisie mumbled to Pat.

'Nonsense. It might have been in the past, but you have a lovely head of hair now. I'd die for curls like that. It must take you hours to rag it and keep it that way,' Pat said.

'Rag it? I don't do anything with it. I wash it on a Saturday and just leave it to dry,' Maisie replied.

'Girls, listen to this. Those curls,' Pat pointed to Maisie's head, 'are natural. Can you believe the luck of the girl?'

The hours ticked by until the all-clear rang out at 1.35am. The captain released them all to their quarters and Maisie raced back to her little cottage. She gave a satisfied smile as she caught a glimpse of her red curls in the mirror and mused over what comments the other girls would have made had they seen her hair when she was little.

The following morning, she sought out the captain and requested a meeting. It was time to find out more about the job she was supposed to be fully aware of, and who was employing her. The captain appeared to have the answers, judging by her statement last night, and Maisie needed to know her future was secure, or to find out her options regarding leaving Holly Bush House.

An hour later, neither she nor the captain were any the wiser. The captain had thought Maisie's recruitment had been organised by one authority but a telephone call proved that not to be the case, and Maisie had assumed she was employed by the group of local government men who'd visited to sort the requisitioning of the building.

It appeared that Maisie had not had her name registered on any legal papers relating to the orphanage, which, as she pointed out to the captain, would account for her empty file.

'This is an unusual situation, Maisie. You need to fetch me your birth certificate for our records. I've also noticed that you're not registered for rations here. In the meantime, I'll make a formal enquiry about the process of getting you listed as a member of our civilian workforce.

You need a salary and food allowance, for goodness' sake,' the captain said and raised her hands outwards in a frantic, frustrated manner.

'When the army arrived, they put me on the new Holly Bush ration list, so I know I'm registered somewhere. Where will I get my birth certificate from?' Maisie asked.

'Don't you have it? Everyone has a birth certificate.'

With a slow shake of her head and a pinching of her lips, Maisie confirmed the negative. 'As I said, my file is empty.'

'Well, who does have it?'

'I've no idea. I can't think who might hold it for me. I've no clue about my parents and my twin has a new family.'

The captain moved across to the door and held it open. 'I'll do my best for you, Maisie. We can get a copy, I'm sure, but it takes so long that you'd be retired by the time it arrives. In the meantime, keep up the good work here. We'll watch over you.'

Smoke spiralled from the dock area. The closer Maisie got to the buildings where Norah's husband lived, the more obvious it was that the bombers attacking had found more than one target. Flames and smoke were the main feature in several piles of rubble.

Norah's home was untouched, but others around it

weren't so lucky. Doubting anyone would be home, but determined to resolve the situation regarding her birth certificate and official status, Maisie lifted the brass lion-head knocker, and gave a hefty rat-a-tat. She went over in her mind what she was going to say. Norah's husband wasn't the most patient of men and she didn't want to spend too long in his company – just enough to find out if Norah had ever spoken to him about Maisie's past. She heard footsteps clip along the hallway and the door creaked open.

'Maisie. What are you doing here?' Norah's husband stared at her. His unshaven face held no trace of a smile.

'I need to ask you if Norah ever spoke about me . . . about me and my brother Jack?'

Fred Bately rubbed his hand across his chin.

'Only that you were a lazy kid, a good-for-nothing. You know how often kind words fell from her mouth. She always was a miserable cow.'

Shocked by his words, Maisie didn't hesitate to nod in agreement. At last, someone else affected by Norah's spiteful nature.

'I can't remember that she said anything about you, not as an individual, like, just moaned on about her job and the kids. She did say that Matron was a sly one, and she wished she knew all the secrets the woman kept about some of the adoptions. Maybe she had a secret story about you. Are you some rich bugger's kid?'

Maisie, partially regretting asking and yet intrigued by his mention of secrets, pushed him for more.

'So, did Norah hint that she'd ever found anything out, that she had a hold over Gloria for something?'

Fred shook his head and yawned. Maisie knew her time asking questions was up.

'I'm sorry to have bothered you, Fred. Take care.'

'Sorry I couldn't help you more. Wait. She did hold onto Matron's things when the old girl died. I kept telling her to chuck them out, but she stuffed them in the shed. I'd forgotten about them. Old papers, I think she said. I'll fetch them. You stay here. Maybe you'll find something useful in one.'

A few minutes later, Fred appeared with two dusty bags. 'They'll need a brush off. I'll fetch a rag. They're not heavy so you can probably manage them home. I just hope they're useful. I don't want them. Not sure why Norah kept them. Hang on.' Fred returned with the rag and Maisie brushed off the worst of the mess.

'Thanks Fred. If I'm the daughter of a rich man, I'll let you know!' she said and picked up the bags.

'You take care. You ain't nothing like she said, you know. You're a good one, I can tell,' Fred called after her, and Maisie turned and gave him a bright smile. His life with Norah had been one she realised she could relate to, and the man had probably suffered just as she had.

Back in the cottage, she lifted piles of papers from the bags and eventually unearthed a file with her name printed across the front. She placed the file onto her small table, unable to open it for fear it might be empty of what she needed so desperately to read. Remembering that Captain Bloom was due to take her usual afternoon walk around the grounds at the exact time of three in the afternoon, she snatched up the file and stood at the end of her small garden waiting for the woman to pass by her gate.

When she spotted her turning the corner, Maisie called her over and showed her the file, explaining how she'd come across it. She invited the captain to come inside.

'I'm not sure why Matron or Norah kept it in her personal belongings, and it has me curious. Why would someone steal a child's file? Because that's what she's done . . . it's not hers to keep. I thought I'd got the only one, but thanks to Norah taking her things, here's another. The only thing is, I'm too scared to look. Will you do the honours?'

Maisie placed the file on the table and waited with bated breath for her to open it, and maybe discover more of Maisie's past.

'There's also an envelope with my initials on it and I can't bear to open that either. Silly, I know,' Maisie said.

Captain Bloom said nothing. She opened the file and

shook her head. 'There's nothing here to do with you, just adoption papers with the orphanage address filled in the appropriate boxes. She picked up the envelope and slit it open. She pulled out the contents and laid out some small pieces of paper, a few folded sheets and a faded photograph.

'It appears to be a collection of notes from someone named Juliana,' Captain Bloom said.

'J,' said Maisie. 'J is my middle initial. It's on the file I've got, too. Do you think my middle name is Juliana? Maisie Juliana Reynolds?'

The captain picked up another piece of paper.

'This says James.'

A hitch of excitement caught in Maisie's throat. Her hands flew to her mouth then she reached out for the paper.

'James? Do you think it's my father?'

Captain Bloom picked up the photograph. It was a woman, thin and wiry, and not smiling at the camera. She held a baby in her arms. Beside her there was a pram.

From her pocket, the captain pulled out a small magnifying glass.

'Handy for splinters,' she said when Maisie raised an eyebrow.

Peering through the glass, she moved the photograph around.

'If I'm not mistaken, there's another baby in the pram. Look.' She handed the magnifying glass to Maisie, but Maisie shook her head.

'I can see them without it and you're right! There's a little hand and a foot peeking out from underneath the blanket. Are they twins, do you think?' Maisie asked, her words high-pitched with excitement.

'Hard to tell, but logic suggests it is a picture of you and your brother. James is the formal version of Jack,' the captain said and tapped the photograph. 'What we do need is your birth certificate and that, I'm afraid, isn't in here. For a file with several years' worth of recording a child's life, there's very little written down, except how badly behaved you were. And that I find hard to believe.'

She gave Maisie a brief smile, but Maisie couldn't muster one up in return.

'Cheer up. I will help you apply for your birth certificate. Keep the rest of the things, but I don't think you'll get very far with so little information.'

Maisie gathered up the pieces of paper, placed them into the envelope, and pushed the file into the dresser drawer. She propped the photograph on the mantlepiece.

'I'll leave it there. If it was in my file, it has something to do with me. I don't own a photograph of anyone, so I'll pretend it's my mother until I find out the truth.'

CHAPTER 13

Maisie stared at a letter handed to her by Pat. She turned it over and over, stroked a finger across the envelope, and studied the stamp.

'Well, aren't you going to open it, my lovely?' Pat's soft voice encouraged.

'It's the first letter I've received since I was twelve,' Maisie whispered.

'Really?'

Maisie shrugged one shoulder. 'My friend Simon wrote once, but that was it. I don't know anyone else to write to me – except Harry Cameron . . . Cam . . . he's a Canadian soldier who promised to write, and I think he's actually done it,' Maisie said as she waggled the letter in the air.

'Ah, the soldier you kissed at the party. We saw you,' Pat giggled as Maisie threw her an embarrassed look.

'I'm off to pack. I'll leave you to it. When I get to my new posting, I'll write to you Maisie. I'll write so often you'll be fed up of receiving letters!'

Pat laughed again and gave Maisie an affectionate peck on the cheek. Ever since the night of the shelter, and the captain's encouragement of the nurses to befriend Maisie, Pat had kept a friendly eye on her.

Once Pat had left to pack, Maisie made use of a comfortable chair in the main sitting room. Two of the four new patients were able to eat in the dining room – or NAAFI quarters, as the captain liked to call it – and the other two were sleeping on the far side of the room, their snores competing with each other to be the loudest.

Maisie opened the envelope with care and slid out the letter.

Somewhere in England
April 5th 1941

Dear Maisie from the orphanage,

Forgive the opening, I couldn't resist. As promised, I'm writing to you, but cannot tell you much about what is going on around me.

The birds are singing outside and the grassy banks with spring flowers are far more welcome than the damp air we've had over recent weeks.

153

I heard Southampton has taken quite a bashing again from enemy planes. My hope is that all the folks I met while stationed there are safe.

What I wouldn't give for a smoked meat sandwich and a butter tart from my mother's pantry today. Our ration truck failed to get through, thanks to fires and bombed roads. We're told we might have to stretch one day's food over three days. The guys are not happy, as you can imagine.

Not sure what you want from a letter, from a virtual stranger who stole a kiss, so I will share a little more about myself and my home.

We have a dog called Bob, and an overflowing henhouse. My parents work hard and although we suffered during the Great Depression, Pops found a way to keep his engineering business afloat. Mom baked bread and sold it at the market. She gained a good reputation and funded us through school.

Aside from sailing, one of my hobbies is skiing, and the other is birdwatching. I find peace in seeing an eagle soar to the tip of a redwood tree and sit majestically overseeing the land below. It's a sensation I can relate to – the soaring, not the perching on a tree. I am not built for perching, nor do I have the grace and balance of a bald-headed eagle.

I love to carve wood. The smell of a sliced pine is nothing that can be described on paper. Maybe you will get the opportunity to smell one and understand what I'm trying to express.

If you want to reply to this letter, give it to Charlie; he's trustworthy and has access to the garrison. They'll get it posted on to me. It will be read before it arrives, so make sure no sensitive information is passed along.

Your friend, Cam
(Harry Cameron)

Maisie folded the letter and placed it back into its envelope. She slid it into her pocket and gave a satisfied smile. Cam had remembered to write; she hadn't put him off with her silly antics after the dance. As she moved around the building changing towels and linen, she tried to compose a letter in her head. By the time evening fell, Maisie had formed a draft letter, and sat down in her cottage to write a reply.

Holly Bush House
April 20th 1941

Dear Cam,

Many thanks for writing to me. It was quite something to receive a letter along with the other people here, and a pleasant surprise.

You are quite right; Southampton has taken a beating. The docks, a church, the factories, all burned and badly damaged.

I'm afraid this will be short as my life is simple. I've nothing to share about my background except that I was left here when I was four. I came here with my twin, but he was adopted, and I haven't had any news about him since. I now think my middle name is Juliana as I found a file hinting as much. Sadly, I have no birth certificate, and the captain in charge here is going to look into it on my behalf.

We have a few patients at Holly Bush House. The poor men are nervous wrecks and have nightmares. One thinks he's in charge and shouts out orders for us to run for cover and hide. He scares me witless when he does, but we have to duck behind the sofa until he's satisfied. I should imagine he was a fine protector of his men on the frontline.

The nurses are kind and I'll miss them when they're shipped off. We are to get civilian support from the Voluntary Aid Detachment as their replacement. It gets a little confusing with all the comings and goings, but I'm reassured that this will be the last of the changes for the house. I don't mind too much as it adds variety to my life; it's no longer boring, that's for sure!

The Forgotten Orphan

There is great excitement here as one of the nurses is getting married. I'm not certain I'd take the risk. Who wants to get married with this war raging around us? I'd be frightened my loved one wouldn't return. I'm worried about you and we've only just become friends.

I love the little cottage the captain allocated to me when she reorganised the placements. I'm not so annoyed with her now. I've a garden area, and I see that you and I have something in common. I've got a henhouse with four chickens and a cockerel. They scrap around and keep me in eggs. I got them when one of the nurses suggested that with such large grounds, we should turn part of it over for vegetables, and have a few hens. My friend Charlie's uncle keeps chickens, and I think Charlie got a little carried away when he arrived with a truck load of manure, twenty hens, and a cockerel. The captain insisted we cook four, I took on five, and the others are penned in the new victory garden. I've never had pets before and they give me someone to talk to when the others are busy. I must sound crazy, talking to chickens. Crazy Maisie. I named one Cam in honour of my new Canadian friend who stole a kiss. I bet that will make you smile.

Thanks to you, I've started writing poetry to pass the time in the evening – the ones when we're not *shivering in the damp shelter or on duty. I can't write in the shelter; the light is bad and the others chatter away. It's distracting which is annoying as we spend hours in there until the German planes finish trying to destroy us.*

It's time now to go and play a game of some description with a couple of patients. I like to get involved when I'm not working. It gives the nurses a break and I feel like I am doing something worthwhile.

> *Stay safe and my very best wishes,*
> *Maisie*

PS: I've included my first poem. I can share it with you as you are not here to see me blush. And as you made me blush with your kiss, I think it's acceptable to share my words.

Regardless by Maisie Reynolds
They drop the bombs, regardless –
Regardless of where they fall.
They aim and fire, determined –
Determined to destroy us all.

We won't give in, regardless –
Regardless of where we fall.

The Forgotten Orphan

We aim and fire, determined –
Determined to destroy them all.

With each blasting sound I hear,
Or when the sounds of violence cease,
Regardless of the outcome,
I pray for tomorrow's peace.

Handing the letter over to Charlie made her feel a little self-conscious, but she resisted removing the poem, or asking for the letter back. She had to find the courage to open up her small world and embrace communication with new friends. In true style, Charlie teased her about writing to strange men and goaded her by saying he would steam it open before posting it, but he stopped when he noticed he'd gone too far.

'I'm sorry, Maize. I'm a fool. Of course I'll deliver it intact and I truly hope he replies. He seems like a decent chap and obviously makes you happy.'

Maisie nodded the affirmative. 'He's made me feel special, Charlie. I didn't tell you but once he walked all the way here from the barracks just to see me. He said he was lost, but I don't think he was, especially after he, well, you know . . . kissed me at the party. Am I imagining this and being foolish?'

'Well, I wouldn't walk miles out of my way for I girl

I didn't think much of, so I think it's safe to say he's keen,' Charlie said.

'Thanks Charlie, and thanks for taking the letter.'

'Anytime. Take care and I'll see you again soon. Keep writing those letters; he'll appreciate them on a miserable day.'

Writing to Cam gave Maisie new courage, and that evening the enemy left them alone which meant that she sat in the comfort of her home compiling new poetry instead of crouching in the damp storeroom. Her mind relaxed and the words flowed. The sense of relief she felt when committing her feelings to paper and storing them in a pretty box one of the nurses had given her, helped Maisie release a small amount of pain and resentment from her past. She found a pretty pink ribbon and tied it around Cam's letter. It filled her with hope, and she kept her fingers crossed for another.

CHAPTER 14

'I've got you. Hush now.'

Maisie offered soothing words to a soldier who was hellbent on banging his skull against the wall. She flinched each time he bashed against her hand. This was not the way she'd planned on spending her nineteenth birthday.

It had started with a game of chess. One player shouted his annoyance and the young soldier's head had jerked up from the game and suddenly he was calling for back-up and support. He insisted the enemy was out to get him. He screamed out loud, his voice filled with terror.

Maisie, who had been mid-discussion with a local volunteer about cleaning window ledges, ran to his aid the moment he yelled, bounded out of his chair, and dived under the table. Pushing her to one side, he leapt to his feet and ran blindly around the room, growing more and more agitated the faster he ran.

Instructing the wide-eyed volunteer to seek help and escort the other men from the room, one of whom had released his bladder as a result of the loud squeals coming from the distressed man, Maisie continued to try and pacify the poor soldier with soothing tones. It surprised her how much the men resembled the scared orphan children with which she had until now been more familiar. An instinct within her told her to comfort them in the same way. She spoke with a calm, reassuring voice.

By the time help arrived, Maisie was cradling him in her arms whilst he sobbed. He rocked to and fro, and she stroked his hair, whispering to him until his sobs subsided into gentle whimpering noises.

'Hush now. You're safe.'

With a flurry of activity, the in-house doctor and two qualified staff took over from her, and Maisie stood back watching a brave, young man cry like a distressed toddler abandoned by their parent.

'Good work, Maisie. You have the knack of soothing him. Poor lad. He was part of the Dunkirk invasion. Should be thinking of a wife and kids at his age, not how to survive a war. He'll never recover. We can only help calm him down day after day.'

Maisie knew from that moment on that she'd never abandon those in need. She'd continue working to keep the residents and staff comfortable and give support whenever required. Her path was laid out in front of her. Leave and flounder, or stay and be of use and a comfort.

The doctor settled the soldier and Maisie watched his every move. He was a patient man in his late twenties. Two or three of the nurses had laid bets on who could get a dance with him at their evening events, but he was dedicated to his job and kept himself apart. This had earned him the reputation of being a snob, or worse, but Maisie saw only kindness and dedication – qualities to be admired.

The doctor broke into her thoughts.

'Have you thought about training in the QAIMNS, Maisie?' he asked as he washed and dried his hands.

'Training where?' Maisie asked.

'As a nurse, in the Queen Alexandra's Imperial Military Nursing Service. You have the exact qualities they need. You're calm and collected even under pressure,' he replied.

'Become a nurse? Yes, sometimes I think about it. I've often thought about leaving here but I'm drawn to this place now. It was a sad place when I was a child but now it is a home for those in need, and I would find it hard to walk away from the men who deserve our help here. I wonder if it is my destiny, to care for all those who need shelter at Holly Bush House.'

'It's admirable, sacrificing your life for another's,' the doctor said.

'Isn't that what they are doing for me?' Maisie responded, confused by his words.

'Point taken. Seriously, think about a nursing career.'

'I will, thank you, doctor,' Maisie replied.

Her pleasure at the doctor's words continued as she thought about the possibility of training to become a nurse. The doctor had made her feel useful, given her a sense of purpose, and it meant a lot more than he would ever realise.

'Are you sure, Joyce? I'm speechless.'

Maisie looked to Charlie and then back to Joyce. An overwhelming feeling of love for them both caught her unawares, and she rushed to Joyce and embraced her.

'Yes! Of course I'll be your bridesmaid! Oh, my word. I'm honoured. You've made me so happy. It was quite a day yesterday and today feels more like a birthday. Oh, and thank you for this beautiful notebook. I'll record my poetry in this from now on, rather than on scraps of paper.'

Joyce and Charlie exchanged a satisfied smile.

'It's good to see you happy, Maisie. And Charlie tells me you received a letter from your Canadian chappy. Good for you. Writing definitely has brought good things into your life.'

Joyce wrapped her arms around Maisie in a warm

embrace. Maisie valued her friendship and knew Joyce was genuinely happy for her.

'I am content with my lot now, Joyce. Life is choosing a path for me to follow and it makes getting through this war much easier. I had a lovely letter from Cam, and he's shared a bit about his life in Canada. I've written back but I'm not sure whether I'll get a reply. He was probably just being polite and keeping a promise.'

Joyce gave Maisie's arm a gentle reprimanding tap.

'Don't be daft. If he wasn't bothered about keeping in touch, he wouldn't have written to you. You have a lot to learn about men, Maisie. They do or they don't, that's the gist of it with men. Aren't I right, Charlie?

Charlie's shoulders shook with laughter and he held his hands up in submission.

'I suppose so. It's true, Maize, he wouldn't bother writing if he didn't want to.'

'It would be nice if you could see him again, too. It will happen, you wait and see,' Joyce said.

Charlie winked at Maisie. 'She'd like that, I can tell. I bet he'd not say no to another meeting, either.'

'Stop teasing and take her home,' Joyce instructed him and gave Maisie a smile of understanding. Maisie knew she'd noticed her embarrassment. Of course, she wanted to see Cam again, but she wasn't going to tell the world for fear of looking foolish.

She changed the subject.

'You didn't say when you were getting married.'

Charlie shuffled his feet and looked to the floor. A flush rose from his neck to his cheeks. Joyce brushed her hand over her hair and fiddled with her gloves.

'Before you leave, I assume,' Maisie said.

'Um, yes. Sometime before then – before November anyway,' Charlie said.

Maisie smiled at Joyce. 'It will be hard for you when he goes, but my door will always be open for a chat.'

Patting her shoulder, Charlie smiled. 'I knew I could trust you to be her friend when I'm gone.'

A silence fell between them. They all knew Charlie had meant 'when he left Southampton', but the word 'gone' resonated around them, leaving them in no doubt that the war could so easily take him from them forever.

Maisie's heart went out to Joyce. She knew very little about romance and love but she could see that what her friends shared was special. The glances between them, the soft smiles, were not those of two ordinary friends. A twang of envy shimmied through her. Maisie wanted someone to look at her like Charlie looked at Joyce. No sooner did the envy come than she kicked it back and reprimanded herself. Joyce had earned those loving eyes watching her every move because she gave the same glances and loving tenderness in return. Cam sneaked a kiss, and although Maisie hoped it would lead to a romance, she was not naïve. She'd witnessed nurses cry

over soldiers who came and went from their lives sometimes taking with them a girl's dignity and respect when
they were left with the consequences of a one-night stand.

'Right, you two lovebirds, I'm heading back. I'll walk
across the common; it will do me good. You spend some
time together.'

All the way home, Maisie composed her next letter to
Cam, and one to Pat. She formed a short poem in her
head and couldn't wait to transcribe it into her new
notebook. Paper was precious, with every scrap needed
for the war effort, and that made the gift from her best
friends even more special. It would not be wasted.

Life at Holly Bush was generally calm and as she worked,
Maisie could hear laughter and peace ooze throughout
the building. For one brief moment, the war didn't exist.
She thought about the pending wedding, and what she
would wear, and of life after the war and all the losses
that so many had endured. As she meandered through
to the kitchen with a pile of tea towels, she heard a
wailing sound from outside the kitchen door; it sounded
like a wounded animal. She opened the door and saw
the patient from the previous day crouched on the floor.
He was dressed only in his pyjama bottoms, which she
noticed were soaking wet. Her heart broke for him when
he leaned back screaming with his hands clasped over
his head. Maisie looked at his forlorn and bewildered

face that was contorted with pain. Another member of staff tried desperately to coax him inside, but he lashed out in fear. Maisie grabbed a dressing gown and fresh pyjama bottoms from the pile of clean laundry and draped the dressing gown around the man's shoulders.

'Fancy a walk, soldier?' she asked, offering a smile to the exhausted-looking nurse in front of him.

'Nurse is going to take a break and we'll get you into these dry trousers and have a stroll around the gardens. Do us both good. A bit of fresh air. Sound good to you?'

Maisie bent low and lifted the man's chin so he faced her. Dark rings looped his eyes and his pallor lent a ghostly shade to his skin. She hated to think what he'd been through to suffer so much in his mind. She touched his elbow and with gentle pressure raised him to an upright position. She gave soft encouraging instructions for him to remove his wet clothes and put fresh ones on and, after a few short struggles, he was dressed and leaning on her arm. She'd worry about washing him after he'd calmed down. They stood side by side watching the chickens scamper up and down their enclosure. The soldier twitched and jerked at loud noises, but eventually they managed to walk the perimeter of the gardens, twice. Colour formed in his face as the warmth of burning energy pinched his cheeks, and his interest in flowers became a verbal event after she pretended not to know the names of some; it was evidence that he'd once been a keen gardener. An idea formed and by the time they'd returned to sit and enjoy the company of the others, Maisie knew what she had to do to help the man, whose name she had learned was Billy. The courage of taking charge of the children after Norah died had instilled a new confidence in herself. No longer did she feel misplaced within the walls of Holly Bush House, and thanks to the urge to support Billy she actually felt more at home, rather than waiting unsettled for a result of some kind. Her daily routine had purpose and a positive outcome for another person. Her whole being had a sense of belonging and an even greater need to offer comfort to tortured souls.

Cam's friendship had settled her mind, she no longer wanted to go running off to find a new home, a new job. Holding Billy in her arms made her realise that her life was right where it was meant to be, caring for those who needed it, and waiting for a man who might return to steal another kiss. She hadn't planned to be the girl-in-waiting, but as she glanced across Billy's face and looked at Holly Bush through his eyes, she saw the grounds in a different light. They'd comforted her during her sad times and she'd planted roots of her own there. Plus, if her twin was ever going to look for her, this was where he'd look first, she felt sure of it. It was also where Cam knew to find her.

For now, this was where Maisie felt she needed to be.

*

Dressed in his new Engineers uniform, Charlie stood with Joyce who wore a smart green suit with a jaunty hat laden with the last of the brightly coloured flowers from Holly Bush gardens. Beside them, in a simple dress of cream and green floral printed cotton, Maisie smiled for the camera.

The flowers in Joyce's modest bouquet were tied with a length of ivy, and in her own hair, Maisie had formed a small spray with a white rose as the centre feature. Maisie had taken great pleasure in arranging the flowers and figuring out what would be ready in time for the wedding. Billy had settled into a potting shed they had created from an old garden lean-to and he quietly nurtured some of the more neglected parts of the grounds. His nerves settled more day by day, and his attention to detail when cleaning the tools put Maisie's cleaning skills to shame. When she asked him to be in charge of producing pretty wedding flowers for her friend, his joy was apparent and his enthusiasm tenfold.

'All done,' Charlie's dad announced, and the newly-weds abandoned their formal poses to mingle with their guests, leaving Maisie standing alone.

She looked around the room at the guests all sporting their Sunday best and smiling as if the war didn't exist. And for that day, it didn't. All talk about Germany invading Russia was soon quashed by Charlie's mother and those who wanted to continue their conversations took them outside. Inside, the room became stifling so Maisie went into the garden for air and to enjoy the warmth of the sun. The perfume of bruised lavender wafted her way and Maisie sought out the shrub, teasing her fingers along a stem and inhaling the cleansing fragrance. Voices chatted excitedly around her and a comforting feeling of wellbeing enveloped her. It was the perfect day. The smiles on Joyce and Charlie's faces beamed with happiness.

'Well, well, well, it is her. I'm sure it's her; red hair like that can't be found anywhere except this corner of the world. Holly Bush Orphanage, Shirley, Hampshire, to be precise.'

A well-groomed sailor strode Maisie's way, his smile beaming out friendship. Although much taller and broader than when she last saw him, Maisie recognised him immediately.

'Simon!' Maisie cried and with no hesitation, ran full pelt into his arms.

'Hello, Maisie.' Simon held her tightly and twirled her around.

Easing herself back, she stared at him. The teasing of facial hair hinted at a moustache across his top lip, and his hair, still white, was clipped close to his head.

'What are you doing here at Charlie's wedding?' she asked.

'I'm not at Charlie's wedding, I'm at Joyce's. To be precise, I'm at the wedding of the sister of my best friend . . . if that makes sense.'

'Her brother invited you? I didn't know you knew the family,' Maisie said.

Simon nodded. 'Me and a couple of other lads from the ship. We're on shore leave for a couple of days, and when he mentioned the wedding and invited us along, I jumped at the chance. Free beer is always welcome. I was going to pay the old place a visit tomorrow. Is it still standing? Never thought in a million years you'd be here, and still with a gorgeous head of hair. Less frizzy, but not faded one bit!' He lifted a curl with his finger and Maisie heard him expel a soft sigh. 'How've you been? What's my Maisie been up to all these years?'

Hooking her arm through his, Maisie felt a warmth inside she'd not felt for years. Happiness. Contentment. Excitement. All rolled into one. Simon was back.

'We've a lot to catch up on. Come on, let's get that beer for you,' she said.

Throughout the remainder of the day, Maisie hung on every word Simon said. His guardians had lost interest in him when he'd struggled to cope with learning a trade. They'd encouraged him to leave home and he'd taken work where he could and lived in hostels. The outbreak of war had given him the opportunity to settle into something more worthwhile. After relaying his life story, Simon listened to Maisie's.

'You never left?' he asked. 'That's quite something, Maisie. Why are you still there?'

'I want to help the poor broken men who have been brought to us to learn to live again. I've helped one man already and his flowers are the ones here today at the wedding. I try not to get too attached but when they're crying in your arms, it's hard not to comfort them. It's the least I can do.'

During the wedding breakfast, Simon, filled with beer, staggered around with his friends declaring his love for Maisie. Shocked by the change in him, but flattered by his attention, Maisie accepted the sloppy kisses he dropped on her cheeks or forehead. She sipped from his glass and enjoyed the intimacy of the act. She noticed Joyce frown her way a couple of times, but Maisie chose to ignore her and enjoy the attention for a change.

The wedding celebrations finished before the blackout to enable everyone to get home safely. With Charlie and Joyce spending one night together at a hotel before he left to join his unit, Charlie's mother had arranged for Maisie to be driven home by one of the home guard before he went on duty.

'Don't leave me Maisie. Stay, talk with me. Don't leave me lonely,' Simon pleaded.

'I have to go, Simon. Rules and regulations. You know how it is. They still exist at Holly Bush,' Maisie said and tugged her hand free from his firm grip.

Simon continued to make a fuss about her leaving, but when Joyce's brother pointed to a full crate of beer and suggested they head back to the house of some friends, Maisie knew her time talking about their past was over. She said her goodbyes and watched as Simon sauntered out of Charlie's home without looking back.

The intimate moments of sipping from a beer bottle, of holding hands, of Simon tucking flowers in her hair, were hers alone. They were a fabrication of her past and they were suffocating her present. For a fleeting second, she felt a pang of guilt for sharing those moments with Simon, and not giving Cam a second thought. Simon's presence had brought both happiness and conflicting emotions. He was rough and ready in his handling of her, and his bullish ways were in stark contrast to Cam's gentle ones. Cam had never known her as a little girl, he'd never witnessed her tears of frustration because no one loved her, but Simon had and today, she realised, he'd taken advantage of that. Cam treated her with delicate respect, and he teased her gently, properly, never going too far. Maisie knew in that moment that her heart was set at Cam's door. She wanted to be treated as the woman she had become, not the twelve-year old girl clinging desperately to a scrap of human kindness. If their paths crossed again, she'd put Simon back into the box of her past and not encourage him into anything more intimate.

CHAPTER 15

'That's right, an inch apart.' Billy's voice was soft yet authoritative. He found new confidence in teaching her how to grow their produce as they worked through a tray of vegetable seedlings.

The warmth of the summer sunshine touched Maisie's shoulders as she bent to plant out the small plugs under his guidance. Working with Billy, Maisie set aside all thoughts of war. They had both settled into a peaceful working relationship and Maisie's appreciation of the outdoors grew. Her mind took in the tranquil moments and she penned them into her precious book when she was off duty.

The sound of tyres on gravel distracted her. She looked up to see Charlie's father pull up in his truck, and Charlie jumped out and ran to her.

'Quick visit. Came to say goodbye, Maize. Joyce

sends her love and says see you Sunday for tea at her mum's.'

Charlie scooped her into his arms and held her tight. It was the most affection he'd ever shown her, and Maisie found it hard to speak. His going to war meant it was the first time she'd have to wave off someone who was dear to her and a pang of anxiety spread through her. Trying not to show her upset, she wiggled her way free.

'Put me down, you silly thing.'

Charlie stared her in the eye and his face took on a serious expression, one she rarely saw him wear.

'Thanks for looking out for Joyce . . . for my wife.'

'Your wife. It sounds so strange, and yet, so right. I'll look after her, don't worry yourself. Stay safe, and don't stand upright. You'll be an easy target at that height.'

Maisie chose humour to cover her sadness and earned herself a gentle thump of the arm.

'We've brought someone with us. He's hungover and waiting for us to say our goodbyes. He's a bit of a strange one and normally I'd hold him off at arm's length, but when he said he'd known you since you were little and used to live here, I made an exception.'

Maisie peered around Charlie's arm, and Simon waved from the back of the truck.

'Don't let this one overshadow the Canadian. Cam's

the reliable sort,' Charlie whispered as he pulled her in for another friendly hug.

'Thanks, Charlie. I'll be fine. You take care.' Maisie gave him a brief peck on the cheek, and waved to Charlie's dad, as Simon got out of the truck and joined her in waving them off.

'Lovely family. Good friend to you, I hear. Nice,' Simon said.

'Enjoy the beer?' Maisie said with a wide grin.

'Too much. Good job I'm not sailing today,' Simon replied and turned to face the main building. 'Nothing's changed. Still large and grey. Still looks like the old workhouse. The garden looks good though. That your chap over there? The one having a rough time?'

Simon waved to Billy.

'Want a cuppa?' Maisie asked.

Simon screwed up his nose and shook his head.

'No ta. Let's have a stroll around for old times' sake.'

'The old tree is still there,' Maisie said and pointed beyond the building towards the oak tree they'd sat under as children.

'Let's go and sit a while. My head's killing me.'

Enjoying the welcome shade of the tree, they sat and reminisced. The sadness of Charlie leaving was replaced by the joy of having another friend beside her again.

'Why did you stop writing, Si?'

'Matron told my guardians it was for the best if we

didn't communicate anymore. It was upsetting you far too much.'

Maisie gave a sharp intake of breath.

'That old witch. I begged her to find you. She told me you'd moved and I was to forget you. I kept writing to your old address but I bet she didn't post the letters. I had no money for stamps and she took the letters off me saying she'd drop them in the postbox!'

'It wasn't great with them . . . the new parents. They were just biding their time until I left. Not sure why they took me on, to be honest, but they claimed they knew my mother and wanted to do right by me.'

Maisie jumped to her feet.

'Come with me. I've got something to show you.'

Entering her home, Simon looked about.

'Cosy. You live here on your own?'

'I do. It's small, but it's my sanctuary after a day over there,' Maisie said, nodding her head in the direction of the main house.

'I couldn't imagine living here again. Too claustrophobic. Not this place specifically, but the whole way of life. The Navy is tough but I have support. Here, all I got was grief. I don't think I've ever been so miserable as I was living as an orphan.'

'You were luckier than me, that's for certain. Thank goodness we had each other for those few years. It's an unbearable life to live alone.' Maisie let out a sigh.

'I bet,' Simon said.

'Look. In my file. This is the picture I spoke of last night. Two babies.'

'Yes. I see. I wonder why Matron kept it with your things. Might be your mum with her other kids.' Simon peered closely at the photograph.

Maisie said nothing.

'Sorry. That was clumsy of me.'

Simon sat on one of the seats. He patted the cushion beside him. Maisie glanced at the clock. She'd completed all her chores in every house and no one ever chased her for jobs. She was a free agent for the rest of the day.

'Come and sit down, Maisie. Let's catch up some more. Snuggle up like we used to in the dark days.'

Maisie shook her head. 'I'll sit here. I've a feeling it will be safer.' She laughed.

'Spoilsport. I'm famished; have you got anything to feed a starving sailor with?'

Maisie cooked him an omelette and they shared a bottle of beer that Simon produced from his kit bag. It hadn't occurred to her that the day had drifted into night as they sat chatting. She'd unconsciously drawn the blackout curtains, but never registered the time until she yawned sometime later and glanced at the clock. It was nearly midnight! But Simon showed no indication that he was about to leave, nor mentioned where he was staying.

She rose from her seat.

'I'm tired,' she said and yawned again.

Simon stretched his arms above his head and arched his back.

'Me too. We've done a fair bit of chatting.'

'It's late. Where are you staying?' Maisie asked and looked towards his kit bag.

'My leave finishes midday tomorrow,' Simon said.

Maisie cocked her head to one side.

'That's not what I asked. Where are your lodgings?'

Simon shook his head. 'No lodgings.'

'Well, where *are* you going to stay?'

'Here. Where else?'

The hairs on Maisie's arms tingled upright. She could see by his face that he'd planned to stay with her all along.

'You can't stay here. I'll get thrown out. Rules. I can't just have sailors dropping by and staying over. Think about it.'

Maisie pointed to his bag and then to the door.

'You need to leave. Sorry Simon, but that's the way it is.'

'Come on, Maize.'

'It's Maisie to you. Only Charlie calls me Maize.'

Still seated, Simon patted the seat again.

'Sit down and we'll work something out.'

Maisie turned away and went into the small porchway to the staircase.

'I'll fetch you a blanket and pillow. You can stay there until five. I'll wake you and you will leave by the side entrance, across the allotments.'

Simon gave a belly laugh and flung out his arms.

'As bossy as always. I might have changed, but you haven't. I used to listen to every word and do as I was told, but tonight . . . tonight, I want to stay with you, to hold you, and take with me part of you. War is cruel, Maisie. I could be dead tomorrow.'

'And?' Maisie asked, a bitter taste forming in her mouth. Suddenly, Simon sickened her and she needed to get rid of him. She'd clung onto a childhood friendship that had nowhere to go, and it had to stop before it became an ugly nightmare.

Shoving back his shoulders and giving her a look of deliberately not understanding, Simon took a step towards her.

'And I want us to share moments we'll treasure forever.'

'Forever? Moments to treasure? Really, Simon? You are a sailor and, as naïve as I am, I know when I'm being led up the path of morning regret. My nursing friends warned me about men . . . about *boys* like you. One also taught me about the dangers of falling for sweet-talking servicemen. Sleep or go, Simon, they are your choices, but do not abuse the friendship we once had by ridiculous propositions of making memories before you ship out. As I say, sleep or go. Goodnight.'

Maisie gave Simon no further opportunity to speak and instead climbed the stairs to bed. His silence said it all. His interest in her as a young childhood friend no longer existed. He wanted to move into her present and she wasn't prepared to let him. Her desperate weakness of wanting to be loved meant she had to step away, to let him go. It wasn't him she wanted, it was the boy he had once been, the reminder that at some point in her life she had meant something to someone, that she had lived and felt something.

She heard movement, and then the familiar creak of her front door opening and click as it shut. The crunch of his feet on the pathway told her he'd chosen to leave by the main entrance.

Simon was gone, gone from her life, and Maisie knew it was forever.

'Ah, Maisie. You have a visitor. I've put him in the quiet room; there's nobody in there as the men are all eating breakfast.' A male orderly, who some suspected was a conscientious objector but who was nonetheless good at his job, found Maisie storing fresh linen in the laundry cupboard.

'Visitor?' she asked, but the man had already left by the time she'd climbed down from her ladder.

Patting her hair into some form of neatness, and removing her working pinafore, she wondered who else could be seeking her out. With trepidation, she stepped inside the room and found herself face-to-face with Cam. Her heart upped its pace.

She went to speak but he raised both hands in a semi-surrender position.

'I'm sorry I didn't ask permission to visit you . . . again, and I'm not lost this time, but it is all a bit last minute.'

Maisie indicated a seat across the room but Cam remained standing.

'I can't stay long. I have to leave this afternoon and don't know when I'll be back. I couldn't leave without trying to steal another kiss.' Cam laughed and took a step towards her.

Emboldened by his forward proposal and with the knowledge that she might never see him again, Maisie raised her eyes to his and gave a soft smile of encouragement. Simon had taught her a precious lesson. Cam meant more to her than a friend. *This* was a relationship she wanted to develop. Adult Maisie was ready to embrace him into her life.

'You don't have to steal, Cam,' she said, her voice barely a whisper.

He stepped forward and Maisie stood there, unsure what to do next but before she could make up her mind, she felt his arms fold around her and his breath flutter across the top of her head.

He stroked her cheek and ran his finger across her lips. Maisie lifted her face to his, indicating permission, and he accepted it in the form of a kiss so firm she had no doubt about what he might feel for her. Maisie returned the passion until they drew back from one another, breathless. They stood in silence. Eventually, Cam reached out and took her by the hand.

'I want you to know I won't – don't – have a girl in each town I visit. Maisie, I want you to be my girl. My someone to think about when times get tough. Someone I carry deep inside here, someone to give me a reason to live,' Cam said and patted his chest over his heart.

Maisie's heart skipped a beat. Her moment had arrived. She had met the man she wanted to share her life with. Oh, she knew that the war and the fact he was not a British citizen might prove a barrier at some point in the future but now wasn't the time to fret over that. Maisie pressed herself back into his arms and raised her face to his for another kiss.

When they pulled back from the soft, tender embrace, Maisie smiled at him.

'You know where I am, and if you can, write to me. Let me know you're safe. Always let me know you're safe. I'll stay here. This is my place until the war is over and you'll know where to find me when you're on leave again. I'll wait for you, Cam. I'll be here. I'll be your reason.'

Cam embraced her again. 'I'll come for you. I promise, Maisie.'

Maisie nodded. She knew tears were close and she didn't want to make a fool of herself. She wanted Cam to remember the image of her smiling back at him.

'I think you should go now, Cam. I've work to do and I'm sure you have a lot to do yourself.'

'Don't dismiss me, Maisie.'

'I'm not dismissing you, Cam! I'm protecting you from these blooming tears. See, now they've started. Kiss me and go, but make sure you keep your promise. Stay safe and come back to me, Cam.'

Maisie stood at the bottom of the driveway and watched Cam walk away. She imagined his back at the sink once again, and shivered with pleasure. Cam's presence caused a need in her to blossom that she couldn't describe. Simon unsettled her, worried her with his presence, something Cam had never done. Knowing she'd made the right choice, when Cam turned and waved, she blew him a kiss. He was her man, and she prayed he would come home safely.

CHAPTER 16

Activity in the main convalescing building was frantic. A member of staff had forgotten themselves and left the radio on, and two patients heard the news of Japan attacking Pearl Harbour, and the United States entering the war. Britain declared war on Japan, and the two former soldiers raced around issuing orders to prepare for attack. This in turn set off a flurry of fear amongst other patients and the bedridden. Those whose minds could no longer cope with the outside world, hid under beds. The building entered a state of chaos.

Maisie joined in with the care and comfort by leading Billy off to the potting shed; it was his safe haven where she knew she could leave him alone. As she strode back to the main building, she was called by one of the volunteer nursing aids, to sit at the bedside of one man in building three. He was determined to get out despite having lost both legs, and the staff member was needed elsewhere. The men called out to her from their beds and Maisie pacified them as best she could. The noise reverberated from room to room in the house as the news filtered through.

Maisie's hatred of the war grew the more every day. Across the sea, in enemy territory, there probably sat a girl nursing a wounded man much as she was and feeling the same way. Everyone's lives had been touched in some way. But feelings of helplessness and fear were no longer in her repertoire; their places had been taken by courage and strength. Understanding the details and logistics of where the fights were going on in the world was of no interest to Maisie. Her battle was here, at Holly Bush, helping to rebuild the lives of the soldiers in her care. The aftermath of war was her battlefield. It was wrong to ignore what was going on and she never shied away from listening to the news or asking how Britain fared, but Maisie couldn't allow herself to focus on the rotten core of it all. If she did, she knew she would start down the rocky road of fear and she couldn't bear to lose Cam at the start of what promised to be a wonderful romance.

For two hours, medical staff checked and monitored the distressed men and Maisie assisted wherever she could. By the end of the afternoon, some form of normality had returned and Maisie was given instructions to take the radio home with her to prevent the patients hearing it and suffering further panic episodes.

The following morning, she was instructed to take a break away from Holly Bush House as a reward for going above and beyond her duties; she also needed recovery time, she was told. Maisie decided to take the opportunity to visit Charlie's parents and arrived just as Charlie's dad was leaving for duty.

'Hello girl, come for a natter with Joyce? She's inside. Wife's at work. Joyce is lonely; she'll be happy to see you.'

Maisie, puzzled as to why Joyce wasn't at work, knocked on the door.

A pale-faced Joyce answered.

'Maisie. Come in. Lovely to see you.'

Joyce moved slowly into the kitchen, and Maisie joined her. The house smelled of disinfectant and fresh linen. Maisie watched as Joyce slowly folded clean bed linen and was surprised to see that she didn't present as her usual bustling self. Maisie picked up the corner of a sheet and helped with the folding.

'Are you ill, Joyce? You don't look well,' she said.

Joyce dropped her hands to her abdomen and curved them over a small mound.

'Kind of. I'm pregnant and am constantly dizzy or sick.'

A wide smile lit up her face, but soon left as she went pale and reached out for a chair.

Maisie rushed to her side and guided her into a seat.

'A baby! What wonderful news. I bet Charlie is thrilled. Oh, congratulations.'

A sudden wail of distress came from Joyce and it made Maisie jump. She watched as Joyce pulled a crumpled handkerchief from her apron pocket. She blew into it with such force Maisie feared for the baby.

'Why all the tears? Surely you're happy, Joyce. It's a baby. It's a shining light in all the gloom nowadays. You clever things. Congratulations!'

Joyce gave a huff of a laugh. She stood up and went to the stove, switched it on, and indicated to Maisie to sit down.

'I'm happy. Of course I'm happy. Charlie doesn't know I'm suffering. I've written to him but I haven't mentioned how unwell I am because I don't want him to worry. He's got enough on his plate. The Engineers will be moved because of Britain declaring war on Finland, Romania, and Hungary, according to his dad. What with yesterday, and the announcement that we are at war with Japan now, I don't think he'll ever come home!'

A further bout of sobbing ensued, and Maisie found it hard to control her own tears. She put her arm around Joyce to comfort her and thought of Cam, and what it might mean for him.

'I've got news of my own. Cam – my Canadian friend as you call him – well, we kissed. It was a while ago, but with Charlie leaving I didn't like to talk about our relationship as it might have upset you,' she said shyly.

Joyce grinned. 'At last. But, don't get carried away when he comes home. Bide your time for such things. Get married and have a life together after the war. It's heartbreaking doing it this way.'

Joyce stroked her bump absentmindedly.

'You regret marrying Charlie?' Maisie asked.

'No, silly. I regret falling in love with a man who had to leave and fight a war. What people don't know, is we had to get married 'cos I was pregnant. Sadly, I lost it, but this one is hanging on for dear life, thank goodness, I just wish it didn't make me feel so sick. After Charlie's last leave I had an inkling I'd fall again, and well, here is the evidence.' Joyce patted her pregnant belly again, her joy evident.

Maisie felt her face flush.

'Oh, I see. The baby is why you married. But you would have married him anyway, so what's the problem?'

'Not being together. That's the problem. I miss him so much.'

No longer wanting to see Joyce in such distress, Maisie suggested they go for a walk. Joyce declined.

'The air will do you good.'

'I'm not strong enough to get to the end of the road. I keep fainting. Charlie's mum got me a piece of liver the other day because she thinks I need iron in my blood. I tried to keep it down, but this little one threw it back. I'll be fine, Maisie. Come and see me again, but don't sit here waiting for another smile. I've not many to give at the moment.'

Maisie leaned over and kissed Joyce on the cheek.

'Maybe you'll give me one for Christmas. Keep your chin up, Charlie will get more leave before he's shipped out, I'm sure. And you'll have him fussing over you for days. I hope you feel better soon, and I'll drop by in a few days to check. It's a bit busy at the house, but I've always got time for you my lovely. No, stay there. I'll let myself out. Take care.'

On her way home, Maisie fretted over Joyce. She'd lost a baby and never said; it must have been a sad time in her life. Goodness knows how alone she must have felt with Charlie away. Maisie made a pact with herself to be a better friend and visit Joyce more often. She'd hate to be in the same position. Her thoughts turned to Charlie. He was a kind and loving soul and must have been heartbroken at his wife's news. Men so far away from home must be suffering similar heartbreaks. She wondered if Cam ever received bad news from Canada. Being so far away from home must be hard.

Once she arrived back at Holly Bush, Maisie picked up her pen and scrawled a letter to Cam. She wanted to reassure him that she was there for him, that she was still waiting for him, and he could think of her if he needed some comfort while he was away.

Holly Bush House
December 15th 1941

Dear Cam,

I have good news to share. Charlie and Joyce are having a baby! Isn't that wonderful news? A new life is forming amid the horrors which surround us to give us all hope.

How are things with you? All is well with me, but I'd be happier if you were here so we could chat and relax together. I light the fire and often imagine you sitting in my little cottage, cosy and warm, rather than out there fighting for your life, and for all of us really. Have I ever told you I am grateful to you for protecting us? My real-life hero jumping from planes.

It is very sad about Pearl Harbour. I wonder what will be in store for us now.

The day you left, I meant to tell you that an old friend of mine from the orphanage came to see me. Simon has changed. He's not so kind-spirited as I once thought he was. It's funny how life changes us. I used to be a timid girl and now I have the courage to do things I'd never dreamed of doing, such as kissing Canadian soldiers – well, one soldier. I mean it. Only you, Cam. I promise. I'm waiting for you.

Take care and come home to me soon.
Merry Christmas when it arrives.
Maisie, with my love

CHAPTER 17

1942

As pretty as the snow might look, Maisie hated how it ground everything to a halt. She trudged miles on slippery pavements and her legs ached. Charlie never made it home due to drifting mounds blocking roads, nor could the postman could make it to Holly Bush, and it was a frustration for all.

Although this winter wasn't as severe as the past three had been, the snow was a hiccup in Maisie's daily life. Billy still insisted on tending his plants in the potting shed, and Maisie's time was often spent persuading him not to freeze to death.

Before the bad weather had set in, a letter from Captain Bloom had arrived, as well as a short one from Cam. In the warmth of her home, Maisie finished the last of her darning for the staff and patients, then opened her letter from Cam to re-read it before settling down to write one in return. She had three to post once she was able to get out to the post-box.

Europe
December 19th 1941

My dear Maisie,

I'm still alive and I have survived many experiences I would rather not repeat again. One of which is getting my leg caught in my parachute strings on a practice jump. Dangling upside down from a tree with only a squirrel for company wasn't the best half hour I've ever spent.

It is my hope you receive this letter but with the situation we find ourselves in, I won't hold my breath.

Should you receive it, I wish you a very merry British Christmas and send you a kiss as my gift.

Thank you for sharing your magnificent poems. You have talent. Keep writing!

Any news on Charlie?

Any more news on chasing down your birth certificate? I find it a strange situation. Your life story fascinates me. Mine is mundane in comparison.

To be fair, I've not a lot to write and tell you. Well, I have, but it would all be censored out.

Please, take care of yourself and stay safe. I long for the day when we can be together again. I'm going to be bold here and put in print the words I want to say out loud.

I love you, Maisie Reynolds. It happened faster than I'd ever expected, but there's no denying the feelings I have for you and I know it's a love I want to share with you. Always yours,.

Cam

> *Holly Bush House*
> *January 10th 1942*

Dearest Cam,

Thank you for your last letter. It did make me giggle. Just the thought of you dangling from a tree was funny enough but to be watched by a squirrel, well that had me laughing.

Things are not too bad here, although I have very little time to myself nowadays. Our workload has increased so much; it's heartbreaking.

I had a letter from Captain Bloom and she's

struggling to trace my birth certificate. I'm beginning to wonder if I ever had one – the mystery child.

It's a frustrating process without one though. The Red Cross is taking over Holly Bush and increasing the nursing bed capacity. Captain Bloom recommended I stay to assist the patients. She wrote a letter of reference and mentioned the difficulty with my certificate. They seemed satisfied by her letter as I've received the relevant forms, and confirmation approving my post as a nursing assistant.

From what I gather, the only thing which will change is my uniform as I do everything the others do anyway. I will get to study first aid and basic nursing care. I have never thought of myself as a nurse, but I'll get a taste of it with the Red Cross training.

Billy, our recovering soldier, is potting on so many plants we'll be self-sufficient with a large variety of vegetables come spring. I've a horrid feeling the enemy pilots will be guided to bomb us by the mass of bright flowers he has plans to plant out in the warmer weather. Keep your eyes open as you float down! It does my heart good to know I've helped someone find a way to escape from their nightmares. He's not fully recovered, and will remain here for the foreseeable future, but he's improving.

The Forgotten Orphan

The hard days for me are when I think about you. I worry you will be shipped back to Canada one day and I'll never hear from you again – or if you do write, I'll never see you. I have days where I long for your arms to hold me. I keep wondering whether there is a magic spell to make the world right again so we can be together. I look to the stars at night and make wishes. Silly I know, but it makes me happy. You make me happy. I dream of the time you stole a kiss and of those I gave back with no regret. How I'd love one of your kisses right now.

Stay safe, my love, and don't forget to stay out of Hitler's way!
Maisie

CHAPTER 18

'Ah, Maisie. Post arrived this morning. There are a couple for you,' one of the staff members called over to her as Maisie walked past the office. She took the letters and looked at the postmarks. She noted one was from Cam and her heart skipped a beat of excitement. The other one wasn't handwriting she recognised and carried a local postmark.

'Oh, and a man named Fred Bately arrived with a bag for you,' the staff member continued. 'He said you'd know what it was about. Some dusty old thing. Billy's taken it and put it in the potting shed.'

'Thanks. He's the husband of someone who used to work here. He must have found something that he thinks I should have.'

Offering up a grateful smile, Maisie slipped Cam's

letter into her pocket to read later in peace and tore open the other.

Maisie,

I am sorry for being a complete buffoon at the wedding and at the cottage. I'll be deep at sea by now and won't be back for several months. Not only am I writing to tell you I'm sorry but also to say that I worked alongside a chap who said he was from Southampton area. We got chatting and it turns out he knew us both, but I don't remember him – Alec somebody or other. I told him about you and Jack, and he said he's sure he came across someone several years back at naval college who mentioned having a twin in a Southampton orphanage. I asked him to hunt him out. He couldn't remember his name but thought it might be Michael something. Anyway, I'll not get your hopes up but thought I'd let you know.

In my thoughts,
Simon

Maisie reread the letter and scrawling handwriting. It touched her that Simon had put the effort into apologising, and also that he had sent her a note about the men he mentioned. It wasn't a letter to excite her, as so many boys had come and gone from the orphanage over the years, several sets of twins amongst them, but she thought it kind of Simon to write and tell her anyway.

After her busy shift, Maisie stood proudly waiting for a signature to sign her off on her bandage wrapping technique. As praise was heaped upon her, Maisie realised it had never happened much in her life at all. Unsure how she was expected to respond, she thanked her tutor and smiled.

'You have a good work ethic, Maisie. You think. You see something is wrong and you work it out . . . and you have the patience to finish it. You should be proud of yourself. It's fine to feel a little pride for one's achievements. Well done. Now, go home and rest. You've earned it.'

Wasting no time, Maisie raced back home to change her clothes. Curiosity about the contents of Grace's third bag and Cam's letter called to her, and she rushed through her basic chores before tugging the bag inside. She wiped it clean and tipped out the contents.

For a woman who'd been responsible for so many children, Gloria had very little to show for her years as Matron at Holly Bush. No pictures or letters from children settled in new homes, and not one memento from her own life.

When she'd finished sorting through the contents of the bag, the only items remaining on the table were a key and a box. The box had once housed toiletries and had no need of a key. Several pieces of yellowing paper sat in the bottom of the box and Maisie picked her way through in the hope of finding something of use.

Pulling out each piece, Maisie laid them on the table in the hope that they might link together in some way.

Wicked
Cruel
Hopeless
Unhappy

The first two words she could relate to Gloria, the others to herself. But where did they actually feature in Gloria's past? Who were they from?

Unable to find answers, she switched her attention to the key. It was too large for a jewellery box, too small for a pantry or door. It reminded her of an office cabinet key but Maisie knew that all the cabinets belonging to the old orphanage had been sorted, emptied, and reused. She had done most of it herself.

Putting aside the key, along with a fountain pen and ink, and a silver photograph frame, she tucked the papers inside her file and set about removing the remaining unwanted items from her home. Cam's letter begged to be read, but Maisie wanted to be relaxed and settled before she absorbed his words.

As she carried the last box into the storage unit behind the main building for disposal, Maisie spotted a nurse burning unusable bandages in an old drum converted into a brazier.

'Rough night, Coleen?' Maisie called out. She and Coleen had shared one or two shifts together over the past month, but they'd never had the opportunity to spend much time chatting.

'Very. Jimbo had terrible nightmares again and undid a few stitches.'

Coleen poked more bloodied bandages into the fire with a stick. Both stood silently watching the smoke spiral skywards.

'He's had it tough. Losing friends at sea, and then his family in London – three children, his wife, and mother. It doesn't bear thinking about. I've my parents and no siblings, and so far they've been safe in the countryside with my aunt.' Coleen chatted as they watched the fire burn itself out.

'I've no one either. Well, that's not strictly true. I have a twin brother, but they separated us when we were four,' Maisie said.

'Really? That's so sad. Do you see him much?'

'Never. I remained here,' Maisie made a wide sweeping movement with her arms,' and no one told me where he went. I tried to track him down but got nowhere. It's sad but there's nothing I can do about it now.'

'And you never thought of leaving?' The nurse stared at her, wide-eyed.

'Often. Especially when I felt abandoned and thought no one cared. I'll be honest with you though, since the place has changed hands, I'm doing better now than I ever was. I love what I do here. I feel part of something special.'

'You're the something special, Maisie. I've seen you work. You're good with the men. A calming influence. And we love having fresh sheets on our beds without having to wonder where they came from! You work so hard, but I've never seen you have fun. Why don't you ever come to the dances with us?' Coleen asked and checked the fire.

'I don't like to ask. I'm shy in that way,' Maisie said.

'Well, stop being shy. You really have no need to be nervous of us. You're part of the team, remember. Don't hide away. You might meet a knight in shining armour to whisk you away.'

'I have one – I think. Cam . . . he's a Canadian paratrooper.'

Coleen let out a low whistle. 'If you're gonna catch one, catch a good one, I always say. Good on you! You kept him quiet.'

Maisie laughed. Coleen was bright and cheery, just the person to buoy someone up when they needed it most. Her voice lifted at each end of each sentence and Maisie asked where she came from. Loughgall, County Armagh was apparently a quaint place which grew apples, and Coleen intended to return once she'd finished battling Hitler, to make and drink cider.

'We're going to a dance over at Aldershot next month. A hall outside of barracks this time, one where the forces and locals can mix. They've started holding regular get-togethers, and they are such good fun. I'll speak to the others and tell them you're coming with us. No arguments. If your man comes home, he can come too!'

Pushing the ash around, Coleen nodded her satisfaction.

'That's all out now,' she said of the smouldering pile. 'I'll catch you tomorrow and fill you in on the dance arrangements. Take care.'

Maisie rushed back home in high spirits. She boiled the kettle and filled her hot water bottle, tucked it under her covers, and drew the curtains. Downstairs, she made the room cosy and settled down to read Cam's news.

She looked over the envelope for clues of where he might be stationed but there was nothing.

The Forgotten Orphan

Still somewhere in Europe
February 14th 1942

Dear Maisie,

How I wish I could hear your voice again and see that sweet smile. I want – no, I <u>need</u> to hold you in my arms and know all is well in the world. I know our friendship – relationship, call it what you will – is new but I feel I've been waiting for someone like you to walk into my life. The war changes our perspective on life and I've a clear vision of what I want when it's over. You. I want you in my life. It's wrong of me to ask that you wait for me, but knowing that you might keeps me going.

Happiness is so rare nowadays and thinking of you makes me happy.

Letters from you make me happy, and as you can probably tell, happy is the word of the day for me. That's because we all made it home after our last mission. Usually, at least one or two don't make it, and then we're made to feel vulnerable once more, but this time, all my brothers came home with me and we celebrated in British style, with a cup of tea.

Well done Captain Bloom for recognising your

skills. You will be an asset to the Red Cross. I keep an image of you in my head, one where you are studying or writing poetry at your table. My busy bee.

I promised to write to you, but I never know what to say. I feel we have a deep friendship growing, thanks to our kisses, but we know so little about each other, so here's a little more about my life in North Vancouver, British Columbia, Canada.

Today, I think back to swimming in Deep Cove, and sailing there with my father. It's such a great place to enjoy summer. Eating lobster and clams with my cousins on a summer evening at Granville Island is a time I'll never capture again. Those cousins are now scattered around the world, fighting the enemy, or looking out for their own children at home.

One of my most treasured times was when we visited an old friend of my father's in Tofino, which is a place on Vancouver Island. Never have I felt so welcome, and my schoolboy history lessons faded into nothing when I met the men from an indigenous tribe who were so old and true to Canada. Pops would spend hours trying desperately to communicate in their native tongue, and they would tease him with wonderful humour.

The Forgotten Orphan

I made a summer holiday friend there, and we spent time in the waters fishing. His tribe were true Indian natives and had an incredible knowledge of living off the land and were expert whale hunters. My friend and I kept to trout fishing – much easier on the arms. Such happy relaxing days. They carved wood, and I still have a small totem pole he made for me in my room back home.

If only mankind could get along like children do and stop trying to dominate and obliterate each other. Forgive me, I am reminiscing a lot these days, holding on to boyhood memories. Most of us are. I confess, some days I am scared, scared of what's to come. I can only dream of the good things in life; I dream of you.

Stay safe. I send my love in this letter.
Happy Valentine's Day.
Cam

CHAPTER 19

'If we tuck it in here, and add a tie-back, it will make it like this one here.' Maisie pointed to a magazine Coleen had brought, along with an old dress she had decided to make over. She'd come to beg Maisie to help her re-make it in a more up-to-date style.

The two of them had already spent much of their free time together, including an evening at The Forum cinema. Coleen had introduced Maisie to the joys of new musicians and singers by insisting her gramophone, along with her collection of records, were to live in the cottage. She said it was the only place where she got the opportunity to listen to them without someone asking her to turn it off or down.

Maisie absorbed each new experience and couldn't wait to share it all with Cam in her letters. After Coleen left armed with a new outfit, Maisie sat down and wrote a new poem and included it in the letter.

Holly Bush House
March 15th 1942

Dear Cam,

How I enjoyed your last letter. Canada sounds like a wonderful place and somewhere I think I would like to visit. Your memories are good ones to hold on to. If only I could share memories of my childhood with you, but alas, you have seen more of England than I have, and I really do not have anything interesting to look back upon. Meeting a handsome Canadian paratrooper is the most exciting thing to have happened in my life but I cannot share it with you as you were there!

My days are not so lonely now I've a companion. Coleen is a nurse and we work most shifts together. She's Irish and great fun. She teaches me so much about life outside of this place. We listen to music and she keeps me updated with the latest fashions. I sew much better than her (she said that; it's not me boasting) and we recreate outfits by copying them from magazines. I am now a great fan of Glenn Miller, and The Beverley Sisters. What wonderful uplifting music they share with us. My feet tap even if I try to prevent them.

It might seem silly to you getting excited over songs, as you jump from planes and fight the enemy every day, but it gives me something to hold on to during the times I'm alone and to fill the space you left behind.

Joyce's bump is growing fast, and I've the honour of being the child's godmother when it arrives about August time.

I have been sent more things which once belonged to the old matron of this place. I have the pen I am using to write this letter, a key, and a box which has no keyhole. I can't think what the key might belong to, but she had kept it secure inside a little box, so I assume it is important to someone. I've not thrown it away in case I find the rightful owner or a keyhole it fits. It's an odd thing, throwing away keys. I can't bring myself to do it. I had some from broken cabinets in the orphanage and I put them in a tin inside a cupboard. What use are they? I think I'll give them to the metal collection to be made into bullets or something useful.

The weather is improving – windy but not so cold. I don't suppose you would appreciate windy days in your job. I still cannot imagine how anyone could jump from a moving plane. You are so brave.

The Forgotten Orphan

I'm going back to Aldershot soon. There is a dance – for adults this time – civilians and servicemen and women mixed. Coleen insists I join them. There are hundreds of Canadian soldiers based here now, but never fear, I only have room for one in my life.

Another poem for you to enjoy.

Winter Died Last Night

It brushed my skin – the warmth
Of a gentle breeze alerts me,
Winter died last night, yet
No mourning will you see.

A blade of grass, a satin petal,
Oh, new life, a simple thread.
The birth of Spring renews me,
Winter passed away; it's dead.

Spring arrives full glory,
It carpets the world with green,
Bursting buds and rainbows –
We forget Winter has ever been.

Stay safe.
With my love,
Maisie

Saxophone music blasted from the hall and loud laughter reached Maisie's ears before she'd even stepped down from the truck.

Coleen shook out the creases from her outfit, and Maisie touched the curls at the base of her own neck – just for something to do. Her fingers trembled as she readjusted her skirt and removed her gloves. She knew she'd made the right dress choice as it felt comfortable around her bare legs which she'd painted with cold tea and which now sported a false seamline of amazing accuracy, drawn with care in eyebrow pencil by Coleen. The navy dress with a Peter Pan collar was another updated outfit which had been donated by one of the other tiny-waisted girls.

According to Coleen, the dress fitted and draped in all the right places. When Maisie first saw herself in the mirror, she was surprised by how glamorous she looked compared to her normal appearance.

'We're sure to have fun. Look at all those handsome faces,' Coleen said and linked her arm through Maisie's.

Maisie looked, but wouldn't have said the grinning faces staring over at them were particularly handsome. Happy, for sure – and some she would describe as leery – but in her mind, none were as handsome as Cam. Her heart fluttered at the thought of his good looks.

'Tonight might be your lucky night, Coleen. A husband might lurk amongst that lot,' Maisie teased her friend and laughed. More laughter came when one of the soldiers shouted over the noise and called them twins.

She and Coleen were the opposite in height and shape. Coleen had more flesh on her bones and was much shorter than Maisie. She was a pretty girl with red hair, but nowhere near as red as Maisie's. They'd both joked that Maisie might have Irish blood running through her veins, but Coleen said she'd never seen anyone with such deep colouring in Ireland. Another girl wondered if it was Scottish blood, as she had once nursed a Scot with the same thick mane.

The thought of having a Scottish mother or father appealed, but before she could ponder the idea anymore, Coleen was nudging her inside the hall.

Maisie gasped. The room looked different from when she'd last stepped inside. Bright bunting decorated the walls and lights draped with a coloured cloth gave the room a completely different feel compared to the afternoon of the children's party.

Male voices boomed out deep resonating laughter, a total contrast to the poor men recovering at Holly Bush. Maisie's ears tingled with the happy sounds. A Glenn Miller song she recognised came on and she watched the floor fill with gyrating bodies.

'Wanna dance, Red?'

Maisie looked up at the tall soldier grinning at her with anticipation and gave a polite smile.

'I . . . um . . . thank you, but I don't.'

Without waiting to see if she'd change her mind, he headed towards another female victim.

'Your loss,' he muttered.

Coleen and Maisie giggled together as they watched him walk away with a cocky swagger.

'Where's your sense of adventure, Maisie?' Coleen said, composing herself as a group of men looked their way.

Maisie played with the fringe of her evening bag, a gift from Joyce.

'The moment they use the name Red, I freeze. It's the name for a film star or something, not me. Besides, I can't dance, which might prove to be a bit of a problem out there.' Maisie pointed to the dancefloor at the many bodies performing their skills to a new jive.

Coleen nodded and shouted above the music which had now been turned up more than a notch.

'If Hitler can't see us, he'll hear us! You have film-star quality about you, Maisie. Use it. Flaunt it. Have fun. Life's too short.'

Before Maisie could reply, Coleen was swept off her feet by a very enthusiastic Canadian who was not taking no for an answer.

'What, no dancing for Maisie from the orphanage?'

A familiar voice cut through the vibrant tones of the saxophone and Maisie's insides fluttered with excitement.

She turned to see Cam standing beside her, his eyes gleaming with amusement.

'Cam!' Maisie shouted out, looking at him in shock.

'Hello Maisie. Well, at least that's who I think I'm talking to. Look at you!' Cam let out a low whistle of approval and chuckled when Maisie gave him a twirl.

Cam winked approvingly and grinned widely. 'How's things?'

'Good. Better now you are here. What a wonderful surprise! When did you get back? I never dreamed you'd be here. I thought you'd be dangling from the edge of a plane or somewhere more glamorous.'

Cam raised his glass to her.

'Aldershot isn't glamorous? Well, well, who'd have thought.'

Maisie gave his arm a light punch.

'Stop teasing me.'

Cam made a melodramatic pretence of being injured and laughed.

'You wound me. Stop it, you cruel woman.'

Maisie's heart flipped as she enjoyed their banter. She longed to experience another of his kisses but held back, not wanting to make a fool of herself in case he rejected her. It was far more public than at the children's party or the room where they'd last kissed. Maisie was determined to enjoy every second they had together but she also didn't want to put him off by being too forward.

She sensed he was enjoying the moment, too. Kissing could come later.

'No woman out there for you to dance with, Cam?' she teased.

Cam stared out across the room, making a game of seeking out a companion.

'No. She might be standing right beside me though.'

Before Maisie could say anything, Cam had grabbed her bag, placed it on the table beside him, and pulled her onto the dancefloor.

'Cam, no. Stop. I can't dance.'

Fixing his eyes on hers he shook his head, and she stopped resisting.

'I'll lead you. Relax. Let me hold you. Like this, yes, that's right.'

Cam's arms held her in the waltz position, and he tapped her right foot with his.

'Slide it, lift, and tap gently down.'

The warmth of his breath against her ear and the firmness of his hold brought Maisie's heart rate to a racing level. Her mind filled with unexpected questions.

Was this passion? Was it lust? She'd heard about lust from her friends' giggles and chats. Maisie concluded that what she felt when Cam held her close was most definitely lust. His body melded with hers at one point and she made no objection.

Coleen moved past them with her partner and stared

open-mouthed. She winked at Maisie who felt the blush of pleasure burn into her cheeks and was thankful that the lights were dimmed. At one point, Cam pulled her so close they danced chest to chest. She sensed that Cam also felt that there was more between them than friends who'd shared stolen kisses. They were two people who'd written the words but had never been able to act them out together. Neither of them let go; they clung to each other in silent declaration that they were a couple.

They stared into each other's eyes as they moved carefully around the gyrating enthusiasts. She snuggled close, inhaling his scent. It stirred her innermost feelings, and when she glanced up at him again, he winked and ran his tongue across his lips. It was the most intimate experience of her life, and Maisie couldn't resist stroking his neck as he rested his lips on her forehead.

Throughout the evening, Cam and Maisie were glued to each other. They talked and enjoyed several intimate dances, but she drew the line at the livelier ones, protesting that learning to dance one style was enough for this evening. Coleen and her new friend, Ted, joined them and the four of them laughed the night away. Maisie had never experienced an evening like it and occasionally sat back just listening to them talk about their travels and lives before the war. Ted was the son of a farmer and intended to return to take his place at the head of the business once it was all over.

After a while, Maisie realised that Cam didn't speak about his future plans the way he had in his letters. He told them of the past, of waterfalls and logs, of pine trees and raccoons, but always with a wistful, distant look in his eyes. His homesickness was apparent . . . and it scared her. What if Cam became so homesick that she no longer featured in his plans of a life together? What if he just upped and left when his job was done? No matter how many times she'd given herself a good talking to, Maisie always had a niggling pang of insecurity when it came to Cam. How much of herself should she invest in him? For tonight, it would be all she could give, but would it be enough? Maisie reached out and touched his hand as it rested on his knee. He turned and looked her full in the face.

Maisie held his gaze. For a fleeting moment she wanted to reach into his mind and soothe any troubled thoughts he might have.

Coleen and Ted were too involved with each other to notice, and Maisie let the stare linger. Cam's hand slid out from underneath hers and he stroked her fingers.

'You have beautiful fingers,' he said and wrapped his own around hers. Lifting them to his lips, he placed a soft kiss on each one.

Maisie said nothing. She just let the warmth of his touch send shockwaves around her body.

As the pleasant tingling sensation increased, Maisie

thought more about Cam's nature. He had a gentle, kind manner with no hint of aggression if something didn't go his way. He treated her with respect. His attention was solely on her but at no point did he make her feel uncomfortable and he never took advantage. She'd witnessed other girls removing the wandering hands of servicemen from buttocks or breasts but Cam never overstepped the mark.

The silent moments between them were filled with unspoken words. The conversation was soft and relaxing, amusing and fulfilling.

When it became clear that the end of the evening was only a few dances away and the slower paced, more romantic tunes filtered through, Cam encouraged Maisie to her feet, and they swayed in unison around the floor. He stroked her cheek with a tenderness that indicated their friendship had progressed to a different level.

'Never stop writing to me, Maisie. I couldn't bear it,' he whispered.

Maisie laid her head against his chest. 'I won't. I promise,' she replied.

No sooner had the tender moment passed, another emotion hit Maisie tenfold: fear.

From the corner of her eye, she spotted a staggering Simon across the room, and the menacing look he gave her as he puffed on his cigarette communicated a message loud and clear. He was not going to ignore her and Cam.

As she went to pull away from Cam, Simon took his first step towards them.

'Cam, please let me go and walk right out of the building. You're not safe. My friend Simon is heading our way and I've a horrid feeling he's drunk. I've seen that look on his face before when we were children. He punches out for his own way. Something has made him angry, and I've a feeling it's you.' Her words came thick and fast, and she took steps to make sure a gap separated them enough to end their intimate time together.

A puzzled Cam looked at her and then turned around. But it was too late. Simon had lashed out and his fist caught Cam square in the jaw. To Maisie's horror, he did it again. She screamed.

Ted and several friends crossed the dancefloor along with several other servicemen. It happened so fast that it was almost a stampede. The music stopped and several girls ran to surround Maisie. Chaos ensued.

Simon hit out at anyone in his path and took another swing at Cam.

'Leave my girl alone.'

His voice was slurred and threatening. Maisie knew she had to speak out or it would end in a bloodbath. She stepped out of the circle of protective girlfriends and spoke with a clear voice, although she shook inside, both with anger and disappointment.

'Simon, this is Cam, my boyfriend. Please, stop.'

Simon scowled at her and took another swig from a beer bottle.

Maisie looked at Cam nursing his jaw. He stood there, tall and dignified.

'Leave us alone, Simon. Leave *me* alone. You can't treat me like this; it's ridiculous.'

Simon threw the bottle to the ground where it shattered before stepping closer. Maisie held out her hand to Cam to prevent him from moving. Simon swayed and steadied himself against the table. He tapped out a cigarette from a box and after a few attempts lit it and puffed heavily on it. No one moved. Everyone was waiting for the tension to ease and for Simon to lose interest and walk away. Maisie decided on another approach to calm the situation.

'How have you been, Simon?' she asked and added a smile.

Simon peered through glassy eyes and took another drag on his cigarette, releasing the smoke her way. Maisie took a step back and Cam placed a steadying hand on her back.

'Shut it. I've been watching you behaving like a dockside whore. Good job I was here to stop you making a fool of yourself.'

Simon staggered towards her as he spat out his words and Maisie ducked away.

'I've known him for nearly two years. He's not

someone I've just danced with tonight. We've been writing to each other and he's important to me – not that it's any of your business,' Maisie finished.

As she regained her balance, she saw Cam stretch back his shoulders and adjust the sleeves of his jacket.

'No, Cam. Don't get into trouble because of him . . . because of me,' she pleaded with him and threw a look of help in Ted's direction.

The main doors burst open and several more alcohol-fuelled soldiers staggered inside, all spoiling for a fight. Most chose to support Simon and with a whoop and a shout, punches were thrown and tables were over-turned.

Coleen put her arm around Maisie.

'Let's leave them to it, Maisie. I've seen this before. Tension and frustration at this awful war has to come out somehow. There'll be bruised eyes and hangovers tomorrow, but it will be forgotten by dawn.'

Although she wanted to leave, Maisie knew Simon's temper was at its maximum level. She'd seen him get fired up as a child and she remembered how pushy he had been that evening in her cottage. He'd lashed out regardless of the consequences. She knew he would punch and fight it out until blood was drawn. She'd ignored this side of him back when they were children because he'd been her only friend.

Cam didn't stand a chance. For some reason, Simon

considered Maisie his property and seemed to want to fight for her despite her objections. He was an intensely stubborn man on a mission to destroy all enemies. Maisie had seen it before; it was a basic instinct in a lot of orphans who'd lived at Holly Bush. She'd seen both boys and girls fight for what they wanted until knuckles bled. The less you had, the harder you fought to keep it. Tonight, his fists pummelled at anyone within range and Maisie stared on in dismay.

He'd ruined her special evening. Why hadn't he come over and asked her for a dance if she meant that much to him? Why had he felt the need to rant and rave with violence at the forefront of his mind? Eventually she had enough. Simon's behaviour was beyond acceptable and she wanted him gone from her sight.

'Stop it! Come here, Simon. We need to talk.' Maisie shouted across at Simon.

He swung a potluck punch at the soldier nearest to him and swaggered over to her.

'Come to your senses, Maisie Reynolds? Realised what a real man can give you after all?'

Simon's words slurred into one another and Maisie looked at him with disgust.

'How dare you ruin our evening. Who do you think you are coming back into my life after all these years and hurting people who mean something to me? You always have been and always will be a puffed-up bully.

A fist fighter with no care for anyone but himself and I want you gone from my life. Our past is evil and gives me dark nightmares. I don't want that dragged into my future by you or anyone else. So, as I say, go get out and stay away.'

Simon took staggering steps closer and Ted and friends pulled him back from reaching out to Maisie. He glared at her and Maisie shivered.

'Get him out of my sight,' she said to Ted.

Simon struggled against the restraining arms of the men hauling him across the room. His language was a disgrace and Maisie held her breath as Ted and friends dragged him through the double doors of the hall and out into the night.

Maisie turned away from the scene. She was hurt, and very aware that her face was flushed with embarrassment as she looked at the man, still nursing his jaw, who'd brought her nothing but pleasure. She reached out to touch it and he clamped his hand over hers in such a protective way that her breath caught in her throat. He loved her and she him; this was his declaration.

Unaware that tears had formed, Maisie felt the tickle against her skin as they dripped down her face. Cam leaned in and dabbed them dry with his handkerchief.

'He's not worth the tears, Maisie. I've known – I *know* – many men like him. Aggression is their sport. He hasn't hurt me. He's only angered me because he's hurt you.'

The few lingering women backed away and Coleen blew her a kiss.

'We'll leave you with Cam to talk in private. I'll wait outside with the others,' she said.

The atmosphere in the room had changed; the evening was over. Maisie's resentment of Simon grew. He'd ruined the evening for everyone, not just her and Cam.

'I must go,' she whispered.

Cam pulled her closer.

'I can't bear to leave you, knowing he's following you,' he said, his voice raspy with desperation. 'I'm so angry that I can't stay and protect you.'

Maisie put her finger on his lips.

'I don't need protecting. This is Simon and this is his way. You have to understand, we had nothing as orphans except each other. An outsider would never understand.'

Cam reached out and stroked her shoulder, but Maisie flinched away from his touch.

'That was years ago. I don't want to be an outsider in your life. If not for the war, I never would have met you. We lived thousands of miles apart and led different lives. You need to let go, Maisie. You don't belong to the orphanage anymore. Simon has no claim on you. You're a nurse now with a new life and it's time to leave the past behind.'

Cam stroked her cheek again, and Maisie felt the fight

leave her body. Cam had a stronger hold on her than she'd imagined.

'I can't give up on him. We've only just found each other again; he needs my help.'

'You need to walk away for your own safety. Listen to me. He'll try to drive us apart, but I'm telling you Maisie, this is meant to be – *we* are meant to be.'

Cam's lips brushed the tip of her nose, her forehead, but then, before he could reach her lips, she moved out of his reach.

'No. We can't. He's powerful. I can't let him hurt you again. I've seen his temper in full – when we were children. Maybe I don't deserve happiness? There must have been a reason I ended up at the orphanage. You're too good for me. Perhaps we should not see each other again. End whatever it is we are starting,' Maisie said and burst into tears.

Cam took her hands in his and squeezed them tight.

'I'm not letting you go, Maisie. You're safe with me.'

Maisie drew in a breath as Cam traced a finger down the front of her neck and nestled it at the top of her breastbone. He tapped out her heartbeat on her skin and she felt it like an echo of her soul. She'd never experienced such a tender expression of desire.

'I have to go or I'll miss my ride home. I'll write to you. Please be safe, Cam. Thank you for a wonderful evening. I am so sorry Simon—'

Cam drew her against him and placed his lips on hers. His kiss was hard and bruising with its passion. Maisie relaxed into it and when he drew back, she sighed. But then she shook her head when he moved forward to kiss her again. She saw the hurt expression filter across his face. 'If we carry on, we'll never stop. As wonderful as that might be, I think I'd better go home. Come and see me before you leave again.'

'I'll try. I can't promise. We're on a tight turnaround. Maisie, if I don't return, please know that you are loved. Deeply.'

Cam's words and his kiss were more than Maisie could deal with and she let her tears flow. Unable to compose herself, she shook her head and walked away.

'Just stay alive for me, Cam. Stay alive.'

'I'll keep coming back to prove I am, Maisie. I will. As long as you wait for me . . .' he called out after her.

Cam's words lingered behind her, but Maisie didn't dare turn around. Noises from outside indicated the scale of the aggression had risen. She sighed. All because of Simon. Some friend he turned out to be, another orphanage let-down.

'Get her home. I'll find you again,' Ted called out to Coleen who'd raced to Maisie's side.

'I'm so sorry. I'm so, so sorry,' Maisie said to her friend.

'Don't be silly. It wasn't your fault. You did nothing

wrong. The difference between man and boy was pretty obvious tonight. Let's get you home.'

The truck ride home was head-spinning for Maisie. The other girls wanted to know about the mysterious sailor who'd thrashed his way through a group of strapping servicemen. Maisie hated the fact that they seemed to admire Simon's behaviour. All except Coleen – she expressed her disgust at what he'd done and how he'd treated Maisie. After all, he'd ruined the evening for everyone.

Back home, Coleen hugged Maisie tight.

'Sleep and don't fret.'

'Cam was lovely, but I'm scared I'll lose him, too. Everything in my past is a mess and I'll ruin what Cam and I have between us if I don't keep Simon at bay.'

'Cam is still lovely and no you won't, unless the war takes him from you. A blind man could see he's hooked and going nowhere. Stick to your guns and keep writing to him. It's part of your war effort duty, don't forget. Keeping up the spirits of the troops is important. Government's orders.'

Maisie raised her eyebrows.

'Simon will ruin it all if he keeps turning up like that. Cam won't like him trying to pull us apart.'

Coleen huffed.

'He'll get bored of it all when he finds a girl willing to bend to his demands. Simon is the past, don't let him ruin your future. As I said, focus on Cam. I can't wait to see Ted again. Now, there's a man. Get some sleep and remember the nicer parts of tonight. Who knows where they might take you . . .' Coleen gave her a wink and Maisie pushed her towards the door.

'Keep your innuendos to yourself, you. Sleep tight and I'll see you on duty tomorrow,' she said and clicked her door shut, turning the key in the lock. But sleep was the last thing on her mind, and she allowed her tears to flow.

What if Cam never came back to her? What if he was killed?

CHAPTER 20

Weeks passed and to Maisie's relief, she heard nothing more from Simon. She received a hastily scribbled message from Cam in which he reassured her that all was fine and he longed to hold her again. The note brought about more tears and Maisie found it incredible that she could produce so many over the simplest of things.

Coleen would often bring up the events of that evening until Maisie asked her to stop; the painful experience of the dance was something she wanted to forget.

Ted and Coleen's friendship had developed into more and on occasion Maisie felt a twinge of envy. Ted was a generous man and Coleen declared her love for him at every opportunity.

A friend of Ted's was introduced with the very

obvious intention of distracting Maisie from Cam, but she found nothing interesting about the man and eventually Coleen gave up trying.

Life took on a pattern of work and minimal leisure activities. The warmer, lighter evenings meant she spent more time with Billy and his plants or knitting baby clothes with Joyce. Maisie often wondered if she'd ever knit for her own child. She watched as Joyce settled into pending motherhood with a calm approach and she admired her for it. Maisie had been certain she'd be a nervous wreck, given how unwell she had been feeling in the early months of the pregnancy. And then there was the news Charlie dropped in her lap.

He'd asked for a transfer and had trained to join the bomb removal squad. Maisie and Joyce both wrote to him pleading for him to transfer back to the Engineers, but he told them both he wanted to do more than tinker with engines. He wanted to save lives.

Joyce expressed many opinions about Simon's behaviour whenever she had the opportunity. She told Maisie she'd written to Charlie about the party after Maisie had told her what happened, and Charlie wrote back with firm advice. Joyce spoke with her brother Eddie to warn Simon it needed to stop.

During her time spent alone, Maisie concentrated on writing poetry and she noticed her poems were increasingly filled with angst and wishful thinking. Her limited experience of romance didn't appear to be an obstacle when she wanted to express her inner thoughts.

For Cam:

Your Gift

My world is small, but you opened a door into a
space beyond my thoughts.
Tender words and a fleeting glance of apprecia-
tion fill a void,
I love when silence becomes the loudest word
between us.
My world is small, but you opened my mind to
appreciate thoughts beyond friendship.

For Simon:

The Inside of Me

A bomb explodes and intensifies the rage inside,
I run yet find I have nowhere to hide.
The enemy is at my gate and I fear my past,
Troubled dreams set to last.

For Gloria and Norah (and maybe my parents, whoever they are . . .):

The Forgotten Orphan

The Forgotten Orphan

Your claws grate against my skin,
You destroyed me,
Took my strength and sapped my history.
What use is my past without answers?
I must let the questions wither and die,
I am not them, I am I.
Never Forget.

As she read over the poem she had written with Matron in mind, Maisie thought about the mysterious key amongst Gloria's things. What did it open? Was it significant or meaningful to Maisie? Should she just throw it away?

Captain Bloom had come to a dead end in her search for Maisie's birth certificate and she indicated there was nothing more that she could do. In her letter she included a few ideas of where Maisie might go next to find answers, one of which was a trustee of the orphanage.

Maisie heeded the captain's advice and sent a letter. As more weeks passed without a reply, she came to the conclusion that the person in question no longer lived at the address she had managed to find or wasn't interested in her request.

Joyce's brother sent a message to say he had news relating to Simon and would visit the following week if Maisie agreed to meet with him.

'He's in a lot of bother,' Eddie said as he settled into a seat.

Maisie, not surprised by his statement, encouraged him to continue.

'Simon's always fired up – looking for trouble. Picking fights. Did you know he was on the run? Why he came back to the area and started a fight in a military camp is beyond us. The man's a fool.'

'He came to see me,' Maisie said.

Eddie shrugged his shoulders and shook his head in disagreement.

'No. That's just it. He didn't know you were going to be there, right? If he'd wanted to see you, why not come here to Holly Bush House? No, he went to that dance because he knew the Canadians were there and he wanted to start some trouble. Seeing you there just gave him the excuse he needed to swing a punch. We find him hard to live with onboard ship. Argumentative should be his middle name.'

Maisie pinched her lips together. Eddie was right; Simon wouldn't have known she was there.

'Where is he now?' she asked.

'Prison. He's been arrested for two other offences and sent to naval detention quarters.'

Maisie stared at him in disbelief. 'Surely not! Where's the prison?'

Eddie rose to his feet and Maisie got up too and followed him to the door.

'I'd better be going,' he said. 'I'm not sure where they've taken him yet but I'll let you know when I find out. I do know this; he'll be a changed man when he comes out. They're dreadful places with severe punishment methods. He's got to earn his bed and bedding which, knowing Simon, won't be his for some time yet. He's not allowed letters, so save your ink. Move on, Maisie. He's bad news.'

With a swift shake of her head, Maisie walked alongside him as they made their way along the driveway.

'I remember the day he left. He was taken in a car and driven out of my life. It takes a lot to get over that sadness. He was one of the lucky ones, but for some reason he doesn't seem happy in life. He was always a rebel – I just thought he'd grow out of it.'

They stopped at the entrance to the road and Eddie turned to face her.

'When he comes back here – and I'm sure he will – be careful. My sister loves you and I'm saying it because we care, but I repeat, Simon is bad news.'

'Thanks Eddie. Thanks for coming and telling me.'

Back home she set out more feelings on paper.

Glynis Peters

<u>Solitude</u>

Alone. Locked away, but not forgotten.
Words to comfort are unavailable,
But written here, on this page.
Quiet. Locked away, sombre reflection.
Words for life lessons must be pondered,
Until settled mind erodes the rage.

Twirling her pen around in her hand, she decided to write to Cam to tell him of Simon's situation before heading over to the main house to start her shift.

Holly Bush House
May 31st 1942

Dearest Cam

Life has its strange moments and its wonderful ones. The evening at the dance had both. Thank you for taking care of me, and for making me feel special. I'm saddened by what happened but I have news which might put your mind at rest because you will know that I am safe.

Simon is in prison. Apparently, he had another couple of charges against him, all for violent behaviour, and was on the run the night of the dance. According to Eddie, Joyce's brother who works with

238

Simon, he was out for a fight and hadn't come to the dance in search of me.

I'm told he cannot receive letters in prison and won't even have a bed because it has to be earned. The Navy prison rules are tough. Eddie said he'd also be a changed man when he is released. I can only hope so, and pray he stays away.

Yesterday, we experienced a sight and a half. Planes filled the sky as they headed out to destroy the enemy. The noise was incredible, and I must admit it was a bit exciting. We could feel the thundering shakes in the soles of our feet as they flew overhead. Charlie's dad said they were headed for a city called Cologne in Germany, and I think with such a force heading their way, the enemy can do nothing but fear and respect us from now on. I think it's sad, but I'm told it is necessary for survival. I looked to the sky and wondered if you were in one. I often do that when a plane flies across the water. I get a little scared about you jumping out of them.

We've also had a few more bombs dropped here and, as always, they've created problems for the city. Thankfully, we're fortunate at Holly Bush House and have so far been spared. We are filling up with injured men, but I'm pleased to say that many are returning to the arms of their loving families soon. Although, goodness knows how some of them will cope as they'll never find work again. It breaks my heart at times. I'm not sure what's worse, shattered limbs or shattered minds.

I urge you, stay safe, my love,
and come back to me.
Maisie

CHAPTER 21

The line of black-coated mourners moved slowly towards Joyce, her in-laws, and the rest of her family. Maisie stood beside her friend and kept hold of her trembling hand. Each time someone offered their condolences, Maisie felt Joyce's hand tremble and she feared it would never stop shaking.

When the devastating news came that Charlie had lost his life dismantling a faulty wire on an unexploded bomb, Maisie's world fell apart. She now understood the loss of a family member, how the heart twisted in on itself and burned with pain inside.

When Joyce and Eddie came to tell her the news of his death, she and Joyce sat alone holding each other, drawing comfort in the fact that Charlie had died quickly. It broke Maisie to see Joyce's tormented face. A widow with a baby on the way by the age of twenty-four. How did you come back from that type of despair?

By the time they returned to the house, they were wrung out emotionally. Eddie beckoned her over to him.

'All right, Maisie? Sad day. Sad day. Here's to Charlie, God rest him.' He lifted a bottle of brown ale in a toast. 'I've a bit of news for you. My mate has a delivery job with the Navy and knows Simon. He reckons he saw him all pale and thin walking around a prison yard in Portsmouth. Fresh air and exercise ain't a treat there, so he's done something to upset someone . . . again,' Eddie said with an air of disgust.

'He's ill?'

Despite her anger towards Simon, she didn't like the thought of him suffering.

'I'm not sure if he's ill, or just sick in the head. I bet he was sporting for a fight again. He won't win one in there. We hear all kinds of horror stories. Steer clear, Maisie. Walk away. Even I would be better as a fella for you than that one, and you must admit, I'm not your type – and don't be offended, I don't mean anything by it. I'd need a stepladder to kiss you.'

No matter how he tried to lighten her mood, Eddie failed. Maisie offered her thanks for the information and watched as Joyce whipped off her coat and stroked her pregnant belly.

'Come on, everyone. Smile. I can't have misery when it comes to memories of my Charlie. I have to hold it together for this little one. You all toast my man and his bravery whilst I'm putting my feet up. I need to lie down; it's been a long day,' Joyce said, and embraced the mourners one by one.

Maisie's stomach churned. The last thing she wanted to do was to sit listening to tales of her dear friend, it was too painful to hear them and remember the happier times. It pained her to see his parents suffering the loss of their son. A panic set in and she said the first thing she could think of which would get her out of the house.

'I've got to go back on shift, Joyce. I'll come and visit soon. I wish I could find the right words to help you, but I feel useless . . .' she said and snuffled back her tears.

Joyce leaned in and gave her a kiss.

'We must try and be brave. No more tears. Charlie would be upset if he thought he'd made you miserable. We'll get by so long as you come by regularly and cheer us up, you are far from useless.'

'Take care and I promise, I'll try not to cry next visit.'

Back home, Maisie changed into her uniform and folded away her mourning clothes. Although not actually on the working rota, she felt the need to occupy herself to prevent the tears flowing every time she thought of Charlie. She took herself over to the main house where she was joined by Coleen in the kitchen.

'I won't ask how it went. Got a letter here for you. I was going to bring it over later. Looks official.'

She handed Maisie a buff envelope. Turning it over in her hands, Maisie stared at the postmark: Colchester, Essex.

'That's odd. I don't know anyone from there. What could it be?' she said.

'You won't find out if you keep staring at the thing. Open the envelope and be surprised. It's an army camp in East Anglia, that's all I know,' Coleen said.

'I don't think I can cope with anything else today. If it is bad news I'll break. My nerves are fragile, Col. What with Charlie . . .'

Coleen took the letter from her.

'I'll look after it until tomorrow. You can take some time to read it then. Switch the urn on for tea and we'll play cards with the lads, or you go outside with Billy. Don't think about this – see, it's not arrived yet.'

Slipping the envelope into her white apron pocket, Coleen patted Maisie's arm with a reassuringly friendly firmness.

Maisie made no objections to her friend's decision. It was sensible and thoughtful. Maisie was so tired she knew thinking about the contents of the letter wouldn't keep her awake. Hitler's bombs wouldn't disturb her sleep tonight. She needed to heal and recover from the pain of the day. A sudden urge to write and tell Cam about Charlie took hold and she snatched up her pen.

Holly Bush House
July 25th 1942

Dear Cam,

Today was one of the most painful I've experienced. We said goodbye to Charlie. We buried him. Sadly, he tried to detonate a bomb to save a family home. He got into the house and dragged them all free. Four of them. He then went on to do what he was trained to do and apparently, he called out a warning to a colleague that the wiring looked different. They were his last words.

As you know, he was a brother to me, and I am numb. My duty now is to give comfort to Joyce and help her when the baby arrives.

I can't wait to see you again. I need to see you again to make life bearable once more.

Stay safe.

With love,
Maisie

Winds blew across the garden and Maisie watched a piece of stray paper fly free. For a fleeting moment she wanted to be that piece of paper. The war weighed heavy on her shoulders and she wondered if she would ever laugh again. Pretty dresses and a new pair of heeled shoes hanging in her wardrobe were going to waste. Coleen couldn't do enough for her, but Maisie's mood had reached rock bottom. Apart from attending work that week, she'd not done anything else. Food choked her and the thought of stepping outside of Holly Bush House made her tremble, but she'd done it and would forever regret the journey.

It started the day after Charlie's funeral, when she'd opened the letter Coleen had handed her. Inside was quality paper and neat handwriting. It was from the wife of the gentleman that Maisie had written to seeking information about where to obtain official papers relating to the orphanage. She'd not expected a reply, only hoped. Now, she wished she'd never written.

> *S. R. Whiting*
> *Itchen House*
> *S/Hampton*
> *July 16th 1942*

Dear Miss Reynolds,

My apologies for the late reply.
My husband received your letter whilst serving

in Africa, and sadly did not return home to us. His belongings, however, did survive and amongst those was your letter to him. There was also a part reply to you drafted out in his writing case, and I've written it out into a more legible copy for you. It is my hope that his memories assist you in your search.

My regards
Sylvia Whiting.

Dear Miss Reynolds,

When I received your letter, I will admit to being rather puzzled by your request.

I see your residential address is still the orphanage, and you make no mention of your brother, James. Your twin. You were both entered into the care of Holly Bush Orphanage when you were about to turn four years old. I remember the day well as I was there for a meeting about another private matter. I wonder if your hair is still as red. You were a sweet child. Your brother was far livelier, and as I understand it, took a lot of persuading to get him inside the car, let alone the orphanage. It saddens me that you were separated. You were born together and should have been raised together. I did argue your case, but it fell on deaf ears.

With regard to your question about a birth certificate, a woman named Juliana Reynolds will have the answers you seek. She had a local Southampton address, and if I recall it was rooms above an ironmonger's in the high street. She is registered as your mother and when I heard of her dilemma, I agreed the funding for your care.

I am wondering if Matron Mason withheld the information due to the unfortunate circumstances surrounding your background. My advice is . . .

Immediately after reading the half-finished letter several times, Maisie felt gut-punched. Gloria must have known their mother's name – maybe even met her. Jack's real name, unsurprisingly, had been James. Was her real name Maisie? She now had confirmation that Juliana Reynolds was their mother, but was she the woman who took them to the home?

She recalled a large woman holding Jack's hand and watching them walk down the corridor together whilst she sat alone on a seat outside Gloria's office crying out for him to come back.

Questions raced through her mind. She went to the photograph propped above the fireplace. This had to be a photograph of her twin brother and mother.

Had Gloria Mason known the answers to all of her questions? Why had she hidden them from Maisie? Her cruelty of depriving a child the comfort of family was beyond comprehension, but only a heartless woman would split up twins.

Anxious and desperate to learn more about her past, she took a half day's leave and made her way to the city. Maisie despaired at the sight of flattened buildings and the once proud and beautiful architecture, now caved in and useless. Holy Rood Church tower was the only part of the beautiful church remaining, and Maisie stopped to pay her respects. It was a sad sight, and as she looked further down each street she passed, the view was the same: total devastation. Hitler had not held back on his bomb quota.

The further she walked, the more it became obvious that the blitz had destroyed the majority of the city and the further she searched up and down, the less evidence there was of the main street that had once existed. She walked along Above Bar Street and approached several people as to the whereabouts of the ironmonger's, but most were demolition teams from outside the city, and couldn't help. Eventually, a man with a barrow who was clearing a pathway said he was local born and bred.

'I'm looking for the spot where the ironmonger's shop was – well, the room above it is what I need.'

The man removed his tin helmet and scratched his scalp in thought.

'The ironmonger's? Scrap junk shop, more like. It was over there. You ain't going to find any room there.' The man pointed across the street at more rubble and debris. Large chunks of building lay beaten by the enemy.

'Oh,' Maisie said, her voice flat with disappointment. Realistically, she knew she would find nothing, but a spark of hope still fired her up inside. 'I'm told my mother lived there. Above the shop.'

The man's smile twisted into a black-toothed sneer.

'Oh, them. You'll find them down on the docks. Working.'

A cold shiver struck Maisie as he continued his sneering smile. Maisie thanked him and picked her way through the bomb sites towards the docks. Was her mother alive and nearby? Today her life could change forever.

Along the dockside she saw people moving around from one side to the other, men and women in various forms of work. One woman walked past her with a tray of pies, and the smell teased Maisie's taste buds, but she knew she could never eat one; her stomach was tied in knots, twisted up with nervous energy. Where on earth would she start looking for her mother?

She stopped person after person for over an hour to ask about Juliana Reynolds but received nothing but negative replies. Maisie had to conclude that her mission was hopeless. The docks was a large place with extensive damage, and she needed a plan so as not to waste what was left of her day. She strode to the end of burned-out warehouses with only their blackened frames on show, like large skeletons of nothingness. She stared into the hollows of what had once been and tried to comprehend the what was now. How could the city come back from such devastation? Talk she'd heard on the radio suggested that other cities had endured the same level of devastation. How could the country keep moving forward? Surely food would run out and building supplies would be in short supply?

Maisie shook off the negative thoughts and concentrated on finding her mother. She worked nearby; the man had said so. If it took a lifetime, Maisie would come each day and spent her free time searching.

She glanced at her watch and was disappointed to see it was nearly time for her next shift. With reluctance, Maisie turned around and headed home. The next time she came she would bring the photograph and hope someone might recognise the young woman in the picture.

CHAPTER 22

For two weeks, Maisie walked around the docks. Both Coleen and Joyce pleaded with her to give up her search. Their fears were for her health and mind. Coleen forced her to eat a bowl of porridge and Maisie only did so because her friend had used her precious milk and sugar allowance to make it and refused to leave until the bowl was empty.

'I'm worried about you, Maisie. Is she worth it, this woman who not only gave you away, but her other baby too? Make a new life. Stop living in the past. It's making you ill.'

'I need to find out who I am,' Maisie replied.

'Well, don't make yourself ill doing it. I hate to say it, but it might be for nothing.'

'But I still need to know.' Maisie's arguments never

altered, and Coleen gradually gave up trying to persuade her from her search.

Both Joyce and Coleen offered to go with her, but she refused. If the answers she got were not the ones she was hoping for, she didn't want witnesses.

One morning, Maisie decided to walk around a different area of the docks. It was a hot spring day with a hint of summer and a welcome breeze filtered between the ships docked on the quayside. A pretty shimmering silver haze danced on the usually dull grey-brown water, and she stopped to look whenever it caught her eye. Courage skipped around her insides, teasing Maisie into a tranquil mindset one minute, then trampling all pleasantries the next when she remembered why she'd set out to walk the docks that day. Maisie pushed her sun hat more firmly onto her head; her neck was hot where the bottom curls refused to stay tucked inside. She gripped her handbag tightly as she marched between stacked boxes and army vehicles lining the edge of the walkway. Soldiers whistled. Dockers called out to her to be their sweetheart, but Maisie gave them no attention in return. She was determined to find her mother. She manoeuvred past a group of men standing idle against packing crates, when one gave a low, elongated whistle.

'Well there's a sight for sore eyes. Not seen you for a while. He's down the other end, love.'

The man pointed to the end of the walkway. 'At the bottom end. They moved offices.'

The other men in his company gave loud raucous laughs and made comments about his choice of words. Maisie tried to ignore them and walked away.

'Where you been? I'll give you a look tomorrow. Oh, sorry love, you ain't who I thought you was . . . but you'll do.' The man winked and stepped in front of her. He wasn't threatening in his behaviour but it still made Maisie uncomfortable.

'I'm not sure what you mean. You must have me confused with someone else. I've come to see the ships. Who do you think I'm here to see?' Maisie asked. She kept her voice casual despite the trembling inside. This man seemed to have confused her with someone who resembled her. Could it be . . .? Could it actually be her mother?

'Your sister's bloke. But he's down the bottom now.'

Maisie shook her head and smiled.

'I don't have a sister.'

The man drew on his pipe and scratched his chin.

'She's got the red hair like you. I just thought . . .'

Maisie gasped.

'Someone else has red hair like mine?'

'Not quite as red, but she's the spit of you.'

Maisie's heart pounded. A sister! Finally, this felt like progress. Her chest heaved with anticipation and anxious excitement.

'I've no idea who you're talking about, but I'm keen to find someone who can help me with . . . well, something to do with my mother. I was told I'd find the person here. Maybe it's the same person you've mentioned. Where will I find them?'

The man pointed ahead.

'Take a left behind the temporary huts down there, and walk into the yard. He's hard to miss. Big guy. Usually works from the hut with a splash of red paint on the front. Strange . . . I thought you were family. Mind how you go, lady. If they ain't who you think they are, don't hang about, that's all I'll say.' The man gave her a nod goodbye.

With a swift smile of thanks, Maisie headed in the direction the man had pointed, keeping her eyes open for another red-headed woman. She entered the yard and saw several men standing around smoking, passing packages back and forth. They grinned at her as she walked across the yard towards a hut with a large red paint mark splattered across the front.

To one side of the building, a man with a large protruding stomach that stretched a shabby waistcoat to its limits stopped talking in order to look Maisie up and down. She stopped in her tracks, his face not encouraging her to venture closer.

'Who the ruddy heck are you?' he bellowed at her, waving a dirty, stodgy hand her way.

Another man cursed and nudged his fellow loiterer, and so it went on amongst the group of roughly ten.

All heads turned to face Maisie and she felt a burning flush rise to her face.

'I . . . I'm looking for someone,' she replied, determined not to be intimidated.

'Who?' the man asked, puffing on his cigarette and exhaling the smoke slowly.

He unnerved Maisie with his menacing stare. The men gathered around him watched her every move, but she stood her ground, not willing to show how terrified she was inside.

'I'm actually looking for my mother. She's got red hair, the same as me, I think. I've got a name written down but not sure if it is my mother's: Juliana Reynolds. She had twins twenty years ago.' Maisie's words came out in a rush.

'Ain't here no more.'

The large man spat on the ground.

'So, you know her?' Maisie asked, trying to keep the excitement from her voice.

'Sort of,' the man said and winked at the others who let out loud, deep laughs.

'Where is she? I must speak with her. I've been in an orphanage for sixteen years. Did she have hair like mine?' Maisie knew her voice sounded pleading, but she no longer cared. This man might have the answers she sought.

'Went with the business in town. Bombs hit and she was gone. Not a bone left unbroken. Ruddy woman left me without a penny to me name. You might be a blessing in disguise. A replacement sent from heaven.'

He turned to the gang of men with a leering grin, waggling his tongue between his stained teeth and they all laughed again.

Maisie cringed inwardly and made a pretence of getting her handkerchief from her bag. From the corner of her eye she noticed a woman look her way; she stared Maisie up and down then walked over to the men and draped herself around the large man. He clutched her buttock and gave it a squeeze.

'Found a replacement for Red, Jock? I'll get her working tonight. She's a good match,' the woman said, then sneered at Maisie. 'Needs a bit of padding up top, but what's below is more important. She'll earn you top-drawer money.'

Maisie thought she might faint and gripped her bag tighter. The realisation that her mother – or sister, perhaps? – might have been a prostitute clawed at her insides. She must have been a desperate woman who had given up her children in order to survive.

'I'm not here to work. I came looking for my mother. If any of you know anything, I'd appreciate answers. Am I the daughter of Juliana Reynolds? I'm Maisie Reynolds and I was placed in care aged four. The matron, Gloria

Mason, wouldn't tell me a thing and it's taken me years to get this far so please, if anyone knows anything, please will you tell me. I need to know where I came from.' Maisie took a deep breath after giving such a long speech in the firmest voice she could muster.

She shifted from foot to foot in nervous anticipation of answers, but no one spoke; they all simply stared at her.

'Please. Anyone?' She looked around but most of the men turned and walked away.

Jock and the woman stood looking at each other, then Jock nodded.

'Gloria. That old hag? She's my sister. And pretty Juliana – Red – was her girl. Which makes you, sweetheart, her granddaughter, and my great niece. Welcome to the family,' Jock said and laughed. He gave the woman a slap on her backside and then he walked away. 'Sort her out, Doris.'

Maisie felt her body sway. The shock of his words was beyond comprehension. Utterly unbelievable. She took a moment to compose herself before stammering out her question. If she'd ever thought Gloria Mason an evil woman in the past, the feeling of betrayal she experienced now only confirmed that the woman was one of the cruellest people she could imagine.

'Gloria Mason was your sister? I'm her . . .?'

Jock turned around and walked back to her. Maisie

tried not to gag at the sweaty aroma he wafted each time he moved an arm. The man was a revolting specimen.

'Jessie Reynolds is her real name. She changed it when she applied for the job and made herself look respectable. Too old to work the streets and she got in with some army toff who fell foul of her blackmailing. She was a nasty piece. Made our lives hell with her preaching. Yes, you are blood and I can see the joy in your face. Gonna be sick? Go over there,' he said.

Maisie stood there taking it all in, her legs trembling with shock. She straightened her back and tried to focus but waves of nausea prevented her from moving.

'Listen. I don't need more hungry mouths to feed. I didn't like your mother. She was a mouthy bitch, but she performed well and earned me a good few quid. If you want a job, you've got one. If not, clear off. There's nothing here for you. Tell my sister she still owes me.'

'She's dead. Heart attack,' Maisie said bluntly.

'Good riddance. If you lived with her, I feel for you. Evil flowed through her sanctimonious veins. You're penniless, I suppose. You can start work tonight, if you want.'

Stunned by his suggestion, Maisie shook her head.

'I don't need work. My life is a good one. I want to find my brother, my twin, but there are no birth certificates. Nothing.'

'Double the trouble came to Red's door and she couldn't hack it. She gave them over to my sister to get rid of 'cos round here, if you ain't working, you ain't earning, and she lost me a fortune,' Jock said, hissing through his teeth. 'Being her girl, you can repay me. Work off the debt.'

'I'd rather die.' Maisie made a move to walk away, but Doris put a restraining hand on her arm.

Doris looked to Jock again.

'What about Red's box? Give the girl her box and let her go. She's no good to me. I want willing girls. This one won't earn you a penny. You're not a cruel man, Jock. The tin will be thrown away, so give it to her. Do right by the girl. Let her have her cheap beads from her mother.'

Jock's face changed several shades of scarlet before he turned on his heel, went inside the hut splashed in red paint, and returned with a small tin box.

'This is all we found. Everything else was lost in the bombing. Doris is right; I ain't a cruel man. By rights this is yours. She had no money so don't get excited. Just some cheap beads in there. Fond of cheap beads, she was.' He tapped the tin.

Maisie reached out and took it from him, avoiding contact with his filthy hands. The smell he emitted brought back memories of the room she and Jack huddled in together before Holly Bush. She looked at the people milling around them. She had been born in squalor, there was no doubt in her mind.

'Her mother took the money when they had a fight over the babies. As I said, horrible woman. If you ain't going to work for me, you ain't any use. I don't need family. Don't come back. And unless your brother is good with his fists, I don't want to see him round here either. So when you find him, don't bring him here.'

Maisie nodded. Tears welled and she felt a tightening in her throat. This man was a relative. He was as unpleasant as his sister but at least he had the decency to do right by her and let her leave with something belonging to her mother. Had Juliana Reynolds been as cruel as Gloria or had she been a victim of her mother's bullying ways? Maisie wanted to believe the latter. She straightened her back and looked him in the eye. She had no intention of ever returning to the place, but she wanted to remind Jock of her existence and of the consequences of his forceful nature.

'After you drove my mother to give up her children, your sister made my life hell. She cut my head to pieces with a razor to rid me of my hair. She never held back with her punishments. Now I know why. I'm the child of her prostitute daughter and my curls reminded her of that every day. But why didn't she tell me who she was?'

'Twisted bitch. She preferred torture to nurture, that one,' Doris said.

'Did Juliana have any more children? Do I have siblings?'

Jock shook his head. 'Good Lawd, no. I don't think I have any more kids – Red certainly didn't. No, the hag sister wanted any babies born round here for the orphanage so Red made sure she didn't produce any more. She wasn't going to feed her mother's pockets. The old hag took a couple of Doris's babies though. Earned her good money. Not fond of kids are you, gal? Doris here filled her spot once you were born. Wouldn't let me near the girl again, would you my lover?' He grinned at Doris who shrugged a shoulder back at him.

A cold bucket of water couldn't have hit Maisie any harder and her body trembled with shock. The man was her great-uncle *and* if she'd heard him correctly, her father!

'You're . . . my father?' she whispered, nausea raging around her insides.

'No! Listen carefully. I shared a bed with your mother, and she gave birth to two bastard children. I am no father to any kid round here. Now, unless you have any other business here, I suggest we part ways and forget we ever met. Bugger off now. I don't need any more trouble.' Jock's voice changed into a deep growl. Maisie noticed his features harden and then he walked away.

Doris lingered, obviously wanting to speak without him around.

'Take the tin and clear off, dearie. Don't come back. He'll work you to death if you do. And the water will be your grave. And as for finding birth certificates, good luck. As I say, get going or you'll join a few in there.' She nodded her head towards the quayside.

Before Maisie could ask any more questions, Doris walked away.

Gathering her composure, Maisie placed the tin under her arm and left the yard. As she passed the quayside, she wondered how many poor young women never got the opportunity to walk free from Jock's clutches.

A wave of sadness swept in, but as she thought of Jock it fizzled into a raging anger. If a bomb dropped on him now, Maisie felt it would be the kindest act the enemy could do for her. She fully intended to honour his demands and never enter that part of the city again.

She powered along the dockside so fast people swore at her to slow down but her mind was in turmoil.

She called in to Joyce's place on the way home, attempting to control her anger and upset, but she couldn't shore up her emotions any longer once she saw her friend and she flung herself into her arms.

Joyce moved her to a chair and stared at her in disbelief as Maisie relayed what had happened. Maisie's anger had subsided, but large, sad tears dripped over her lashes.

Joyce patted them away with the corner of her pinafore, with all the tenderness of a mother. 'Go home, Maisie and rest up. Look at you, you're as white as a sheet. Then you must do what is best for you, but don't go near that man again. Promise me.'

Drying her tears, Maisie picked up the tin. 'I promise. I bet the key I've got fits this box. I'm glad I didn't throw it away. I wonder what joys it holds for me, more exciting information about my great-uncle – or is that my dad?' she said, her voice heaped with resentment.

Joyce sighed. 'I doubt he's your real dad. He's probably saying that to get rid of you. You're vulnerable, Maisie. You could be in danger if you go back.'

Maisie dried her eyes and went to the door. She stepped out into the sunshine; the walk home would help her assemble her thoughts.

'Believe me, I'll not go back. He made my skin crawl. Just the thought of what he said makes me cringe. Pure filth.'

Joyce gave a theatrical shiver and pulled a face of disgust.

'Sadly, I doubt my mother was any better. She gave

us up to Gloria, which shows how much she cared about us. It was all for money. Rich parents paying for children a mother didn't want were the ideal outlet. Gloria got stuck when it came to me. No wonder she despised me. You can't sell an ugly orphan. No, don't worry about me Joyce. I just want to get home and see what she *did* value in life. I'll come and let you know in a few days. Please, don't worry about me. I'll never go near the man again, I promise.'

CHAPTER 23

With a shaking hand, Maisie put Gloria's mystery key into the keyhole. A positive click released the lid and it rose a fraction.

The waning sun still shone through the window and glinted on the surface of the tin. Maisie touched the lid, hesitating for fear of what she might find.

'Right, Maisie Reynolds, this is either something important or an enormous let down. Deal with it and cope. Jock is nothing to you. The man is evil; you can't possibly be related.' Maisie chatted away to herself, trying to retain some composure as she lifted the lid of the box.

Inside, she saw a small silver ring in one corner, a layer of yellowing papers, and a photograph of two children. Toddlers. She turned over the picture to inspect the back and saw a scrawl of poor handwriting

The Forgotten Orphan

Julie and James Reynolds.
Twins, born Southampton, July 2nd 1922.
Gone but not forgotten.

'How dare she! How dare she declare us as gone? I was here, so close to her, and she must have known! *We* were here, together, Jack and me. Only for a short time together, but we were here. We existed.'

A major surge of emotion brought Maisie to her knees.

'Who had the right to give me this name, and not let me be Julie?' she cried out.

There was a banging on her door and she felt the sudden rush of warm air as it was pushed open, but it didn't stop her from pulling at her hair and slapping at her legs. She thrashed and screamed into the arms that held her. She knew it was Cam by his familiar smell and soft voice.

'Maisie. My Maisie. Who's hurt you? Calm down, I've got you. Hit me, not yourself. What's going on?'

'I'm not your Maisie. I'm Julie. Nobody's Julie. I hate her, I hate her.' Maisie continued thrashing out and screaming. The more she struggled, the more Cam held her close. He settled down on the floor beside her and held on to her until she could no longer cry out and her sobs hiccupped into breathless sighs.

'I take it this photograph has something to do with your distress. Did you find your parents? Has somebody died? Talk to me, Maisie. Let me help.'

With slow jerking movements, Maisie tugged herself free from Cam's arms. She moved to the chair by the window and looked at him. He was so handsome, and his face showed genuine concern.

'That photograph is of me and my brother. James – or, as I know him, Jack. The one up there,' she pointed to the mantlepiece, 'that's us with our mother, Juliana. I hate her. She gave us away and for the worst possible reasons.'

She directed her gaze at the box.

'Inside that box are the only possessions left of my mother's. I met my father and would rather have been told I was the child of the devil. As for my grandmother, Gloria . . .'

Cam expelled a loud breath and Maisie pursed her lips and nodded slowly.

'Oh, yes, my grandmother was Gloria Mason – or, should I say, Jessie Reynolds.'

'The matron you spoke of?' Cam's voice was a combination of shock and amazement.

'The one and only. My mother was her daughter, a redhead called Juliana, and, as I understand it, they fought over selling me and my brother. I wonder how much we were worth?'

Maisie heard Cam inhale and exhale, but she held nothing back when she launched into her second speech. She wanted him to know everything about her newly discovered background.

'Her uncle is my father and he sold her for sex. And, lucky me, he offered to set me up in the family business today.'

Maisie looked across into Cam's face and tried to make out what he was thinking, but he remained pale-faced and calm. He gave an encouraging dip of his head for her to continue.

'My mother was a prostitute at the docks and she was killed by the recent bombings. I hate them, I hate them all!'

Cam rushed to her side, lifted her to her feet, and held her close again as Maisie tried to stem the tears. This time she didn't resist.

'Cry, honey, just cry it out. I'll hold you. I'll keep you safe.' Cam spoke softly as she leaned into him for comfort.

Maisie took him at his word and sobbed. Eventually, she settled into irregular sniffles and he gently lowered her back into her seat.

'Have you looked at the rest of the contents?'

Maisie waved her hand in dismissal of his question.

'I can't bear it.'

Cam picked up the box and took it to her.

'Let's do it together. I'll help you. I'm here for you – always, Maisie.'

'Julie. My name is not Maisie.'

Cam said nothing and handed her the tin. He pulled up a chair beside her and sat down.

'Listen. I'm on leave for forty-eight hours and I want to spend it with the girl who's captured my heart, and her name is Maisie. Let's take the next step together.'

He lifted the lid and pulled out the first document.

'This looks like it's your birth certificate. It appears you are Julie Reynolds. Mother, Juliana Reynolds. Born July 2nd 1922. Father not named'

'And we know why that is,' Maisie snapped.

Cam reached out and touched her arm to calm her down.

'This is the past. You'll always be Maisie to me. The kind, loving girl who makes me smile. I'm here for you.'

Cam took up the small ring and held it out to her, but Maisie shook her head and he placed it back in the tin.

She curled up in the chair, tugged a cushion to her chest, and watched him.

'Cam. I need to tell you something and please don't interrupt me. Please let me get it out before I lose my nerve.'

Cam stopped what he was doing, went over to her, and sat on the arm of the chair.

'Fire away, I'm listening.'

A shyness came over Maisie, but she so desperately wanted to get her deeper, more intimate feelings for

Cam out in the open. She clasped her hands in her lap and fidgeted her fingers against her palms. It was time. Time to let the woman she'd become express her innermost thoughts. She wanted to wash away the horrors of the docks and understand the true meaning of love. Of being held by a man who loves you. With Cam she knew it would be pure and meaningful. Time was not on their side or she'd possibly have waited, but the moment felt right and Maisie wanted to commit to him.

'Cam. I fell in love with you the first time I saw you and now I know what true love is. I know this is what I'm feeling because I cannot imagine there can be a deeper love. My emotions about my situation are in a mess, but just seeing you here, at the time in my life when I need support has made me realise you don't care about who I was, only who I am. You are still here despite my ranting, and I love you for that. I want to . . . well, I want to *share* myself with you.'

After rushing out her words, Maisie took a deep breath and gave him a brief smile, but his face expressed nothing.

Cam sat in his chair in silence, unmoving. Maisie couldn't bear to see his reaction and so turned her head to look out onto the garden. When she spoke to him again, it was in a soft, calm voice.

'You came through the door just when I needed you the most and listening to you take control and calm me has made me want you in my life the way I've never wanted anyone before. You could have walked away, and I would understand if you left because I've become a complicated person with a very unrespectable background. Part of me thinks you should walk away, but the other part desperately wants you to stay. To stay with me, to be with me . . . in the physical sense, not just the emotional. I want to wake with you by my side.'

His sudden gentle touch didn't startle her; it gave her hope. She felt the warmth radiate from his hand onto the back of her neck. It was soothing and she gave in to his strength as he scooped her into his arms and lifted her from the chair. He sat down with her on his lap and cradled her in his arms. Maisie could hear his heart pounding in his chest. It was a comforting sound. His lips brushed her forehead, and she dared not move in case the peace she felt at that moment melted away. She closed her eyes as he whispered his love for her and promised he would always help her through all the tough times when they came her way. Maisie wanted time to stop. A blackbird chirruped in the early evening and neither of them stirred.

Several hours later, Maisie lay beside a softly snoring Cam. He'd taken her to a place of wonderment and drawn from her a passion she hadn't known her body was capable of. It wasn't the typical rushed wartime passion, nor the experimental fumbling she'd heard

Coleen and her friends speak about during their evenings together. It was love, and it had depth and meaning.

They'd explored a path of togetherness and vowed they'd stay loyal to each other for as long as the war allowed.

CHAPTER 24

Maisie made a slow recovery from the mental anguish she had experienced down at the docks but she thrived on the many hours that she and Cam spent exploring each other's bodies and meeting each other's sensual needs. When she was with him, all thoughts of her terrible family disappeared.

On the day he left, she broke down and became inconsolable. Coleen reported her in as sick and for four days she spent her spare time comforting Maisie.

During that time, Maisie wrote to Cam and found comfort in her poetry.

Holly Bush House
August 2nd 1942

My Darling Cam,

The Forgotten Orphan

I am so glad you did not see me after you left. Red eyes, swollen with tears, is not a pretty look.

Once again, I dream of the day you will be back in my arms. It is so lonely without you around. In two days, you showed me what I've been missing my whole life, and how wonderful it is to be a woman so loved.

You make me laugh, you comfort me, and you show me how to be strong. Is it so very wrong to fall in love so soon? I once asked myself whether we were simply snatching moments and fooling ourselves. I don't think so; this feels real and, as you once said, meant to be.

My Pain

It hurts – my silent love
So quiet as it mourns your
Arms of strength and warmth.
It hurts – our missing love
Lost in the dark days of war,
No reassurances of a future.
It hurts – the everlasting day
When arms no longer hold me,
Arms of the man I love.

To pass the time, I've put everything into my studies and I am pleased to say I've passed another first-aid certificate today.

Talking of certificates, I am seeking a way of changing my name and obtaining a fresh birth certificate. I cannot bear the thought of a piece of paper dictating who I am, especially when it's a name I do not recognise or want to be associated with. Ever. Does that make sense to you?

Coleen said there are many young men out there willing to take me off your hands should you decide I'm not what you fancy after all. She didn't take too kindly to my reply. It was a bad day and she received a proper telling off. We made up soon after. She realised she'd spoken wrongly, and I confessed to overreacting.

She and Ted are a true couple now. He proposed by letter and they are going to buy a ring when he returns from wherever he's been sent. You can imagine the excitement around here now. Other than that, I have no further news.

I must go on duty now, my love.

Please take care and don't be a hero. Just come home to me.

With my love,
Maisie

Maisie scrawled a heart with an arrow through it onto the paper beneath her signature and sealed the envelope. Before posting it, she pressed her lips to it and hoped Cam received it quickly.

Every day Maisie threw herself into her work and tirelessly cared for more and more patients. She devoted herself to looking after the staff laundry, visited Joyce, and ensured she always had shifts with Coleen. Her friend made her laugh and kept her sane.

She needed her friend during the dark times when she couldn't push the truth of her heritage from her mind. Jock, Jack, Gloria, Juliana . . . they all ruled her past like never before. When Coleen wasn't about, Maisie worked extra shifts to prevent herself from staying home and brooding about it all. When she did take time off, she drew on the memories of tender moments spent with Cam and she wrote endless letters to him expressing her love.

Ted returned to Aldershot barracks and they saw each other as often as they could. Maisie couldn't help but feel envious – and sometimes extremely lonely, despite being surrounded by people for most of the day.

Maisie held Cam's latest letter to her chest. She sat in the late sunshine after a particularly gruelling day at work and savoured the slower pace of early evening. Today, the sound of men crying like small babes ate away at her. She'd never expected to be twenty years old still walking the grounds of the place she had lived all those lonely years, listening to sounds which would haunt her for the rest of her life. In her dreams and fantasies, she'd often imagined pushing a pram with a pretty child in it and coming home to the arms of a handsome man. A man much like Cam. Tall, strong, gentle, and handsome. Simple dreams for the simple life Maisie desired.

She tugged Cam's letter free from its envelope and read it through once again. It held hope and promises of a future she couldn't bear to think would come true. She stored the words away as part of a dream to hold on to, because she couldn't allow herself to believe it would ever actually happen. The war wouldn't allow her dreams of a future anymore. She was witnessing too many of the terrible consequences of war and had come to understood why everyone said that life was too short.

June 29th 1942
Classified Address

My dearest Maisie,

Please do not let the world drag you down once I am gone. You are by far the most beautiful girl I've ever met, and I know I will love you forever. Our time together means so much to me and I swear for as long as I survive this ugly war, I will never forget our night together. You confided in me and shared your personal fears and I shared mine with you. I knew the first time we met there was something special about you, and I am proud to call you my girl.

I have no idea where I will be sent next, nor when I will return to you. I repeat what I always say: please wait for me. Once again, I promise with my heart I am not just passing by and I don't have a girl in every town, as you so sweetly put it.

When this war is over, I will take you away from Holly Bush House. I'll give you the life you deserve. We will live under the shadow of the mountains in Canada and watch the glint of sunlight shimmer over the snowy tips or sit and enjoy the peace of flowing rivers together. I'll teach you how to catch salmon and we'll cook it under the stars. Ours will be a happy life.

My love for you always.
Happy birthday for July 2nd, darling. Although it is bound to be a late greeting.
Cam

As Maisie glanced at her present surroundings, she leaned back and created pictures in her mind of how she thought Canada might look. She couldn't imagine living anywhere other than Southampton, but the thought of moving to Canada with Cam, although scary, dominated her dreams.

Summer rolled along with cinema visits, dance hall events and slow walks with Joyce. On August 9th, Charlie's dad arrived with the news that Archibald Charles had arrived into their lives and all was well with mother and child.

Letter after letter to Cam kept the postman busy, and Maisie pored over the few she received in return. She heard via Joyce's brother that Simon had been released and had been shipped back out to sea. Although she was glad he was no longer a prisoner, Maisie was still unsettled by the news. Simon was no longer someone she trusted.

Watching Joyce with her newborn, Maisie wondered if a mother with so much love for a child was capable of just abandoning it like an unwanted kitten. For some time Maisie suppressed the urge to find out more about her mother. One day, after sharing time with Joyce and witnessing the love she gave to Archie, that compulsion to know more about Juliana was overwhelming, and that afternoon Maisie stood at what had once been the entrance to the docks in the hope of catching Doris alone. She'd stood back in the shadows away from leering eyes, with her hair bound in a scarf and hidden under a hat. She'd given no one the opportunity to report her presence to Jock. But after watching the women selling their bodies, and the types of men purchasing what they offered, it was the cure for Maisie, and she headed back to the sanctuary of her cottage. Any further moments of curiosity were soon quashed by the images she saw that afternoon.

CHAPTER 25

'Silent night, holy night . . .'

Maisie peeked from under her eyelashes from where she stood amongst the group of singers in church. Coleen had approached her about singing for the Christmas service when she heard Maisie singing to a patient.

'You've the voice of an angel. Sing with us on Christmas day. I'll not take no as an answer.'

Maisie sang in church – not for Coleen, but for all the servicemen and women who were away from loved ones. She sang for Cam, for Charlie, for Joyce, and baby Archie. She even included a verse for Jack. He tugged at the forefront of her mind most days. She had written to several district councils around the country in the hope that someone might have news of a child adopted into their area, from Holly Bush House. A few had replied to the negative and others replied that although they had taken children from that orphanage, sadly a James or Jack Reynolds was not one of them.

Back home from church, Maisie set about a new exciting project which would keep her busy for a few weeks. Coleen stood on a chair and Maisie had a mouth full of pins. She pushed at her friend's leg to steady her.

'Keep still,' Maisie said carefully, slipping pins into the hem of Coleen's dress.

'Ah, go on. Sing at me wedding too. I can't have me mammy there, but I can have my bossy English friend.'

Maisie punched the last of the pins into the fine parachute fabric secretly donated by Ted's friend at the barracks. She stood back in the hope that a hint of a wedding dress would stare back at her. She was not disappointed. Deep valleys of pleated cream hung in perfect formation.

'Done,' she declared.

Coleen stepped off the chair, each movement with caution.

'I cannot believe it's nearly ready,' she declared.

Maisie gave a puff of negativity.

'It's not. I've still got to stitch it up.'

Coleen slipped the wedding dress over her head.

'Don't stitch it up just yet. Wait a little. Nearer the wedding, like,' she said with a wink and handed the garment to Maisie.

'Oh, really? I'll cut out an extra panel then,' she said with a flippancy she didn't feel inside.

Another friend expecting a child. Another friend leaving, this time for the other side of the world.

'Come on, Maisie. It's not a disaster nowadays. A lot of girls have fallen pregnant then married. Once our paperwork from Canada and Britain gets a stamp of approval, I'm off. Away from this place.'

Maisie sighed.

'Aw, don't you go disapproving now. I'm a good Irish girl. Catholic. This bebby will be loved. Daddy is well off enough to support us. Blame it on the enemy for me wanting to leave. I can't take another bombing.'

Maisie raised an eyebrow but said nothing.

'And there it is. The silent Miss Maisie disapproval. Be happy for us, won't you?'

'I am. It's just that . . . well, I'm . . . don't you think, I . . . well . . .'

'Spit it out.'

Maisie smiled. It wasn't her place to upset Coleen, nor allow her envy to come between the friendship.

'There's a lot for you to think about. It's a big deal wanting to marry Ted, a Canadian,' she said.

'So? And wanting to marry Cam isn't? I seem to recall he's a Canadian too, and I know you'd marry him like a shot if he asked,' Coleen said sharply.

Maisie ignored the barbed retort.

284

'I mean, what do we know about these men? Ted and Cam? About their way of life. They are in our country at the moment, on good behaviour. What if it isn't like that in their own countries. What if Canada isn't all they make it out to be? What if they have girlfriends or wives out there and are leading us astray?'

Coleen slipped on her everyday clothing and carefully draped her wedding dress over the back of Maisie's sofa.

'I think we know them both very well, don't you?' she teased with a wink. 'Be honest, Maisie, you'd love to be in my position. Come to think of it, didn't close contact with something parachute-related feature in your life one night not so long ago? And I'm not talking wedding dress material . . . Clothes didn't come into the conversation, as I understand it,' Coleen said and sniggered.

Her words left a sour taste in Maisie's mouth. She'd whispered her secret to Coleen and had hoped it would never be spoken of again. She wasn't ashamed of sleeping with Cam. It had felt like a natural progression in their relationship. What bothered her was Coleen's way of making it all sound so seedy.

'Some of us will live with the consequences of our actions, others will do things the right way,' she said with sniping friction and stared at Coleen's stomach. Coleen had pushed her too far with snide remarks.

'Touchy,' Coleen retorted.

285

Maisie knew she'd been unkind and apologised.

'I'm sorry. I'm out of order. I'll confess, I'm jealous of you. I *do* want your life . . . the wedding and a new life. I'm being silly. I wish you all the happiness in the world, Coleen. It's Christmas Eve and peace on earth is all I'd wish for anyone at the moment.'

'Jealousy can be a bit of an odd thing. I'll let you off,' Coleen said, and embraced Maisie.

Maisie ran her fingers through her hair and yawned. Both of them were so tired from the increase in their workload that they often threw words back at one another, but their friendship was strong enough to bounce back.

'No, I'm in the wrong. I'm tired but I have no right to take it out on you. I'm sorry. I'll hand your dress up and get some sleep, I might be a nicer person in the morning. I'll cover it with a sheet to protect it. You'll look lovely.'

Lifting the dress onto a hanger, Maisie hooked it onto the back of the door leading into the small porch.

'I'll give it to you to wear after me,' Coleen said as she pulled on her coat.

Maisie giggled and gave Coleen a hug goodbye.

'I'll see you in the morning. We're on the same shift and I hear we've got a few goodies to feast on. Sleep tight,' she said.

*

Tugging out a sheet from the pile in her ottoman, Maisie heard a noise and guessed Coleen had come back. She often did as she was always leaving something behind.

'Forget something? I'll be right down,' she called out and ran down the few stairs into her main room.

Instead of Coleen, as she'd expected, Simon stood in the middle of the room. His face was grey and gaunt. Her body tensed.

'Surprised?'

'Of course! I was told you were deep-sea. How are you?' Maisie asked, thinking how dreadful he looked.

Simon pulled out a dining chair and sat down.

'Hungry.'

Annoyed at his assumption that she had enough food to feed him, and that he expected her to serve him a meal, she stood firm.

'I'm sorry to hear that. I've only got one egg left. I can fry it for you, but I've no bread until morning. I eat over at the main house.'

She kept the conversation going but noticed his eyes flicker towards the door every now and then.

'I take it prison was not a good experience for you. You look dreadful. Are you supposed to be here or have you got yourself into trouble again?' Maisie said with added sarcasm.

With a movement that startled her, Simon pushed back

his chair and rummaged around in his coat pocket, pulling out a cigarette.

'I'd rather you didn't. The dress,' Maisie pointed to the wedding dress, 'it might smell of smoke.'

Simon looked towards the wedding dress.

'He didn't waste time. Ruddy foreigners.'

'It's not mine. I'm making it for a friend.'

'I need a drink,' Simon grunted.

'I don't have alcohol here and anyway, I think it's time you left. You can't just turn up for a visit whenever you feel like it. I don't like it, Simon.'

'I need a drink. It's Christmas,' he repeated and scowled at her.

Maisie ignored the comment and pointed to the door.

Simon rose to his feet and picked up the photograph of the two small children. 'Yours?'

'Of course not! That's me and my twin – remember, I mentioned him. Please leave, Simon. You are not welcome here. I have a new life and Cam is a big part of that life. Your bully boy tactics won't work anymore. This is not an orphanage anymore; it is my home and workplace. You need to leave, I mean it.'

Simon suddenly pushed back his chair with such a force that it clattered to the floor. Both of them stared at it and before Maisie could speak, he was out of the door and racing along the pathway.

Shaken, Maisie locked her door and pushed a chair against it, making a silent plea that Simon never returned.

'Merry Christmas!'

Joyce and Charlie's parents greeted Maisie with flushed faces and enthusiastic hugs.

'Merry Christmas! I see the sherry has ventured out of the cupboard whilst some of us were hard at work this morning,' Maisie laughed as she slipped off her coat.

Joyce put her arm around Maisie's shoulders and guided her into their front parlour.

'Come and help yourself. Mum has laid out a spread in your honour. We have a feeling my brother has a few friends with light fingers because they've brought us illicit gifts, but we're not complaining today.'

Maisie stared in surprise at ham slices, a fruit cake, and other treats she'd not seen for a long time.

'Is that a banana?' she exclaimed.

'We all had one as a Christmas present. This one is yours. We certainly didn't ask where Eddie got them but we'll hide the skins as deep down in the compost heap as we can,' Charlie's dad said and everyone laughed.

The evening passed with carol singing and more merriment and as Maisie left the house, she heard more happy sounds of families taking a brief moment in their lives to forget fighting enemies and enjoy the company of each other. A twinge of sadness shimmied through her as she thought of Cam. Was he enjoying a Christmas meal with friends, or was he across enemy lines, trying to bring about a peaceful New Year?

CHAPTER 26

1943

Holly Bush House
January 1st, 1943

My dearest Cam,

Christmas came and went with a little drama but no let-up in the war, as I'm sure you are fully aware. Silly of me to mention it! Merry Christmas, my darling.

I sang in church on Christmas Eve with the choir and I sang my heart out for you. It was followed by a brief visit from Simon, who is out of prison.

He saw Coleen's wedding dress and assumed you and I were getting married. It was a bit of a weird moment to say the least. I think he'd been drinking.

I sent him packing and fingers crossed he'll not repeat the visit.

I'm making a christening gown for Archie out of leftover material from Coleen's dress. It's sad Charlie isn't here to see his son. Going by the babe's measurements, he's going to be tall like his daddy.

Oh, Cam, life just doesn't seem fair. Simon runs amuck without a care and we are fighting a war that keeps us apart. Dear Charlie lost his life fighting for us and Joyce seems content enough, but it must hurt her to be so alone.

Oh, guess what I had as a gift from Joyce's brother – a banana! If I could have eaten the skin I would have done. It was a delicious surprise. I'm sitting nibbling on a large piece of Christmas fruit cake Charlie's mum sent for me and am feeling rather spoilt. I am relaxed and comfortable but always feel there is something missing. Oh, I know. It's you!

I long for the day when we can relax and enjoy our love with no interruptions by this wretched war. My love always,

Maisie

Holly Bush House
January 8th, 1943

Dearest Cam,

I pray you are safe. Thank you for the Christmas drawing. You are very talented, and the little Robin is perfect. I hope he always keeps you company.

Ted and Coleen had a splendid wedding day and Coleen has applied to return to Ireland to be with her family until after the baby is born, then she will move to Canada. I'll miss her so much.

I haven't had time to write poetry lately. I've been so busy with making baby items for both Joyce and Coleen.

As always, I send my love. I look forward to your next round of leave. I miss you so much.

Maisie

The months rolled by and April arrived with startling speed, bringing with it sporadic bouts of spring sunshine and drizzle. Maisie's heart ached with wanting news from Cam, but letters often arrived months after being written. She'd taken to sending him several in a week, whenever a thought came to her, she shared it as it made her feel closer to him.

Gardening with Billy was a relaxing activity for Maisie. Both were keen on growing their own food and they were succeeding in abundance. When the first of the lettuce leaves broke through, there were great celebrations that the slugs had left them alone. The simplest things brought so much joy to Billy and it rubbed off onto Maisie. She found his company suited her need to unwind, much more so than going to dances with the nurses.

As the months moved along into a hot summer, Maisie's concerns for Cam grew. Planes flew back and forth, but fortunately Southampton suffered no further heavy attacks. Maisie wished she could find out where Cam was but she had no connections to anyone who could help her. Ted didn't have a clue – although she suspected he was holding back protected information – and Charlie's dad pointed out that they were hardly going to hand over sensitive information to a girlfriend.

She'd still had no news from Cam other than the Christmas drawing from 1942, which sat in a frame on her dresser next to her bed. On her twenty-first birthday, a day which slid into the rest with no great fuss, she and Joyce spent an hour together and a handful of colleagues presented her with small posy of flowers.

Her shifts were longer each day as more and more injured men needed her encouragement and support to get well again. But their screams or prolonged silences stayed with Maisie long after she'd settled down to sleep. At one time Cam's past letters kept her company and soothed her but the frustration of not knowing if he was injured or dead meant they'd become painful reminders of what might have been. Maisie feared she was losing hold on her dream of becoming his wife and found it hard to hold back her dread. Work became her main focus.

One afternoon, she sat recording the successes of a patient who was recovering well, when she heard a colleague calling her name. She rose from her chair and peered out into the corridor. A nurse pointed to the front entrance.

'You've a visitor. A sailor. Says his name is Michael Weatherfield and he's been sent by a friend,' she called with a beaming smile and pointed outside.

Curious, Maisie walked down the corridor and turned into the entrance porch. She suspected that Simon was in some kind of trouble and wanted her to bail him out. His unpredictable reappearances in her small world felt very much like an invasion.

She smiled at the sailor in front of her. 'Michael Weatherfield? I'm Maisie Reynolds. Is this about Simon?'

The man could only be described as handsome. He was certainly physically attractive, standing there with his legs astride, his arms behind his back, looking clean and tidy in full uniform. His face was cleanshaven and looked fresh and healthy. His smile was wide and there was something familiar about him. Maisie gave a small frown.

'Yes. Simon sent me in this direction, via another shipmate. I ignored the message at first, but something my parents told me before I left home resonated with me, and a letter to them from a local government department confirmed it all for me. I think I'm your brother.'

Warily, Maisie forced a smile back onto her face. She looked him up and down.

'Gracious,' she said, not entirely convinced of his story. If Simon had been involved, she wasn't sure she could trust what she was hearing; he was not a reliable friend.

'What makes you think that's the case?' she asked, her voice blunt and suspicious.

'My parents told me I was adopted. They said, with me going to war, they felt it only fair I went knowing the truth about my background. Apparently, I lived here for a few months before they took me in. It was before I'd turned five. When I told my shipmate, it filtered along the line to a chap who'd also lived here, and well, the official letter asking whether I would be prepared to be found by a sibling arrived and here I am.'

The sailor took a step forward and Maisie stepped back, clutching her chest. She closed her eyes and tried to control her breathing. Opening them again, Maisie saw tears nestling on the man's lashes and, before she could speak, he spread his hands out in front of her.

'You found me,' he said.

'Jack . . .' Maisie whispered.

Her brother smiled. The familiarity of his features suddenly became obvious. He had her smile, her eyes and lips, but his hair was sandy rather than deep red. 'I only know the name Michael, but Jack sounds right when you say it, so we'll go with Jack.'

Neither could move.

'I think we need to talk,' Jack said, his voice soft.

'I'm just about to finish my shift, so I'll let them know I'm off duty and meet you back here in a minute,' Maisie said and rushed to sign herself off.

The nurse who'd announced Jack's arrival stopped her before she left the building.

'Enjoy your time with your man. I've always had a soft spot for a sailor, and he's a looker.'

Maisie grinned at her. 'I'll pass that along. He's my brother.'

The nurse gave an appreciative smile.

'It's my lucky day. Tell him my name's Christine,' the nurse said.

Outside, Maisie relayed the fact that Jack had caused a stir inside the building.

'Come back to mine. There's so much to say,' Maisie offered.

'I'm so grateful you tracked me down, Maisie. My *sister*, my *twin!* I always felt I was missing a part of me, but never dreamed it would be . . . well, you. Now I'm here, I have vague memories of this place, but I had such a happy life in Suffolk that the memories must have been pushed aside.'

Maisie sighed loudly. 'Lucky you. I'm pleased it worked out well for you.'

Jack stopped in his tracks. 'That was tactless of me. I

saw the address on your letter and realised you've never left here.'

Maisie carried on walking, guiding the way to her front door. 'This is my home now, not the main house, obviously. Welcome.'

Seeing Jack standing in her cottage gave Maisie a thrill. She pulled down the photograph of them as toddlers. 'I have another you can have. This is our mother.'

Hearing herself say the words was strange. Jack took the picture from her and smiled.

'We look like her, don't you think?'

Maisie shrugged. 'I see it now, but when I looked at it before my focus was only on you.'

He looked down at the floor. 'I hate that you had to live all these years knowing about me, remembering, missing me, while I drifted along in a happy daze.'

Maisie held open her arms and Jack accepted her embrace. They clung to each other for several minutes. All the wrongness Maisie had ever felt in her life melted away. She felt whole again.

'You're here now and we've a lot of catching up to do. We've not had a pretty start in life, but you need to hear it, including the reason why we were abandoned. I found out some dreadful things, but I'll not sugar-coat them; it's your right to know, same as mine,' Maisie said.

Moving her back into his vision, Jack held on to Maisie's hands and stared intently into her eyes. 'I'm ready to hear it all.'

For over an hour they discussed her findings. Jack was shocked as she had been and scrunched his eyes together as if in pain.

'If any good is to come from this, it is that you are a determined, young woman and I am thankful you are my sister, or we'd have remained separated. Never again. Well, sadly we don't have long together as duty calls, but from now on, we are a pair again. Two halves of a whole.'

They shared a meagre supper together and chatted about their hopes and dreams, some horrors and nightmares, and Maisie learned that Jack had been renamed Michael Weatherfield. The name didn't sit right with her, and she knew it never would. Her brother's name had always been Jack and for her it would never change.

'Be happy, Maisie. I'll write to you when I can, and please share your news with me, won't you? We have a short sailing this time around, but I've a feeling this war is going to take us more deep-sea than ever.'

'Can I come to see you off?' Maisie asked.

Shaking his head, Jack put his finger to his lips and kissed it, then placed it on Maisie's forehead. 'I'd rather you didn't. Let me remember you here, in your uniform, looking every part a nurse. My sister in her little cottage. Let's take a stroll around and then I must go.'

'I'm far from being a nurse, but maybe one day I'll train. In the meantime, I like what I do here, and I love my cottage.'

They walked around the gardens holding hands, and Maisie was reminded of the times they'd done exactly the same as children before being ripped apart.

Jack broke the silence as they stood beneath a walnut tree.

'Your Canadian . . . do you love him? I mean, the marrying kind of love?' he asked.

Maisie gave a soft, shy smile. 'Yes, it is that kind of love.'

'Well, sister dear, when the time comes, I'll give you away. How about that? Do you think that will work?' Jack asked.

'It would, and it would also make me the happiest bride.'

Jack glanced at his watch and frowned.

'I've got to go. Take care, little sister.'

Maisie felt a moment of anxiety. She couldn't bear for him to leave again; it was too soon.

'Enough of the little, if you please. I might be the eldest, who knows? Can't you stay a bit longer?'

Maisie knew she sounded needy, but the thought that this might be her only chance to know her brother was too much. What if she lost him again? What if Jack never came back?

Jack grinned, but it was soon hidden by a serious grimace.

'No. I'd love to stay but I'd be in big trouble. I promise that on my next trip to shore, I'll make contact and take you back to meet my parents. They'll adore you. I'll write to you when I get the chance and leave details of where you can write back.'

Jack kissed the top of her head. 'Don't watch me go. Stay here so I can imagine you in your uniform, under this old tree. A new image to take with me. A happy one.'

'Stay safe, Jack. Now go and make me proud.' Maisie reached out and touched his hand.

When Jack was halfway up the drive, Maisie called out to him. She'd ignored his request not to watch him leave.

'Hey, brother. I love you.'

Jack never turned around but he raised his right arm above his head in a farewell gesture so she knew he'd heard her.

She looked on with pride as he kept his back straight and walked with dignity. Maisie didn't cry for him until he was no longer in view. When her tears fell, they were tears of happiness.

Dearest Cam,

I had a surprise visitor today . . .
Michael Weatherfield of the Royal Navy came to

see me. I used to know him when he lived here. Back then I knew him as Jack. Yes, I've found my brother! Isn't it the most wonderful news? I want to sing it from the rooftops and share it with the world. We've agreed he's to remain Jack to me, as there are some things in life you cannot change when they've affected you so much. The strangest thing is, that it was Simon who brought us together in rather a roundabout way. I cannot put into words the happiness I feel right now. The joy at knowing I have family and my soul is no longer split in two.

I've so much to tell you about him when you return.

As always, my love,
Maisie

Maisie spent many weeks frantically rearranging the home to accommodate more injured servicemen. She threw herself into the work, giving herself very little time to think about the lack of communication from either Jack or Cam. The war and its reminders brought reality to her door in raw visual waves. The main building and dining quarters were converted from a space for convalescing patients into a proper hospital. The convalescing patients – with the exception of Billy who'd made himself invaluable in the garden, and it was felt that for the sake of his peace of mind he'd best stay – were moved to a nearby mansion house. The owners had opened their doors to accommodate the twenty convalescing men. Meanwhile, back at the newly converted hospital, the injuries which the medical team and volunteers dealt with were extreme. It was sometimes mind boggling how the patient had survived at all.

She recalled the first time she escorted a patient into Holly Bush House from the ambulance. It took all her strength not to faint. The ambulance driver and doctor gave her a swift glance as she allowed a gasp of horror to escape her lips.

'Keep it to yourself, Maisie. He still has ears that work.' The doctor's words were firm with a sympathetic ring to them.

Determined to get through the event, Maisie pulled her shoulders back and thought of the man beneath the blood and gore which smothered every inch of his body.

'Is it, can it be cleaned?' she asked.

The ambulance driver nodded. 'A lot of superficial blood, the rest the doc here will sort out. You'll be up and about in no time mate.' Maisie watched as he redirected his attention back to the patient and doctor.

'He's a sailor caught in the bombings at the docks, hence the reason he's here.' The doctor turned to the patient again. 'Lucky man, Maisie here is one of our best trainees. She's going to put her hand on your stomach now and hold on tight until we get you to theatre. Not going to lie, this is going to hurt.'

He nodded to Maisie and, taking the deepest breath and releasing it slowly, she went to his side.

'Gentle. The long pink tubes are his guts. Lay this wadding across and do not move your hands once we get moving. Understand?' Maisie nodded. The patient deserved her full attention, she was ready to give her all. Her foot slipped and she looked down. Her stomach churned at the sight of black mess mingled with red. She glanced at her hands and saw they were covered in much the same. Her hand trembled as she reached out for more wadding to suppress the continuous surge of blood and protect the patient.

'Focus Maisie,' she said out loud.

'Good girl,' the ambulance driver whispered as he moved to the end of the stretcher.

They struggled their way inside the house and when a nurse offered to relieve Maisie, she shook her head. The patient was hers and she wanted to see him through his care.

'Can I stay with him?' she asked.

The doctor gave the nurse a few brief instructions to prep the theatre, and followed it through to confirm Maisie was more than capable of assisting.

'If you feel faint in my theatre, walk out. I cannot step over you and the staff will simply leave you there. I need you to do exactly what you are doing, keeping calm and clearheaded. Understood?'

'I'm ready,' Maisie said, her voice confident and truthful.

They entered the theatre and once the patient was on the table Maisie rushed to wash her hands. A fresh apron was handed to her and she followed each instruction shouted to her with perfect precision. The sailor fought for his life and his country; she would honour him by fighting by his side until recovery.

Only once, when the doctor pulled the full intestines out to inspect them, did she feel the rush of blood leave her body, but she dug her fingernails into her palm and imagined Cam requiring the same sort of surgery. She'd want a nurse to be in control of her emotions to help him survive.

For four hours she mopped large pools of blood from the floor. Her heart went out to the doctor who worked diligently with patience and calm.

'Last stitch, Maisie. We've done it. Well done team.' The doctor beamed at the people around them.

Back at the patient's bedside, Maisie looked down in wonder. She'd held his insides and he'd survived. She stroked his brow and smiled at the nurse tending to his care. Leonard King was a man she'd never forget and she wished him strength to get through the weeks ahead, before heading home to shake off the horrors of the morning.

To this day it always amazed Maisie how strong her stomach was and how tolerant of blood and death she'd become. She moved through her duties without flinching, comforting those with gruesomely burned faces, limbless bodies, and men whose bodies were pumping out blood faster than it could be replaced. Her strength usually held until she closed the door of her little cottage and was safely in the privacy of her bedroom, curled up like a baby, sobbing for every life lost, and for all the pain inflicted on those who had given their lives and their very souls for her.

As kind as she hoped she was, Maisie had no sympathies for the enemy; she didn't have the time nor the energy. She did, however, have time to be shocked and horrified by the attacks on the Jewish people. Gas chambers and camps were all she heard people talking about and eventually, Maisie had to tune it out and focus upon patient care for the sake of her sanity. It wasn't because she wanted to hide from the news, but it felt like her mind would explode at the horror of it all. She also carried the responsibility of holding onto the secrets that the dying whispered into her ear, but despite how hard she found it, Maisie knew her duty and calling was to ease the pain of others.

CHAPTER 27

News on May 13th, created an excited buzz around the wards when they were told the Germans had surrendered to British and American forces out in North Africa. Although everyone knew the war was far from over, it brought hope that progress was being made.

Sadly, it also brought about a surprise air raid on Bournemouth, with the planes appearing before anyone could sound the sirens. It unnerved the residents of other cities and towns and drowned out any positive news that came their way.

It also brought with it a dark mood for many, and Maisie wept for those they couldn't save at Holly Bush House, but after several days of sore eyes and heartache, she chose to climb from the pit of despair. She continued her job to the highest standard, knowing any death was beyond the medical team's control and

Hitler would not take away the strength and courage of the British people.

When June brought more news of German concentration camps, whispers of the country creating new bombs, and the successes and losses of American bombers targeting Germany, Maisie's heart sank. The house discussed the news of the gas chambers and the diabolical treatment of the Jewish people, until she could bear to hear no more but out of respect for those suffering, she listened. How had human beings become so cruel and hateful towards their fellow man? The war was exhausting her ability to comprehend such cruelty, yet strengthening her commitment to tend to the wounded and feel in some small way she'd thrown her own form of ammunition at the enemy.

News came through in July, the British and Americans had razed the German city of Hamburg to the ground and with it the fear of another retaliation attack for Southampton and other British cities.

Although these were victories, Maisie quietly thought of the innocent victims suffering the same across the water as they were in Britain. She'd taken to leaving conversations which hinted at gloating. Too many lives around the world were caught up in the disasters. Would anyone find peace at the end of it all? How many men, women, and children would be rendered homeless, injured mentally and physically all for one man's greed.

She celebrated the victories with her colleagues but lived with a new fear. The fear of their own deaths.

Maisie's ears tuned into sounds during the night as she sat beside her patients, forever waiting for the sirens to send out their alarm. Her nerves tingled with the thought of having to move such sick people to safe areas, where their chances of survival weakened.

Every day someone read out news of successes and disasters, and more than ever Maisie wanted Cam to be part of her life; to return to her whole and happy, ready to start the rest of their lives free from the war.

In August she found relief from the dark thoughts when she joined Charlie's family as they celebrated Archie's first birthday. It was a day of joy where everyone laughed and giggled with him for two carefree hours. Archie was their sunshine during the dark days of war, his innocence gave them back a small piece of theirs and Maisie left their home with a better outlook on life.

In November, Joyce confessed that she had met another man and that she had feelings for him. Life for Joyce was moving along but Maisie felt like hers was static. Only the determination to give the best of herself to comfort others kept her from being bored of her life. One she described to Joyce as static, but every sensation of boredom brought with it feelings of guilt when so many others were clinging to their lives by a thread.

Letters from Jack arrived which contained snippets about his upbringing. She noted how sensitive he was about always apologising for being adopted and having had a good life when she had had to endure Holly Bush. Eventually, she had to write and tell him to stop feeling so guilty. The past was behind them and they had to focus on what they did have, not what they'd missed out on. They had an opportunity to rebuild their relationship and they had to be grateful for that.

She was touched when he arrived unannounced for a brief visit while his ship docked for a swift turnaround. He brought with him a gold St. Christopher necklace for her and wore a matching one underneath his uniform. It was a symbol that they travelled together, no matter how far apart they had been pulled, and she loved it.

Stepping outside into the sunshine, Maisie felt like embracing the outdoors to reflect on her brother's all too brief visit. She touched her necklace and sent up her usual prayer to keep Cam and Jack safe. She lay on a blanket under the shade of the old walnut tree to rest. She'd worked through the night and past dawn to help a young severely disfigured pilot transition from pain to peace, and she was exhausted.

Her heart ached for Cam's return and she longed for the day when they would be able to enjoy adventures together. She wanted to fish for salmon, to taste maple syrup, to kayak and swim in warm waters, or trek snowy mountains, all the things Cam told her were waiting for her to experience. Now another year older, Maisie was ready for the ties of Holly Bush House to be ripped away, but as she lay watching the branches above sway in the breeze and birds dip and dive while snatching at insects, Maisie knew her commitment to the injured servicemen was her priority until the war ended. As her mind unwound from the frantic activities of the night, she accepted that chasing adventure was a thing of the future, and for now she must focus on the present.

She closed her eyes and allowed the warmth of the ever-rising August sun to tingle her skin. Her thin cotton blouse and skirt were too warm for the time of year, but decency forbade her to strip down to her underwear. Trickles of perspiration crossed her brow, but Maisie was determined to enjoy the listening to the birdsong in the sunshine. The soft breeze blew away city noises and the tinny anti-aircraft sounds which normally drifted on the air. Today, all was peaceful and even if it was to be only for an hour, Maisie was determined to allow the pressures of life to drift away. One cynical nurse spoke about the quiet before a storm and was shot down with terse remarks from the others. In the garden, they all found their own space to breathe and recuperate.

A shadow fell across her, blocking out the sun, and Maisie squinted to see who'd disturbed her. But when she peered through the shimmer, she saw Cam smiling down at her. In one swift movement, she jumped up and into his arms with a delighted squeal, careless of the others and their peace.

She and Cam laughed when a ripple of applause and shouts of encouragement for Cam to kiss her came from the others in the garden. A loved one visiting or returning from duty was always something to be celebrated.

In response to their excited instructions, Cam's lips found hers and Maisie didn't care who watched their lingering kisses. Without speaking a word, they gathered up her things and walked hand in hand to her home. The chickens scattered across the garden, then regrouped around Maisie's legs.

'Poor things. They need feeding.'

Cam put his head back and burst out laughing. He scooped her into his arms and squeezed her close.

'Here I am flying halfway around the world for you, jumping out of planes into enemy territory and hitching rides back to England, grabbing a quick shower and begging a lift before dawn to be with you as soon as possible, and the first words you say are related to feeding chickens.' Cam kissed her cheek. 'I love you Maisie Reynolds. I truly love you for grounding me.'

Although Cam couldn't tell her where he was headed after his six-day embarkation leave, Maisie knew it must be into the thick of things because he asked if he could leave a few personal items with her including letters for his family. It frightened Maisie but she pushed it to the back of her mind, determined to treasure the time they had left §in the best way possible.

She applied for leave and it was granted. Maisie taking time out was a novelty and her shifts were covered quickly with no argument.

She and Cam planned days out together where they went walking and talked for hours. They planned their future and curled up in each other's arms.

As they lay in bed together, there was no shame or embarrassment; they both agreed marriage was what they wanted. Cam warned her he wasn't sure when he'd be free again, and it might take a while to book leave in order to marry, but as soon as he knew, he'd get word to her so she could make arrangements. Maisie only had to inform her senior and request the day off and although both were eager for it to happen sooner rather than later, they agreed they would have to leave it to fate.

Cam told her more tales of Canada, and of where he'd like them to settle and Maisie expressed her fears about leaving England – and Jack – behind. Cam suggested that Jack might enjoy a good life there too, perhaps setting up a fishing business that Cam had always dreamed of owning. Maisie loved him all the more for his considerate offer.

One afternoon, they took a bus to Bournemouth and

to Cam's delight came across many serving Canadians which made him feel closer to home. The beach was surrounded by barbed wire and heavily patrolled. To Maisie's surprise, despite this, it was extremely busy with people enjoying the opportunity of a sunny day at the seaside. A group of GIs threw a ball about, and several young women urged them on from the sidelines. Maisie and Cam found a quieter spot and sat on a blanket together away from prying eyes. They continued their conversations about their future together in the comfort each other's arms, watching seagulls dip in and out of the water. Cam let out a heavy sigh and Maisie moved herself around to look him in the face. She was taken aback by the sadness on his face. He bit his bottom lip to stop it trembling before he spoke.

'I wish I could take you with me, to let you fly free, to float or spin without a care in the world, but not today, not tomorrow . . . not until the war ends. To fly over what I've seen, to drop into the world I have to deal with . . . the danger, the cruelty . . . I could not wish that for you, Maisie.'

Maisie opened her mouth to speak, but Cam put a finger to her lips to prevent her from responding.

'Hear me out. If we can't make wedding vows, I want you to hear my words before I leave you again. I fly into dangerous situations and cope because I know I've got the most beautiful girl in the world waiting for me. Her red hair glistens in sunshine, her smile brightens up the darkest day. I could never wish you the fear I've witnessed or felt; to experience the non-physical pain is not easy. I want only the peace and comfort of love in a peaceful world. I want you to cut and taste my mom's apple pie hot from the oven on a minus ten day. I want you to see my pops whittle wood. I want you to open your eyes on a summer's day and see a tiny hummingbird hovering for nectar. I want only those things for you. It scares me that I have nothing in England to give you. I have only Canada to offer you and I'm afraid you will be too scared to come with me when the time comes, especially now that Jack has returned into your life.'

Maisie waited with patience while Cam finished talking. She knew there and then that she'd follow him wherever he wanted to go.

She reached out and touched his cheek. Wedding vows couldn't have been expressed with any more passion and she wanted him to know how she felt too.

'I have nothing in England to offer you either, except myself and my memories of this place. Jack is back, but after all these years apart, I cannot give up my love for you for my ties with him. And anyway, he's a traveller, so we'll not be apart forever.

Our time has come, Cam – Harry Cameron – my dark-eyed man of the skies. I want to be the woman who drives you forward, who climbs from her bed to work by your side, to feed our children. I want Canada. I want my life to start with you. We can do it; we can build our lives together. And if it isn't meant to be, then we will mourn one another, for in my mind, here in my heart, I cannot imagine sharing my life with another man. You are the beat, the rhythm that gets me through the days when my heart wants to stop, when I want to give up. I want us, Cam. You've made me the woman that I have become. And the sad, lonely girl of the past? Her real life is just about to begin . . .'

CHAPTER 28

1944

'Any news from Cam?'

Joyce greeted Maisie with her usual question whenever Maisie visited. Hooking her coat onto a peg by the door, Maisie took a moment to reply. She'd not heard from Cam since several letters had arrived at once in December.

'No. Nothing since he sent Christmas wishes and asked if I could knit him gloves and socks, so he's somewhere cold.'

Joyce pulled her in for a hug and Maisie relaxed into her arms.

'I'm sorry, my lovely, it must be so hard for you. I'm sure they'll come in a large sack of their own one day and you'll have a reading feast,' Joyce replied, moving Maisie back and offering a soft smile.

Maisie shrugged.

'I sent some to the barracks, but I'm not sure whether his parcel arrived. I hope so. You? Any news on your man?' Maisie asked, eager to change the subject. The lack of communication from Cam unsettled her and she'd rather not talk about it for fear of crying.

Joyce's relationship with her new fellow had developed, and it was obvious to everyone that she was ready to settle and marry again. Charlie's parents had taken a while to come around to the idea, but insisted that she stay with them until her new marriage and life were finalised. Archie was their pride and joy, and Maisie knew they would do all they could to ensure he and his mum had a happy life.

Joyce poured tea from the pot and handed Maisie a cup.

'Not much milk, I'm afraid.' She pulled a face as she took a sip. 'He's coming home in two weeks. I received word from his sister this morning. We'll be getting married in Bournemouth, where he's from, and then we'll be moving two doors up from here. The landlady spoke with Charlie's dad last week and wondered if he knew anyone interested in renting because her tenants were moving to live with family in the Midlands. The wedding will be a quiet affair out of respect for Charlie's parents. I'll let you know where and when next week.'

A shiver ran through Maisie when she recalled Joyce's first wedding day and Charlie's funeral, two such contrasting events.

'That's wonderful news, Joyce. I can't wait to plan mine and Cam's wedding, but it feels like it will never happen. Just like the end of this damn war.'

The friends gave each other a half-smile.

'It must be so hard for you not knowing where he is. At least I can keep track of Fred's ship thanks to Dad and Eddie. I still can't understand your Cam wanting to jump out of airplanes. What kind of craziness is that? Especially when he has someone to live for now. Surely he needs to think about transferring to something else?'

Maisie put down her cup.

'It's who he is, Joyce. I'm not sure I'd want him to do anything else. He loves his job. Yes, he loves me, but I am not crucial to getting this blasted war over with. I'll not have him change for me.'

'Any news from Jack?' Joyce asked, wise enough to steer the conversation away from Cam and weddings.

Maisie pulled a dog-eared letter from her pocket.

'I got this last week. I think he might have sailed to the Mediterranean because he mentioned that he'd left his ship and swam in beautiful blue water, and I remember Eddie saying much the same in a letter to you.'

Joyce nodded. 'Did you know that Eddie's home?'

Maisie shook her head. 'No. Is he injured? Is the ship back quayside?

'No, it's still out there, near Sicily. That's where Jack's enjoying his swim. Eddie finished training for submarines and is joining a new crew next week. Why on earth anyone would want to be cooped up inside a tin can is beyond me. It worries me to the point that I have to stop thinking about it – a bit like you with Cam, I suppose. I wouldn't be surprised if your Jack is possibly heading this way again soon; they've been out there a long time.'

'We'll see. I still pinch myself that we found each other. I just wish this war would end so we can all focus on rebuilding and living our lives in peace again,' Maisie said with a sigh. 'I still find it hard to accept where we came from though.'

Joyce's eyebrows lifted and dropped.

'I can't get my head around it either. What a story you will have to tell your children.'

'There are some things they'll not be told. My parents died, and we grew up as separated orphans; that's all they'll need to know.'

The door flew open and Archie staggered in dragging a cat by its tail. Both Maisie and Joyce jumped to their feet to rescue the poor creature from the clutches of the toddler.

'See the things you'll have to deal with later on

down the line! Yesterday, it was next door's dog getting a few tugs of the ear. Good job it's a patient old thing.'

Maisie laughed and held Archie away from the cat to give it the opportunity to run free.

'Right, Master Archie, I'm off to work. You behave for Mummy and I'll see you soon.' Maisie dropped a kiss on his head and gave Joyce a hug goodbye.

Walking back to Shirley, she stared at the devastation around her and wondered what Canada looked like at that time of year. She envied them if they'd not had to suffer the enthusiastic bombings of the enemy that England had endured. February in England was always bleak, and even more so with so many destroyed family homes lying in heaps on the ground. The idea of eating Cam's mother's hot apple pie on a cold day kept her going.

Once on duty, Maisie collected the post for patient delivery and to her delight saw a letter addressed to her in Cam's handwriting. She avoided the temptation of opening it there and then, and let it burn a hole in her pocket whilst she worked. Once she finished the last of her chores, she battled against the bitter cold wind all the way to the cottage, checked on the chickens, and heated herself a bowl of vegetable soup.

After she'd eaten, she settled down to read Cam's letter.

Glynis Peters

Dearest M,
You are my Valentine and I hope I'm still yours.
Sending kisses and all my love.

The days are long and boring. The training is intense.
Yes, training. Something's afoot and we are being
put through rigorous routines, but no one can tell
us for how long – or where we are to be sent next.
I'm with a great group of five men, three of us
Canadian and the other three Brits. We all have
girls waiting to see us, so it helps to know we are
not alone in our loneliness. Judging by the activity,
I suspect your brother is also busy.

I've sent a few treats in a package but it's anyone's
guess if it will ever arrive. It's bleak and dismal here
and my trek to the post office took me nearly two
hours, mostly across fields filled with cattle.

I've given some thought as to where I'd like to
live when we settle in Canada. I've several options
but, inspired by my surroundings, I think a recent
offer I've received of living in Nova Scotia would
be just the thing. We often took trips with my family
to Green Bay and Blue Rocks, and it is surrounded
by beautiful scenery. My uncle has a thriving

lobster-fishing business at Blue Rocks and has asked me to consider working for him when I return. I won't lie to you, the work will be hard and the place is isolated, so we could agree to try it for a year, for your sake. My cousin Larry was killed in Dieppe in '42 and my aunt and uncle have no other children. We'd inherit the business to continue on the family name. It's a wonderful opportunity.

We could go sailing on the LaHave river. We would need a small boat. Do you fancy building a boat for us to sail? Oh, my darling girl, we will have such a wonderful adventure together. Say yes to Nova Scotia. Say yes to lobsters. Say yes to wide open spaces.

Be my wife. I realise that although we discussed marriage, I never actually proposed! I meant to on the beach that beautiful day we spent together in Bournemouth but never found the right moment. Say yes, say you'll marry me. If only we had a telephone here, I'd make the call and hear you say it out loud. Write to me. Tell me yes.

Another trek in the snow with a tuck and roll session is all I have to look forward to every day. Send me something to change my sorry mood.

Much love my darling,
Cam

The ache inside Maisie's chest was a physical pain as she clutched Cam's letter close. Not a flutter or a twinge, but a full-blown ache as if she'd been punched. She thought of him trudging across snowy Scottish fields just to send her a letter. She was only guessing at Scotland and felt sure it was the place he was hinting about. She read the letter again and imagined the pair of them setting up home; she wasn't sure what a lobster was or looked like, but they seemed to make Cam happy, so she'd be happy for him. She snatched up her pen.

> *Holly Bush House*
> *February 20th 1944*

My dearest Cam,

Your Christmas letter arrived today. I have very little to tell you, but what I do have is good news. Joyce is to remarry in a few weeks but will live a few doors away from Charlie's family. Fred's a good man and Archie will have a father to raise him. We can't be anything but happy for her.

Billy is finally leaving Holly Bush House. He's got a job at a large house and will be responsible for cultivating the fruit trees and vegetable patches. I like to think I played a part in his recovery and it makes my heart sing to see him so happy.

In answer to your questions, yes, yes, yes! Yes,

I'll marry you. Yes, I'll move to Canada with you, and learn about lobsters. Yes, I'll try and make a boat for us to sail in, and yes, to wide open spaces where our children will run free. Nova Scotia sounds so colourful with green and blue bays. I do hope we will be blessed with children. If we have a little girl, I'd like to name her Dee and Charlie for a boy. But first we must get through this war. You must survive and come home to me and we must marry. I am sad about your cousin, but I know you will make your uncle proud. I'll do all I can to make your dreams come true. If we are together, I won't be scared.

There is little news of Jack. Eddie said he's been to the Mediterranean and that's all I know.

I've sent another package of knitted items for you. It sounds as if they will come in useful unless they arrive after April when the weather is warmer! I look forward to receiving mine!

I've written a few words for you. A poem to express how I feel – what I would say if we could speak on the telephone.

For Cam

When I close my eyes you are beside me,
I hear you breathe, feel your warmth.

I feel your touch, see your smile.
When I open them, you are gone,
And I am cold – alone. Lost.
So, I will walk this earth, eyes closed,
Until you return and kiss them open again.

Come home to me soon and stay safe.
My love always,
Maisie

PS: Stay warm, my darling.

CHAPTER 29

'I cannot believe we are wearing nylons to my wedding, Maisie. Your Cam is a lovely man,' Joyce exclaimed when Maisie handed her the gift.

Cam's parcel arrived several weeks after he sent it and Maisie opened it with care. Inside were two pairs of nylons, a bottle of Blue Grass by Elizabeth Arden perfume, and a bracelet formed from twine and small coloured beads with a note to say that Cam had made it during his rest times. Maisie's smile couldn't get any wider as she lifted out each item. The parcel had arrived when Joyce's wedding was only ten days away. Maisie knew a pair of nylons would be the best wedding gift she could offer and chose to give her friend a pair rather than store them away.

The wedding moved Maisie more than she'd thought it would. As hard as she tried, she couldn't put Charlie's face from her mind. When the ceremony was over, they went to Joyce's new home and celebrated with a small supper. Fred was shy, and since most of their family members had been unable to travel or get time off, it had been a small, quiet affair. When Maisie left the newlyweds, she pondered her own wedding, and wrote to Cam with her thoughts.

Holly Bush House
May 29th 1944

Dearest Cam,

Thank you for my gifts! What a wonderful, thoughtful man you are. I made full use of them today when Joyce and Fred said their vows. Archie stole the show as he clapped and chattered his way through the ceremony. I had mixed emotions but couldn't help but be happy for them.

One of the nurses here told me they have family in Nova Scotia after I mentioned you wanted to live there when we are married. Her aunt settled there after the Great War. They write often and said they will mention me in their letters to encourage their relatives to send news for me to read. Isn't that kind?

We are full to bursting with patients now, and beds fill every room in all the buildings. The nurses are pushed to their limits and the assistants like me are encouraged to help where we can in their place. Today I was asked to step in and help a doctor with a surgical procedure. I said yes, of course. If the poor patient was brave enough to fight on my behalf, I felt it my duty to make sure he was given a chance. It was one of the most dreadful things I've ever witnessed. Let's just say that the man will never shake hands again. This war, this dreadful war, needs to end. I must have you back whole and handsome, ready to whisk me away across the waters. I refuse to fly, so do not even consider a parachute with my name embroidered on it as a wedding gift!

I took myself into Southampton today and the activity down there is frantic. Soldiers and vehicles queued for miles. Children were shouting out for gum, so there must have been GIs amongst the crowds. I'd rather have an ice cream again, or a large bar of real chocolate. Gum is a treat, but ice cream and chocolate made with milk are my favourite. Listen to me, moaning about missing sweet treats when people have bigger problems to deal with!

I picked up two packs of cigarettes that were thrown my way but I gave them to my friend after trying one. I coughed so hard I scared her, and she

*took them from me with gratitude. I told her I was
the grateful one. I never want to smoke again!*

*Oh Cam, it's been so long since we held each
other. My arms feel empty. I should imagine it's how
a mother feels when sending a child off to war or
evacuating them, or worse. I try and think of happy
things and hold on to funny events that happen
around me, just to stop the doldrums taking hold
in my head. I've a new book to read, Little Women,
and it is a wonderful story about sisters and growing
up. Am I greedy to want sisters when I've only just
found a brother? I think I'd love to write a book
one day but I wouldn't know where to start. For
now, I'll stick with poetry. My words do become
quite gloomy at times, but it helps me work through
my emotions. If I didn't, I think I'd go mad.*

*I was reminded today of Florence Nightingale,
and of her courage. What an incredible woman. I
wrote a tribute poem and thought you might like
to read it. I think my pen might run dry if I keep
scribbling the nights away, but I have to write. It's
become more than a hobby, more than a young
girl's passing fancy. I learn new words and how to
use them. There's a man who volunteers here; he's
a poet and insists I read my words out loud. He
writes very complicated poems which take me a
while to work out. He is just the sort of man I'd*

The Forgotten Orphan

imagine a grandfather to be like. Another thing I've
never experienced.

<u>For Florence – Respect</u>

Light flickers and shadows kiss,
Tenderness from a loving Miss.
Grace and gratitude entwine,
Amongst twisted bodies line after line.

Patients, patience all are yours,
Defying death behind closed doors.
A no-gun war, no hidden mine,
Just twisted bodies line after line.

A battle daily fought by all,
Woman strong as man does fall.
Respite none, no resting time,
Only twisted bodies line after line.

Touch releases white light sighs,
As yet another brave man dies.
Nightingale sings in silent rhyme,
To her twisted bodies line after line.

What do you think? Am I improving? My dearest,
I'm tired now, so will rest as tomorrow will be

*another busy day. I'm also excited as one of the
wives who will visit tomorrow saves her rations and
bakes us cakes as a thank you. We love her for it!*

Take care, my love. Stay safe.
Maisie

'Maisie Reynolds? Maisie? Telephone call for you.'

Dropping the pile of clean bandages, Maisie ran along
the corridor to the telephone, dread pounding in the pit
of her stomach.

'Hello? Hello?' she called down the line.

'Now connecting you,' came a female voice.

'Maisie? Maisie? Can you hear me?'

Cam's voice echoed down a crackling line.

'Cam! Cam, I can hear you. Where are you, are you
well?'

'I'm on my way back to Southampton. I've a forty-
eight-hour pass and I need to see you. Don't go anywhere.
Wait for me.'

Maisie gripped the telephone handset tightly to prevent
her hand from shaking.

'I'll wait. I'll be here. At mine.'

'I love you, Maisie.'

The telephone line clicked dead and Maisie replaced
the handset. She held her breath, hoping for it to ring
again, but after a while she realised Cam wasn't going

to call back. But he was on his way to her ... She hurried to the main office and tapped on the door.

'Enter.' The voice of the senior sister rang out. Maisie straightened her apron and took a deep breath before entering.

'Sister,' she said as she stood tall in front of the desk piled high with brown files.

'Reynolds. What can I do for you?'

'I know we're rushed off our feet, but I've just received a call to say my . . .' She hesitated then ploughed on. 'My fiancé has a forty-eight-hour pass and will be arriving later this evening, I think. I hope. It is short—'

'You are asking for time off with your fiancé?' The sister nipped her lips together and tapped her fingers on her desk.

'Yes, but I—'

'Gracious, Maisie. You are so formal. You work hard and rarely take time off. I think we can let you have two days' leave. We have a full staffing list at present, so go and enjoy your forty-eight-hours. I've had a call from mine too and he's not able to get leave. Time is precious, so go and make the most of it.'

'Thank you. Thank you. I'll work double shifts when I get back. I am so grateful.'

The sister waved her hand towards the door.

'Go before I change my mind,' she said with a smile, and Maisie didn't need telling twice.

*

By nine in the evening she began to regret leaving work so early. Her mind raced with excitement and time moved slowly. She picked up her book but couldn't read. By midnight, she gave up on waiting for Cam and changed into her night clothes. Disappointment sat heavily on her shoulders as she climbed into bed. In the silence and darkness she no longer fought the tiredness and drifted off to sleep.

A tinny pinging sound disturbed her slumber and awakened at the unusual sound. It came from outside. Pulling aside her curtain a fraction, she jumped back as something clicked against the windowpane. A stone.

She peered down into the garden and in the intermittent moonlight, she spotted Cam about to throw another. She tapped on the window and waved down to him. Jumping from her bed, tugging on her dressing gown as she went, she raced downstairs to the door and pulled it open to let him inside.

'Hello, you,' she said and fell into his open arms.

His clothing felt damp with night dew and she moved away and lit the oil lamp on the table.

'Take your jacket off and hang it on the back of the chair.'

Cam did as she said, and as he did so he yawned. He looked tired and unshaven.

'You're exhausted. Look at you. I've got milk; I'll boil some.'

Cam smiled.

'You spoil me,' he said and bent to unlace his boots.

'It's my duty,' Maisie called from the kitchen.

'I'd have been here sooner except the trucks were held up getting into town. I hitched a lift with a doctor heading this way. He stopped to offer me a lift and we found we were both headed to the same place.'

Maisie placed the mug of warm milk on the table.

'It's warm but not boiling so don't let it go cold. You were walking here? In your condition? You look exhausted, Cam. It's late. Let's head for bed and rest.'

Cam picked up his drink and drank it down in one go.

'Heading for bed and resting is not quite what I had in mind, Maisie Reynolds.' Cam winked.

'I'll pretend I didn't hear that, Harry Cameron,' Maisie said with a giggle.

CHAPTER 30

'Maisie Reynolds – born Julie Reynolds. Will you do me the honour of becoming my wife?'

Maisie looked down at Cam who was on bended knee. The shadow of the walnut tree did not overshadow the sparkle from a round solitaire diamond supported on a gold band nestling inside a green velvet box. It was delicate and pretty and most unexpected. Their last few hours had been spent making love and appreciating the time they had together. Cam warned her he was about to embark on an important mission connected with the activities she'd witnessed in Southampton. Maisie had seen him pacing the garden smoking but she'd thought his edginess in the last hour had been down to the mission; she never dreamed he'd propose, let alone produce such a beautiful ring.

His eager face stared up at her, and although he knew

her answer would be yes, she saw the anxiety of a pending no in his face.

'Of course. Yes! Yes, I'll be your wife. Maisie will marry you, and adore you for the rest of her life, but I suppose Julie will have to sign the papers. It galls me that my marriage certificate will bear that name.'

Before she could utter another word, Cam had slipped the ring on her finger and kissed her lips with a fierceness he'd never shown before. A loud shout and applause came from a window across the grounds, and they turned to see the staff waving their congratulations. An eagle-eyed member of staff must have spread the word.

'We will find a way to get your name changed. You will always be Maisie Cameron to me and that's the most important thing in the world right now.'

Maisie twisted her hand one way and then the other to watch the light glint off the diamond.

'I can't believe you found time to buy me a ring. It's so pretty.'

'It's amazing what you find in Scotland,' Cam said, taking her hand as they walked back to the cottage.

'I was right, you were training in Scotland!' she said.

'Important training,' Cam said, and Maisie noticed him shudder.

'Are you scared?' she whispered.

Cam shook his head.

'Nervous, but not scared. We're about to show Hitler

the door. By the time I've jumped I'll be too busy to be scared.'

The next afternoon, Cam left her with farewell kisses, and a tearful Maisie waved him off. By seven in the evening she stood in the office receiving instructions to join a temporary hospital based at the docks. Their mission was top secret, and they were to support as serving members of a major invasion.

Maisie learned that she was being drafted in as a replacement for a nurse on compassionate leave and was told that her duty was to assist in the care of any casualties brought back from the 'far shore'. She was to ask no questions and not to repeat anything she overheard. Realising that she was about to be thrust into the middle of a major event which could be the downfall of the enemy, Maisie did not falter when she signed official papers signifying her agreement not to share any information and to agree her status as volunteer.

Upon closing the office door, Maisie took a moment to realise that Cam was most definitely part of the campaign. He'd hinted at a big event. Maisie tried not to imagine him parachuting into enemy waters whilst she waited to care for the injured, but a tumble of questions still rolled around her mind, firing off like a machine gun.

Could she do it? Could she wait there without thinking

of the worst outcomes for those she loved? Was she up to the job? Inside Holly Bush House it was different; she knew her skill level and never pushed beyond it for fear of making mistakes. Out there in the mix of such a major event she'd have to deal with far more than she'd ever witnessed. Maisie's thoughts tumbled and turned. Was she capable enough? Would she hold her nerve? What if she made a dreadful mistake?

She stood looking to the skies and thought back over the years and reprimanded herself for her self-doubt. She'd rarely made mistakes with her patient care, so why think she might now. She coped under pressure and thought back to the night she had to take control of Holly Bush when it was an orphanage. No mean feat for a terrified young girl. She had grown up in a way she'd never imagined. The tasks she'd dealt with had certainly given her the strength to face her future. She'd been acknowledged as a tower of strength by many patients and staff, an accolade she dismissed with embarrassment.

Today, Maisie recalled dealing with Gloria, Norah, and the happier times after their deaths when she'd been in charge of the children, like when she released them from chores and gave them time to run about outside and explore, to bring back their findings for discussion. She remembered the Christmas they all received personal gifts and wondered how many still had them. She knew Deedee had a happy life because contact with her parents had never dwindled. Maisie wrote to them about Cam and Jack, and they wrote of Deedee's achievements, from first words to toddling. Maisie reflected upon her handling of the orphanage for that brief period and a fleeting sense of pride came over her. The few remaining residents in her care had left with happy memories to override the miserable ones. Much like her life with Cam and Jack.

By the time Maisie and the other nurses were ready to leave for the docks, and they joined others in the same position for instructions and extra training, Maisie didn't have a minute to herself and all doubts about her ability to perform without faltering fled her mind.

Standing on the western docks battling against the elements, Maisie looked on in amazement at the vast number of vehicles of all shapes and sizes moving along the streets in an orderly queue. The noise of their engines and that of the hundreds of American and British servicemen going about their business penetrated her eardrums until they tingled. She stood, proud of them all, mock saluting those who saluted her as she waited for full instructions from the senior in charge of operations.

She laughed at soldiers who whistled out to her and the other girls around her, and grinned at those who shouted out '*Red, I love you – wait for me*' and other amusing declarations. Nervous energy drove everyone to do their best, and Maisie absorbed each instruction with perfect concentration. Large vessels were loaded with what she learned were landing craft assault vehicles and she watched as they sailed out to the Solent then sat and waited for the signal to leave.

Dark shadows fell as the sky filled with friendly planes. The drone of their engines, their thunderous roar, vibrated across the concrete plinth Maisie stood on for a better view. She experienced a moment of pride, but it was soon stifled by a stab of fear and realisation that Cam could be sitting inside, waiting to jump from any one of them.

She slid her hand into her pocket to feel her ring that was pinned inside. Each time she touched it she thought of Cam and it gave her hope for his return. He was out there somewhere waiting to board a plane, sitting in one, or already fighting it out with the enemy across the water. She had guessed they were headed to France when an orderly mentioned something about Normandy during a training session.

The preparation of the temporary tarpaulin hospitals took days and once the conflict started, they were filled with victims waiting to be shipped out to specialist hospitals – or for some, to the hastily erected morgues.

Every day another batch of vehicles and soldiers arrived to be sent across the water. On British soil, the secret no longer held firm; the word was out with regard to the horrors happening on the beaches. Thousands of soldiers were dispatched to France from Southampton and when a contingent of Canadian units were loaded and sent on their way, Maisie cried as much as if they were the British soldiers she'd sobbed over the previous day. Her depth of feeling for Cam and their plans to settle there once the war was over, gave her a sense of belonging to Canada, and the men reminded her of her promised future. The strength of that promise was now weakened by the grisly scenes she witnessed on a daily basis. If Cam came back to her alive it would be a miracle, but she had to hold on to the faith of a marriage, of children, and of a life chasing their dreams.

Every day she stood anxiously waiting to receive a group of injured soldiers while watching the fit and healthy sail away. *Like lambs to the slaughter* was a term which sprang to mind. Send them out laughing, return them screaming. A conveyer belt of heroes.

For days she did nothing but work, sleep, eat, and nurse. Her wrist ached from writing records and holding the hands of men in agony. Her legs cramped and her back throbbed through standing for so long, but Maisie endured whatever was thrown at her. The more she witnessed, the more she was grateful for the sacrifices made on her behalf. Her colleagues worked at the same dogged pace, each one looking more and more tired and drained, yet, like her, wearing a mask of determination and dedication.

On June 10th, she drew upon a reservoir of strength she never knew she had when stretcher after stretcher was unloaded into their care. She watched a doctor wipe away a tear when a young man thanked him for keeping him alive. Maisie knew the young sapper wouldn't make it through the next hour, but he muttered out his humble thanks until his last breath. The doctor needed a break and Maisie went to him.

'I'll stand by here. I'll mark them up for pain relief and register what I can. Go and get a drink, take a break. If I need help, I'll call someone, but at the moment they are all dealt with. When another group arrives, I'll send word. I can mop brows and hold hands, and that's all they need right now. Go, before I change my mind.'

'It's a nightmare. I've just spoken to a Canadian guy who said their battalions have nearly been wiped out. Heroes, every man out there,' the doctor said, his voice cracking from exhaustion and a parched throat.

Maisie inhaled and slowly let out her breath. His words sent shockwaves through her. Cam! Her knees buckled. Sweat beads formed on her upper lip and she cuffed them away. A panic attack was not useful to their situation. She needed to gain control of herself; as much as she wanted to think only of Cam, there were others in need of support.

'My fiancé is out there, I'm sure of it. He's a para-trooper, a Canadian. I daren't think about it. God this is awful, dreadful.'

Her life without Cam in it was an unbearable thought, and so she pushed it to the back of her mind for fear that thinking about it would make it happen.

'I'm sorry. It was tactless of me,' the doctor said.

Maisie shook her head. 'You weren't to know. Go, get your rest. I've a feeling this is only the start of our workload. Look, more coming.'

She nudged the doctor towards the resting station, urging him forward each time he turned around, guilt and concern written across his face.

'Come back refreshed and stronger,' Maisie called to him, and he waved a feeble hand in the air in response.

Twilight slunk back to allow darkness its place on the quayside as Maisie walked her rounds. Other staff took short breaks or dealt with their patients' needs. It was a well-oiled machine.

Maisie had her two-hour sleep break and rose before dawn. She took a moment to send words to Cam on the morning breeze as she dragged her aching body outside in the fresh air. The sleeping quarters always suffocated her, and whilst she stretched, she recalled Cam talking about wide open spaces. Peace and flowing rivers sounded perfect, but in her present, she knew she'd be facing screams and anguish for the next ten hours or more.

Strengthened by her breakfast and two cups of strong tea, she headed towards her station for the day, accepted her patient care list, and set about her duties. When word filtered through that the troops in France had made headway and defeated large pockets of the enemy, Maisie shared her delight with the others she worked alongside. Something shifted in their mood and a new atmosphere of fresh energy emerged. Hope had arrived. An hour into her duties, she heard someone call her name. An orderly at the end of the receiving tent beckoned her over.

'Maisie Reynolds?' he asked.

'That's me.'

'You're needed in tent two, pronto,' he said and pointed to his left.

Maisie nodded and relayed the message to her colleague that she was required elsewhere. Outside, the scene took her by surprise and she held her breath, unable to release it as she took in the mass of bloodied bodies and walking wounded. Her legs refused to move; it was like something from a nightmare which she knew would remain with her for all her days.

Remembering that tent two had called for her and was obviously short-staffed, she ran the short distance to its entrance. Inside, the system was chaotic, with howling screams of men in agony and staff shouting out orders or requests for help. Maisie grabbed the nearest clipboard and went to receive her first patient.

'Maisie. Here,' a voice called to her and she turned to see Christine waving her over.

'You take over here. I'll see to receiving. I've arranged transport back to Holly Bush House for you.'

With a puzzled frown, Maisie looked at her. Christine gave her a sympathetic smile and looked back at the patient she'd just injected with morphine.

A twisted face stared up at the ceiling, and she just about recognised him as Jack. The label across his chest confirmed it was her brother. A gush of bile threatened to break free as she stared into his burned face. She went to hold his hand but noticed great swathes of bandaging covering them. Christine touched her arm and gave her a soft smile of sympathy; Maisie knew she had to find a new level of strength to get through supporting him until the end.

'Hello, Jack,' she whispered softly.

He twisted his body in agitation and she laid her hand onto his right leg, which was the only place without a bandage.

'It's all right, I'm here. Maisie's here. I'll take care of you. We're going home to rest. Back to Holly Bush House together. We'll be safe there; it's a safe place now. Just rest.'

She dipped a strip of cloth into a bowl of water and pressed it against his lips.

'This will help keep your mouth moist. It won't be long, and we'll be out of here and in the quiet.'

Jack blinked.

'It's noisy. I know.'

The journey back to Holly Bush seemed to take forever, but by four o'clock Maisie had seen Jack transferred into a more comfortable bed in a quiet ward. She left him sleeping through his morphine dose in the capable hands of some other nurses, whilst she took the opportunity to wash, eat, and grab some rest. The staff were under strict instructions to come and fetch her the minute he woke.

At eight o'clock, a tap at her door roused her, and Maisie leapt to her feet and pulled it open.

She squealed with shock and thrust her fist to her mouth. Cam stood in the doorway looking the worst she'd ever seen him. He stared wide-eyed, his face smeared with streaks of blood and what looked like oil. She stepped aside to let him in, and he staggered and lurched towards the couch.

Maisie said nothing. She didn't need to ask how he was; she had a clear visual picture.

He was bruised and battered, haunted by all he'd seen.

'You came back to me,' was all she said.

Cam put his head down to his knees and tucked his arms behind his neck linking his fingers. He rocked backwards and forwards. She heard him sniff away tears and moan. His clothing was not his usual smart uniform, and his boots bore the white marks of dried seawater.

His distress concerned her and she went to him. As she touched his shoulder he flinched away. His action frightened her; the Cam she loved would never flinch from her touch. Seeing him in such anguish broke her in two. She needed to find a way to comfort him but each time she touched him, he reacted as if she'd struck him.

'Cam?'

Nothing.

'Cam, come with me to the main building. Let's get you checked over.'

He shook his head and continued to rock. Maisie had seen this form of distress before and she worried that if Cam were allowed to continue, he'd never stop. His mind was as damaged as Jack's body was.

'If you can't move, Cam, if it's all too much, then take off your boots and rest here. I have to go back to work . . . to nurse Jack.'

Cam's sudden movement startled her. He leapt to his feet and looked around with frantic movements.

'Jack's here? *Here?* Where, upstairs?' Cam's voice became as frantic as his movements. He paced like a caged animal.

Maisie shook her head. 'No. In the quiet room over at the main house.'

Cam's rocking started again; he swayed on his feet.

'Sit down. I'll stay. They know to come and fetch me when he wakes up. He's had plenty of morphine so probably won't wake for a while.'

Cam slumped into the seat.

'It's my fault. He's hurt because of me.'

Maisie frowned. 'I'm sure that's not true, Cam.'

'He saved my life.'

'That I can believe, but you could never hurt him; that's not something I'll accept. Tell me about it.'

Maisie sat beside him and took his hands in hers. She felt his body trembling against her and closed her eyes against the fear that his mind was suffering beyond help. For Cam not to return whole was beyond her comprehension.

'Talk to me, Cam. Tell me,' she said softly.

CHAPTER 31

'We flew over them. Men pushing through dead bodies in the water, wading towards the enemy with their guns held high. One by one they were picked out like tin cans at a fairground. Down they fell.' Cam's voice cracked with emotion as he spoke and Maisie stroked the back of his hand to sooth him.

'The water was a dirty pink where the blood mixed with oil. I dropped down beyond the beach, on the edge of Courseulles, a small town. I managed to achieve my objective, to get a message to the resistance and get out again. I had to head back to Juno Beach, and report back my findings via the wireless.'

Cam took another deep breath and began rocking again; Maisie put her arms tightly around him.

'If it's too much, don't tell me. Don't distress yourself.'

Cam turned to face her. 'I have to tell you. I have to get it out of my head. If you can bear it . . .'

Maisie held his hands. 'I can bear it, if it helps you.'

'I knew I'd not be flying back to England after I found the wireless operator; it was carnage. The only thing I could do was to seek out a ship on its return. As I waded out towards a small temporary landing, we took incoming and the whole thing catapulted us into the air. I heard gunshots and screams as I hit the water. I cracked my knee and elbow on a landing vehicle.'

Pulling him closer, Maisie draped a blanket around him to help with the shivering, although she doubted he was cold; it was shock, she was sure.

'I trod water for a while and clung on to a piece of the shattered platform. The enemy sprayed us with bullets and I watched men sink in front of my eyes. I was helpless. It was helpless. I kept calling out for you. I knew you'd help me.'

Wishing she had a whisky to offer him, Maisie made a note to ask for some when she returned to the main building. Her need to see to her brother was superseded by the desperate state of her fiancé, but she wasn't sure how much longer Jack had to live and a sliver of guilt shimmied through her. She remained silent, but knew she would have to step away if one of the nurses came to get her.

'I wish I'd been able to help you. Go on,' she encouraged.

'The landing crafts were filling with bodies, both dead and alive. I scrambled towards one just as it was shelled. I must have hit my head because all I remember is my mouth filling with water, then blackness.' Cam sighed and rubbed his eyes.

'It's all a bit vague. I remember hearing someone call out, "Hey Canadian," and I came too, but even after that there were moments of blacking out that dragged me under again. A hand grabbed me, and all I heard was me yelling out your name, and as I opened my eyes, a man looked back at me. For a second I thought it was you with your lovely eyes staring into mine, so I screamed for you to save me, to help me. I tried not to, but I couldn't stop. The man told me to keep calm and encouraged me to breathe and stay awake. All I could hear was his voice; the other noises faded away. He kept repeating himself, but I kept screaming out for you. Then it went calm. I enjoyed the calmness and I embraced it, but his voice kept yelling back at me, "Stay with me, stay with me. I'm here to save you. Friend not foe." He told me that his sister was called Maisie and she was in love with a Canadian chap named Cam. He said, "Don't tell me fate has introduced us at a water party courtesy of Hitler? I'm Jack. Soon to be your brother-in-law, I understand." Maisie, he held me and brought me back to life. Your brother saved me, but becau—'

Cam sucked in great gulps of air to try and catch his breath. Maisie left him to speak, not wanting him to hold on to any of his nightmare. Experience had taught her that once it was out, the deep fear and horrors of what men had seen started to lessen and it helped them on their road to recovery. She needed her Cam back, the man as she knew him; it was selfish but she couldn't help it.

'Carry on. Tell me all of it. Fate certainly played a part in bringing you both home to me,' she whispered to him.

After a spate of sobs, Cam continued.

'As Jack reached out his hand, a screaming sound of metal striking metal vibrated around us and his ship started listing. Another explosion ripped Jack from my grip, and I watched him literally fly into the flames that were licking their way around us all. If he hadn't tried to save me . . . Oh, Maisie, forgive me! You can't stay with me now. It's my fault. Just when you found him again . . . How can you even look at me?'

Cam put his hands over his neck again and another bout of traumatic rocking stopped the flow of his words. Maisie wasn't sure how much more she could bear to listen to, but Cam needed to say it out loud. He needed her to hear it, and it was the least she could do to endure watching him fight his pain after all he and others like him had done for her, for everyone.

'Cam, my love, you did nothing wrong. There is nothing to forgive. It was war, awful, terrible war. How could you have known? Don't keep blaming yourself. My darling, I have to go to him now. I have to thank him for saving you. I'll only have him for a short while longer, but I'll have you for the rest of my life. I'm going nowhere, except to my brother's side.'

Cam nodded. 'He deserves everything you can do for him. Go to him. I'll follow soon. I just need to sit quietly for a while.'

'I understand. Rest here and sleep. Go upstairs. Be kind to yourself, Cam. This is not your fault. You deserve my love, too. And you will always have it, do you hear me?'

Maisie out her arms around her fiancé and this time, he let her hold him tightly. She whispered soothing words as his rocking slowed to a stop. 'Go and rest. You are safe with me now.'

Jack's body lay stiff and unmoving. The doctor told Maisie that the morphine had done its job, but that Jack would not need any more. His life was drawing to an end and all they could do was ensure he was quiet and comfortable. Maisie sat beside her brother, only dozing for short periods. Any alteration in his breathing brought her to a state of alertness within seconds.

To her surprise and that of the doctor, Jack survived

the night. Again, with the nurses under instruction to call her if he woke, Maisie returned home to freshen up and to check on Cam.

His clothes were draped over the back of the chair, and his boots stood in one corner. She picked them up and pulled out her boot polish kit. She buffed and shone the boots, removing all traces of the seawater stains. Another reminder of the awfulness they had endured was removed, and the fierce polishing helped her relieve a build-up of tension before she went to her room to check on Cam.

Tiptoeing upstairs, she pushed open her bedroom door and saw him curled like a small boy, hugging the pillow close to his chest and breathing softly. She went to her wardrobe and pulled out a fresh uniform and slipped back downstairs. No sooner had she finished a quick strip wash, she heard him cough as he came downstairs.

'Morning,' she said, not daring to move for fear he'd run or start rocking again.

Cam ran his fingers through his hair and stretched his arms above his head as he yawned. His pale face and gaunt eyes stared back at her; the dark shadow of unshaven growth around his jawline aged him.

'How's Jack?' he asked. Maisie could see the tension in his shoulders.

'He survived the night, and had a calm one, which is good. How are you?'

'Rested. Not sure about recovered. These bruises and ribs will hurt forever, I'm sure,' Cam pointed to large black bruises under his vest and winced when he inhaled.

'Oh, Cam. You've got broken ribs, by the looks of things. Come with me and get yourself checked over.'

Cam shook his head.

'I'll be fine. You go to Jack. I'll come over as soon as I've cleaned myself up and dressed.'

'Is there anything I can do for you?' Maisie asked.

'I'd like a kiss. I need you to forgive me.'

Her heart went out to him. She reached for his shoulders and this time he didn't flinch away.

'I've told you, there's nothing to forgive. It's war. Terrible things happen – dreadful things. It's the enemy who is to blame for Jack's condition, not you. I have to go and say goodbye to him. When I get back we'll kiss and talk for as long as you want, but I never want you to ask for my forgiveness again. Understand? We cannot have this come between us. I didn't know him for long, but I do know that Jack wouldn't want his death to drive us apart.'

Cam kissed her lightly on the lips.

'How can you be so brave, so strong, and so forgiving?'

'I've told you, there's nothing to forgive, and as for me being strong and brave . . . it's all a front. I am scared and weak. I'm about to lose the only family I have, my twin. It's a terrible pain to lose him twice.' She paused for breath and with a clenched fist banged against her heart. 'Deep in here, it's raw. Don't put me on a pedestal, Cam. I can fall off as easily as anyone. I'll be back to see you soon.'

Maisie planted a kiss on his cheek and went to her brother's bedside.

Jack's eyes glistened; pain pushed its way to the surface. He ground his teeth and writhed around the bed, bathed in sweat, panting for breath with rigid jerking limbs flailing in the space above him. He looked like a drowning conductor of a failing orchestra, tortured and incapable of controlling what was going on around him.

The doctor shook his head at Maisie.

'I've given him all I can. I'm sorry.'

Maisie gave the doctor a smile of gratitude and stood beside her brother's bed.

Suddenly Jack screamed out for Maisie to hold him and he pulled her close, staring into her face with such an intensity it frightened her. It sapped her strength to remain detached from his horrors the more he stared. Her heart pounded and she watched his own beat with great intensity against his ribs. She lowered her face to his.

'Fight it, Jack. Fight your demons. Then rest.'

A slight shake of his head was followed by another scream. She touched her palms to the bandages on his cheeks, gently holding his face to prevent him from injuring himself further.

'Sleep, Jack. Sleep, my darling brother,' she whispered.

Instead of closing his eyes, he widened them. Flickering movements of his hands told her that he was struggling to stare up at her but he was determined to show her that he was not giving in to death.

And then she saw it: everything he'd ever witnessed, reflected in his painfully twisted features.

The memories distorted the corners of his mouth, his face contorted, his eyes opened and shut as if he was trying to block out what he'd seen. Maisie saw the torment, and the look in his eyes told her more than his lips ever could. She stroked his cheek bone, feeling the dampness beneath his eyelids as warm tears nestled against his cooling flesh. She absorbed the plea in his eyes, his silent urge for her to keep his secret: he felt guilty for surviving. All her patients had the same look when they returned from the fighting.

'Let's get you comfy again,' she whispered. 'I'll read to you; blink once for the newspaper and twice for a poem from my poetry book.'

Two firm blinks gave her the answer she sought. And it told her that he could no longer bear to hear about the war. It was time for him to rest his memories, to file them away as another soldier's victory. It was time to concede to the enemy's power.

The Forgotten Orphan

'I wrote a poem for you, Jack, about sailors of the past and their love of the sea. Close your eyes and imagine you are out there on calm, blue waters, during peacetime. Go back to the sea, Jack.'

A Sailor's Heart

Mist rolls in on foam-tipped waves,
Eerily silent fleets sail by,
Their elegance and grace are moving,
As their sails stand proudly high.
To the tidal dancing sea,
And the salt within his blood,
The sailor's heart is slave,
When he gives way to his true love.

Halfway through the fifth line of the poem, Maisie noticed a change in her brother's breathing pattern. Shallow breaths rasped around the room, and his pale face drained into a yellowy-grey hue. She laid down the book on the bloodstained counterpane and reached for his hand. Calloused, bruised fingers wrapped around hers with no energy to grip as they once had. She leaned forward to kiss his forehead. His voice, a strained whisper, released one word: *love.*

'And I love you,' she replied.

The soft rattle indicated his last breath and the room

fell silent. Maisie touched her fingers to her lips, ignoring her tears snaking their way down her hand. They fell for her brother and the life they should have had together. They fell for the fallen.

A soft movement from behind her brought her back from her thoughts, and a hand touched her shoulder.

'He saved my life. He pulled me from the water.' Cam's voice cracked with emotion, and Maisie turned to face him.

'He saved you for me. He was sent back into my life for a reason,' she whispered.

Cam eased her close to him and wrapped his arms around her. She could smell the fumes of war on his jacket, but the beating of his heart reassured her it wasn't a dream. Cam was alive, and back in her arms. Two heroes in one room, but only one could share her future.

CHAPTER 32

1945

'I can't believe it's over.' Joyce sat in a chair nursing her baby daughter, a tear dripping from the end of her nose. Maisie dabbed it with a handkerchief.

News of the war coming to an end brought with it bittersweet joy, and as soon as she heard, Maisie ran to see Joyce.

'It must be hard for you. Jack's death feels like such a waste and what with you losing Charlie *and* Fred too . . . it's heartbreaking. I don't think any of us will recover fully.'

Joyce planted a kiss on her daughter's head.

'Thank goodness for my many in-laws, that's all I can say. This little one will keep me busy, and as for Archie, we must make sure war never happens again for his sake.

We have to keep talking about their fathers and what good men they were. They must never be forgotten.'

Maisie sat on the edge of the bed.

'I'll certainly never forget Charlie. It's a lot to try and forget, a friendship like ours. Cam still has those terrible nightmares. Yesterday, it was suggested that he may be medically unfit to jump again, and I must admit, I won't be sad if he is retired out on medical grounds. The wedding date is so close now I can smell it. I can't believe I'm getting married, and I never believed we'd marry in peacetime. Sometimes, well . . .' Maisie took the conversation no further. Joyce knew what her sometimes thoughts were because she had experienced her own . . . twice.

'What are your plans for after the ceremony?' Joyce asked.

Maisie shrugged. 'It depends on what happens to Cam. He's supposed to fly home after the wedding. And as of this week, I am cleared to live in Canada. I've never filled in so many papers. I'm grateful to Charlie's dad for stepping in and helping me.'

Joyce nodded in agreement. 'He was more than willing to fill them in if it made you happy. He's very fond of you. We all are.'

'I'm thrilled he agreed to give me away too,' Maisie said and gave a small smile. 'I'll never forget Jack offering and it would have been wonderful. However, I have no doubt he'll watch over me on the day. How can he not be with me? We are twins, after all. Anyway, I've also applied to go as a Red Cross volunteer to support the men returning to Canada. Obviously, it's a one-way ticket and I'll give up my duties once there. It will pass the time and I'll be of use.'

Joyce handed the baby over to Maisie and sniffled into a handkerchief.

'I'm going to miss you so much.'

Maisie looked down on the child in her arms.

'I'll miss you all, but I have to go. A life in Canada is what we always planned. And in his current state of mind, Cam needs to be back with his family. His idea of us setting up home by a river might have a calming effect on him. I'll be homesick for you, but I've nothing else here.'

Joyce pulled her blouse closed and buttoned it up. She leaned over and took the sleeping baby from Maisie and laid her in her crib. Once satisfied her daughter was settled, she went to Maisie and gave her an envelope.

'If it doesn't work out, you have a home here. Understand? Do not suffer in silence, just come back to us – your non-blood family. Just telegram for the money home, we'll get it to you. Here are a few photographs of us which might be nice for you to put in your new home.'

Maisie enjoyed another hour of chatting with Joyce

and left to catch the bus to Aldershot to visit Cam. She and Cam had enjoyed little time together since the night of Jack's death. Cam had been recalled to duty five days later, and intermittent letters and two telephone calls were the only communication they'd had for nearly eight months. But after presenting himself to the medic whilst in France, Cam had been returned to barracks in England with a diagnosis of exhaustion and fever. Their wedding day was set for June 2nd, and Maisie prayed he'd be fit enough.

The sentry on duty gave her a beaming smile as she walked towards him.

'Here she comes, brightening up my day. What do you want marrying a Canadian when you could have the best of British with me?' he quipped.

Maisie laughed. Each time she visited he said the same. Her reply never altered either.

'And who am I to deprive another of the best? Talking of brightening up, walking out in the evening with streetlights is such a novelty nowadays, so be wary of scaring the locals,' Maisie teased and received a cock-eyed salute in return.

Entering the medical bay, she beamed a smile at the nurse on duty.

'How is he today?' she asked.

Cam was popular amongst the nursing staff for his gentle nature and good manners.

'Better. Much better. Temperature is down and he slept from when you left yesterday at four, until six this morning. He felt guilty but was reminded of why his body shut down in the first place. He's outside having a stroll now.'

Maisie headed out to the back of the units where the nurse directed her and saw Cam walking slowly, drawing on a cigarette. She didn't call out straight away but watched from where she stood. His shoulders were rounded and his steps slow; Cam still looked exhausted, but the fact that he was up and walking was a positive sign.

'Back straight, airman,' she called.

Cam turned and waved. His face broke out into a smile and he strode towards her.

'Slow down, there's no rush,' Maisie said as she ran to meet him.

'I've got energy at last,' Cam said and lifted her off the ground.

'Put me down, silly. You'll have none left to kiss me at this rate,' she said.

'Always,' Cam said and pressed his lips against hers.

When they pulled apart, he tugged at his left ear and looked slightly awkward. A fear that something unpleasant was about to happen gnawed away at Maisie's insides.

'Problem?' she asked.

'No but I have news,' Cam replied.

Maisie linked her arm through his and guided him to a quiet area with a wooden bench. Although not a cold day, there was a slight chill on the wind, and she huddled into him for comfort.

'Sit and tell me your news. I hope it's good, for a change,' she said with false enthusiasm.

'Our wedding. It's going to be a quiet affair . . . just how we want it,' Cam said in a cautious voice.

'Yes. As we both want it. No fuss.'

'I had a call from my mother and after she'd asked about me and the wedding, she told me there were plans afoot to greet you and embrace you into the family. They're going to visit for a month once we've settled.'

'Ah, that's lovely. I'm worried about meeting them but I'm also excited.'

'That's the thing. If there are plans, it means Mom is organising a repeat wedding. She does nothing by halves when it comes to entertaining.'

Cam sighed and looked at Maisie with an apologetic grin.

'Harry Cameron, I've survived a war, dodged bombs, seen many people die, buried a dear friend as well as my brother. I've watched the life drain from you and I'm about to sail across the ocean to live in in a strange country. I think I can fool your mother into believing I'm enjoying the party she's thrown for us, don't you?'

Cam rose to his feet and held out his hands. Maisie

moved in for more than a gentle cuddle. They locked themselves into a hold which meant more than words of love ever could or would. When Cam let her go, he stared her hard in the face.

'And that is why I am marrying you. I've never met anyone with such a big heart. You are incredible. I'm going to be one proud husband.'

The showers of the previous day moved into fair weather, much to Maisie's relief. Dressed in a newly pressed uniform, she looked at the trunk waiting by the door, then back at the image in the mirror before her. Should she change her outfit?

Inside the trunk was the neatly folded wedding dress she'd made for Coleen, waiting to be transported to Nova Scotia. After much deliberation, Maisie had chosen not to wear the dress for her own wedding. Her intention was to create a christening gown for their children from the material, and instead she and Cam would wear the uniforms they were proud to be seen in for their wedding day. It would be the last time Cam would wear his and they thought one photograph of them together at the end of war would be fitting on such a day. Cam's medical discharge letter had arrived a week before the wedding. He had seemed down for a few hours, but after making a call to his parents his mood had lifted. All plans for his fishing project were now his focus.

Outside the registry office he waited with Joyce and Charlie's mother. Charlie's dad collected Maisie and drove her into Southampton. The exchange of vows and rings was over in minutes and a bemused Mrs Cameron stood holding on to the arm of her husband whilst Charlie's dad fussed around taking a photograph.

Back at Joyce's house, they enjoyed beef-paste sandwiches and cups of tea. Joyce had made a small fruit cake and apologised for the lack of icing. Cam said he was relieved as he didn't like it anyway, and Maisie made a mental note never to produce it for Christmas cakes of the future. All in all, it was a memorable day, one Maisie knew she'd treasure. The people she had grown to love were all there and it marked the start of a new life for her.

'Joyce, I have a gift for the children,' Maisie said when Archie ran into Cam's arms for a swing around for the umpteenth time.

'They have no value other than that they belong to me now, and as my godchildren, I'd like them to have a little something. I own very little and these are inherited pieces.'

Maisie handed over Jack's watch that his parents had given her, and the small silver ring she had found in her mother's box.

'I want you to tell them that I love them and one day I will return to visit. I'll send photographs of Canada and write to you often. You know how I love writing letters.' Maisie lifted out another gift wrapped in tissue paper and leaned down to kiss Joyce on the cheek. 'On that note, this is your gift Joyce, with my love.'

She watched as Joyce unravelled the twine and paper. Her friend gasped with delight and objected loudly to receiving such a gift when she held out Maisie's fountain pen.

'It's another inherited piece of sorts. Don't think me deprived, Joyce. My husband bought me the most beautiful tortoiseshell one as a wedding gift, and that's the one I'll use from now on. Write to me about the children and Charlie's parents using this pen. It would mean so much to me.'

When all farewells had been made and promises undertaken not to go to the docks to wave them off because it would only make Maisie cry, Joyce embraced Maisie one last time.

'Be happy, my lovely. He's a good man and I know you're doing the right thing. If he were here, Charlie would give you his blessing too.'

Maisie took a deep breath and smiled at Joyce.

'Charlie would be making plans to get you out there too if it meant he could spend the days fishing.'

Maisie could not believe she stood on the deck of a ship at Southampton docks, a married woman. And all on her twenty-third birthday. Cam's flight home seemed like a lifetime ago, not three weeks, and she'd only received one telephone call to say he'd arrived at his uncle's and all was well . . . and that she'd better brace herself for surprises.

During her ten-day journey to Canada, she played over in her mind what the surprises might be. She knew her husband wasn't going to let her down or allow her to be overwhelmed – he'd promised that much – but as for the rest, he told her she'd have to wait and see; if he told her, they wouldn't be surprises.

The journey was tough going. She worked on a floating hospital, and some of the patients' injuries were nothing in comparison to their seasickness. All strength was sapped from their bodies. Maisie struggled to fight off the nausea and exhaustion herself, all while nursing them through the worst stages. The ship lifted and dropped, dropped and lifted its way into Pier 21, Halifax, Canada. The healthier of the men sang and jollied each other along, and some days the mood was uplifting and joyful. They were going home, and that was something to celebrate when vast numbers of their serving forces had been lost. Maisie had nothing but admiration for them. They told her stories of her new country, what foods and drinks she should try out first, where the best places were in each season and they offered their homes to her and Cam to visit if they found themselves in that particular part of the country.

When it was announced that they'd arrived, the ten days of exhaustive tension dropped from her shoulders. A pleasant warmth welcomed her to the country and Maisie dashed to the deck to witness her arrival into her new homeland. Her heart pounded, her legs trembled, her hands shook, and she staved off bouts of acid that rose each time they dipped in a wave. Back in her cabin, she removed her uniform, folded it neatly, and stepped into a pretty lemon dress with a white belt and a lace collar. She slipped her feet into new white shoes with a small, chunky heel and brushed her hair into shining waves. There was no doubt in her mind that Cam would be waiting quayside for her, and she wanted to look her best.

This is it, Maisie Cameron. Your new life is about to begin.

The war had battered her, the orphanage had taken so much from her, and she had been shocked by the truth of her origins. Happiness had turned to sadness but it had also found a way back into her life. Maisie wondered how she'd managed to survive it all. She knew that until Cam had stepped into her life, her life had been merely an existence, not the vessel of love and hope and joy it was now.

The moment she stepped off the ship, Maisie was caught in a whirlwind of red tape and document stamping. By the time she'd finished answering the last question presented to her, Maisie feared Cam would see a bewildered, exhausted, and frightened woman in a crumpled dress, rather than the confident wife in a pretty frock she'd hoped to present him with. Pulling her cloth bag close to her and trusting that her trunk would be on the other side of the line, Maisie trundled forward. She'd signed off her last patient and from the moment she crossed that line into Canada, Maisie felt proud that her life as an English orphan had all been about bringing her here for this moment, for this man, and for this new country.

CHAPTER 33

'Welcome to Canada, Mrs Cameron!' Cam yelled to her through hands cupped around his mouth.

Maisie jumped and waved when she saw him at the end of a short queue of people ready to exit the vast building after collecting their trunks and suitcases. The queues entering were growing longer and longer, and she was grateful that there were only a few feet between her and her husband.

Outside, he pushed his way through a group of people waiting for their loved ones and grabbed her by the arm, tugging her to his side. He looked so happy and far healthier than when she last saw him in England; she knew they'd made the right choice by not staying.

He stroked her hair, touched her face, and their embrace lasted several minutes.

'Welcome home. Welcome to Nova Scotia. Let's get

on the road and meet the rest. Mom is beside herself with excitement. My parents arrived yesterday, and I've never had so many hugs from my father.'

Maisie looked around at the families and loved ones embracing in much the same way. Tired, drawn faces of the arrivals lit up at the sight of them and she knew exactly how they felt. Loved and wanted. Happy. Grateful.

'Now comes the hard part,' she said and followed him to a large green Ford pickup. He loaded her trunk into the back.

'The family will love you. They love you already for making me happy. I have a surprise too!'

Cam's voice had lost the dull tone that had dogged him during the last weeks and months they'd had in England. His eagerness to please her was almost boyish. His hair was now much longer with curls forming around his neck, and his cheeks and arms were tanned. Maisie saw him as the paratrooper she had first met and beamed a smile at him.

'This is wonderful. It's great to see you so alive again, Cam,' she shouted above the engine noise and wind as they rattled along the coastline. The views were spectacular, and Maisie felt her sense of adventure return. The nausea and anxiety from the ship had dissipated, and she could not wait to start on a new adventure.

'It's you and this country of mine. Both make me very happy,' he said.

As they turned off onto a narrower road, Maisie gasped. The striking landscape before her was nothing like what she had expected. Cam's wide-open spaces were no lie, and they were filled with towering spruce trees. She sniffed the air. Their fragrance and that of the sea was fresh, unlike that of Southampton docks. Cam pulled the car to a halt and jumped from his seat. He ran around the truck to her side and pulled open the door.

'Just take a look down there,' he said.

Maisie peered over the edge of the roadside and looked down on golden-yellow seaweed covering blue-tinged grey slabs of uneven rocks which had formed into fascinating shapes. On the shimmering water, tied to a post, bobbed a small green boat filled with boxes that she assumed were to house the lobsters he intended to catch.

'It's ours,' Cam said, pointing across the water.

'The boat?'

Cam nodded. 'Our wedding gift from the family.'

Maisie looked at his wide smile and hugged him.

'They'll be waiting. But first I have to show you something else. Let's go,' Cam said.

The drive home had been breathtaking for Maisie. Cam appeared to take it in his stride, but she suddenly felt tiny against the vast reaching trees, the enormous rocks and boulders. Houses of varying sizes were fields and fields apart, not row upon row like they were back in England.

'I can see why you want to live here,' she said to Cam as he pulled up outside a large wooden house surrounded by small outbuildings overlooking the water.

'It's very basic compared to what you're used to, Maisie. There's a lot of improvements which have to be made. I know how modern amenities can transform a house into a home, and I need you to be patient and know I'll do my utmost to transform this place.' Cam pointed to the large wooden house, his voice almost pleading with her to like it. Maisie gave his arm a reassuring touch.

Maisie guessed the smaller building set back on its own was the one housing the toilet. Used to emptying bedpans, she took it in her stride that there'd be pots under the beds here until they made improvements.

'My home is with you,' she said, and Cam replied with a kiss.

Maisie felt a sense of release. She was no longer trapped inside the confines of her past. Cam had set her free and brought her to a new world where she would embrace the highs and lows as best she could. There was no going back for Maisie.

They stepped up onto the front porch of the main building and before Maisie had time to turn around and take in the view, Cam had opened the front door of the house, lifted her off the ground and into his arms.

'Time to carry you over the threshold, Mrs Cameron,' he said and nudged the door open.

He spun around with her in his arms as if she had no weight to her body at all. Cam's strength and enthusiasm had returned. Maisie squealed with laughter and it echoed around the walls.

'Put me down, you fool, before you do yourself an injury.'

Placing two feet firmly on the ground, Maisie took a slow walk around the large open-plan room. Maisie saw a basic home in need of loving care. Cam was right; it was different to what she'd been used to in her little cottage, but he'd forgotten that she'd spent most of her life with no privacy at all and very limited freedom.

'There's an upstairs – another two levels; my uncle built this with a large family in mind. They only had one child, and when my aunt's parents died, they moved into their smaller home as it was closer to the water. It's a lovely spot, but this is our place from now on. Another gift from my uncle. My cousin Larry would have lived here had he survived and married.'

Maisie noted the wistful look on his face. It was a brief moment of guilt for surviving the war, and her heart went out to him.

'Oh, Cam. I'm so sorry this makes you so sad. We'll

make it a happy place and we'll make your family proud. They'll never regret this gift. I can't wait to meet them. Take me to them. It's time I met my new family.'

They walked in silence, hand in hand along the water's edge with gulls calling and lapping water adding to the peaceful ambience. Maisie tucked the moment deep inside. She had little doubt there'd be tough times ahead – cold times in the snow, Cam had warned her – but for the short walk to his family it felt like an embrace. A welcome home.

A male voice shouted out in the distance, and Cam squeezed her hand.

'Here we go. Pop has spotted us.'

Their speed increased and Maisie let go of Cam's hand to enable him to get to his father and she watched the pair cling onto each other in loving gratitude for Cam's life. His father looked over at her and the moment of dread disappeared. His smile said it all. *Thank you for making my son happy. Thank you for giving up your home for him.*

'Harry, when you said she was a pretty redhead, you weren't exaggerating!' he exclaimed.

Maisie felt the blush burn her cheeks. Cam's father let go of his son and pulled her close.

'My daughter-in-law. Mrs Maisie Cameron, welcome to your new home.'

'I second that!' another male voice called over to them, before Maisie had time to respond. The man raced towards them and nudged her father-in-law to one side.

'Move over, old man. Let the others have a chance,' he quipped and gave Maisie a brief hug. She immediately saw the family likeness amongst the three men.

'You must be my new niece,' the man said, stepping back and looking her up and down.

'And you must be my new uncle, Bernie!'

She burst out laughing and the others joined in.

Cam looked on and gave a satisfactory nod.

'Time to meet the other ladies in my life. My sister is here and she's so excited for us.'

They climbed a small incline towards a pretty blue house with a sloping tiled roof and an attic window. Maisie could see two grey-haired women seated on rocking chairs on the porch. They made the perfect picture against the blue paint. Both women rose as the group approached the porch entrance, and Maisie could see the shorter of the two was Cam's mother. He had her eyes.

'Mrs Cameron,' Maisie said and held out her hand.

'Mrs Cameron,' her mother -in-law responded, then pulled her close for the obligatory embrace.

'Welcome to the family, Maisie. Welcome to Canada, and call me Mom, you hear? We're all the richer for having you come to live with us. What a beauty you are. Son, you did well. Take care of her, you hear me?'

'I hear you Ma,' Cam teased with a salute.

Maisie's heart leapt and jumped with a sensation that was new to her. She soon realised that it was a sense of belonging to something greater than just Cam: a family. She could now use the term 'my family' in a way she'd never been able to in the past. She would say Mum and Dad, Aunt and Uncle, sister and husband, on a daily basis. Everything she'd ever dreamed of in her life stood before her laughing and chatting together.

Cam's aunt stood back and Maisie looked to her.

'I understand it's you I have to thank for the pretty things inside our new home. In fact, both of you for our beautiful house.' She held out her hand and the woman took it in hers. 'It can't be easy for you. I'm so sorry for your loss, Mrs Cameron.'

With a soft smile, Cam's Aunt Sarah looked at the group.

'Another Mrs Cameron to take the helm. You men had better watch out. Maisie, please call me Sarah.'

An afternoon of drinking lemonade, exchanging stories, and generally getting to know the family ticked by and Maisie relaxed far more than she'd imagined she would.

Cam's sister Emily arrived from a shopping trip, and after giving them both an enthusiastic hug she shyly handed over a beautiful glass paperweight as a welcome gift for Maisie. The gift touched Maisie, and she burst into tears, which sent a flurry of worried family members fussing over her and reassuring her, which in itself brought on fresh tears. It was one of the happiest days of her life, and Maisie allowed it to overpower the sour ones of the past.

By the evening, she and Cam headed to their new home, armed with a basket of food and fresh bed linen. Maisie was exhausted but insisted they watch the sun going down whilst sitting on their own porch steps. She leaned her head against Cam's, and he put his arm around her.

'This is paradise,' she whispered.

'I challenge you to say that in the middle of winter,' Cam laughed.

Maisie snuggled close. 'I'll have you to keep me warm.'

'Always,' he replied and when his lips found hers, Maisie's heart rate rose. She'd witnessed tender glances between his parents during the afternoon, and knew she'd married into loving genes. Her man was hers forever, and although the war had taken a lot away from them both, she knew it had also given her the best thing she could ever wish for in her Canadian paratrooper.

'Time for bed. We've a long day ahead of us tomorrow. Our new home needs the loving touch of a woman. And

I'm also ready for the same,' Cam said and pulled Maisie to her feet.

'I love you, Maisie, and I promise to be a good husband to you.'

Maisie followed him inside and before she closed the door, she looked out at the moon's reflection tripping over the rippling water. She knew it would be a long time before she had the leisure to write poetry again, but the image before her was stamped in her memory forever. Mrs Harry Cameron closed the door on the scene and followed her husband upstairs.

CHAPTER 34

1946

Maisie noticed the first mists of spring rolling around the front of their home. Thick fog often caught her unawares, but today she could see the treetops across the water and shimmering wisps of white straddling branches and filtering through the gaps as if escaping the confines of winter. The longer she stood mesmerised by the scene, the more inspired she became.

With the eagerness of a child at Christmas, she picked up her pen and wrote her first two poems since landing in her new country. It had been a stagnant eight months where creativity was concerned and she smiled when she thought of how the simple words would please Cam. He fretted over her lack of writing, and worried it was due to homesickness or regret. No matter how many times she reassured him, he still felt that he was holding her back from releasing her inner thoughts. She pulled out her poetry book and pondered the title, and within a few seconds the words flowed onto the page.

Misty Morn

Oh, glistening stems of dawn's delight
Bring forth the warmth, remove the night.
Shimmer on leaf and stem,
Shine as nature's precious gem.
Touch gently each floral cup
And offer roots God's ale to sup.
Warm rays, allow them a passage through
To drink the early morning dew.
And on the warmth of their soft kiss,
Rise up to become the morning mist.

Golden Caress

Misty veil lifts, revealing sun-tipped fields –
Aarm, appealing.
The miracle of new day touches all,
The wonder of sunrise –
Bird to bird they call.
Hazy warmth on tender skin,
Let a new dawn show its readiness to begin.

The Forgotten Orphan

Sunset: task is done,
Crimson sky, slow sinking sun.
Rest, restore each golden ray
Then slowly climb and alight new day.
Arouse each bird with a song to sing,
Dawn choruses to ears softly bring.
The joy each morning of a sunshine smile,
The gift to those who watch awhile.

Laying down her pen, Maisie took another moment to watch the mists roll across the water and dance across the grass in front of their house. She adored where they lived and marvelled at how easily she'd made the place feel like home and how quickly she'd settled in to Blue Rocks. She was proud of how far she'd come.

Although it had been tough, she'd survived the sweltering heat of their first summer, and worked alongside Cam during the honeymoon period. Her fishing skills improved each time they took out their boat, and by the autumn – or fall as she'd learned to call it – Maisie had settled into a gentle routine of work and homemaking.

Cam had proved to be a good man, true to his word, and he worked hard to provide her with modern luxuries for their home, producing each one with great flourish. Electricity was one of his main aims for their home, but Maisie knew it would be years before she'd flick a switch for light. She was content with oil lamps.

All was well until the first of the snow fell and the temperature had dropped to a level she'd never experienced before. Although the scenery was transformed into a picture-postcard image, Maisie felt like she'd never feel warm again. Cam had stacked the fires high and she'd huddled around them for a few days, allowing a deep melancholy to set in. She'd tried to hide it from Cam, but he'd often questioned her mood. Not wanting to worry him, Maisie had worked hard to find a way of adapting to her surroundings; she knew she couldn't huddle in front of a fire forever.

Her first trip outside had been to join Cam chopping wood and loading the store with logs. Her arms and legs ached, and her woollen mitts proved useless. They repaired the roof of another small barn, and Cam worked with his uncle to make a large pine table for their home. By the time the temperature dropped so low she couldn't bear to work outside anymore, Maisie retreated inside and felt hemmed in and miserable. Again, she hid her feelings from Cam and kept herself busy. She baked, cleaned, and read endless books, but they didn't satisfy the deep-seated restlessness she felt at being cooped up inside. Even her poetry failed her – a feeling she shared with Aunt Sarah when she managed to walk over for a visit. Her in-laws were planning to move to the bay in the summer and Maisie was delighted that she'd have Cam's family around her, though she wasn't yet sure her mother-in-law would become her confidante in personal matters.

She missed her chats with Joyce and one day, unable to bear the distress she'd stored inside any longer, she broke down to Cam's aunt. To her surprise, Maisie found herself in the presence of someone who listened without judging and from then on, they often talked of such things, about the world and their heartbreaking losses. She trusted Sarah with all her worries and concerns over her mood.

'I know exactly what your problem is, Maisie. You're ready for a family. You're feeling broody, that's what it is. I have a feeling a baby will make the winters more bearable. I know Larry made me feel complete,' Sarah said.

Maisie didn't argue but she could not imagine bringing up a child in such a climate. Also, she was worried that she and Cam would never have children. They'd certainly tried hard enough. Sarah laughed and told her to relax and let nature take its course – and not to worry about children in winter because they loved the snow. They learned to endure and thrive.

Maisie smiled remembering Sarah's words as she marked the day off on the calendar. Quietly, she approached the barn where Cam was working on new railings for their porch. She stood in the doorway and watched as he stroked the wood to a smooth grain. She'd experienced his gentle touch the previous evening, and a shimmer of pleasant memories shimmied through her. Stepping inside, she smelled the sliced pine and an overwhelming feeling of calmness enveloped her. A sense of belonging.

'Hello, you,' Cam said as she entered.

Maisie nodded. 'Hello, you. I've come to ask you something.'

'Fire away,' Cam said and stopped what he was doing.

'I was wondering if you could make a crib before next year's snowfall?'

Cam stared at her as Maisie placed her hands over the front of her coat and smiled back at him.

'About Christmas Eve would be handy,' she said and giggled.

With one wild whoop, Cam was at her side and lifting her off her feet.

'I love you, Mrs Cameron. Thank you. Thank you for making me the happiest man alive.'

Maisie kissed his cheek.

'Thank you for my family, Harry Cameron. And thank you for loving me.'

THE END

ACKNOWLEDGEMENTS

Where do I start?

My family, friends and Team Glynis aka One More Chapter and HarperCollins (worldwide), are in my thoughts always, but even more so now as this book was written during the Covid-19 pandemic, when my mind was mush. You've all pushed me forward to become the best I can be when the odds seemed stacked against me.
Thank you with love
Stay safe.

Terri Nixon, Christie Barlow, and Deborah Carr What a journey we follow together – Authors of The WGW Society will reunite before 2020 fades away –

I hear the champagne corks popping as I type!
Thank you for being my sounding board during
lockdown.

To you the reader.
Without you, I am nothing. Thank you for your
continued support.

To those who fought for freedom during WWII
You have my gratitude and respect – always and
forever.